Mackenzie was everything a man could hope for, her body the lush wellspring of femininity.

He groaned at the sweetness of her untutored touch. He wanted her, wanted to sink inside her and unite them in a way that had nothing to do with centuries of civilized thought and everything to do with primal urges that connected them to the earth itself.

Then memories and feelings whirled in his mind. . . .

"No!" He sat up and clutched his head. "God, no!"

"What is it?" Mackenzie gasped.

He heard her fears and the beginnings of shame. But he couldn't tell her what he'd heard, what he'd seen. He was a madman, seeing beings who weren't there, hearing voices in his head.

Then a worse thought than insanity gripped him. Because if he wasn't insane, there was another, infinitely more fing explanation. . . .

Dear Reader,

This month starts off with a bang—and with a book that more of you than I can count have requested over the years. *Quinn Eisley's War*, by Patricia Gardner Evans, finally completes the cycle begun in *Whatever It Takes* and *Summer of the Wolf*. Quinn is a commanding presence, and every bit the American Hero he's featured as. This is a story torn from today's headlines, and yet timelessly romantic. I have only one word left to say about it: enjoy!

The rest of this month is pretty spectacular, too, but what would you expect when we're celebrating the line's tenth anniversary? It's hard for me to believe we've been around that long, but it's true. And because it's your support that has kept us flourishing, it seemed only fitting to reward you with one of the best lineups we've ever published. We've got *Ironheart*, the latest in Rachel Lee's bestselling Conard County series; *Somewhere Out There*, the followup to *From a Distance* by award-winner Emilie Richards; *Take Back the Night* by yet another award-winner Dee Holmes; *To Hold an Eagle* by yet *another* award-winner (Does this tell you something about the line?) Justine Davis; and *Holding Out for a Hero*, the first of the stories of the Sinclair family, by Marie Ferrarella, another of our bestselling authors. In short, we've got six books you can't resist, six books that belong on your shelves—and in your heart—forever!

We're also offering a special hardcover tenth anniversary collection featuring the first books some of your favorite authors ever wrote for the line. Heather Graham Pozzessere, Emilie Richards and Kathleen Korbel are regular fixtures on bestseller lists and award rosters, so don't miss your chance to get this once-in-a-lifetime collection. Look for details at the back of this book.

And, of course, I'll expect to see you back here next month, when Silhouette Intimate Moments will bring you more of what you've come to expect: irresistible romantic reading.

Leslie J. Wainger
Senior Editor and Editorial Coordinator

SOMEWHERE
OUT
THERE

Emilie
Richards

Silhouette®
INTIMATE MOMENTS®

Published by Silhouette Books New York

America's Publisher of Contemporary Romance

SILHOUETTE BOOKS
300 East 42nd St., New York, N.Y. 10017

SOMEWHERE OUT THERE

Copyright © 1993 by Emilie Richards McGee

All rights reserved. Except for use in any review, the reproduction or utilization of this work in whole or in part in any form by any electronic, mechanical or other means, now known or hereafter invented, including xerography, photocopying and recording, or in any information storage or retrieval system, is forbidden without the permission of the publisher, Silhouette Books, 300 E. 42nd St., New York, N.Y. 10017

ISBN: 0-373-07498-0

First Silhouette Books printing May 1993

All the characters in this book have no existence outside the imagination of the author and have no relation whatsoever to anyone bearing the same name or names. They are not even distantly inspired by any individual known or unknown to the author, and all incidents are pure invention.

®: Trademark used under license and registered in the United States Patent and Trademark Office and in other countries.

Printed in the U.S.A.

Books by Emilie Richards

Silhouette Intimate Moments

Lady of the Night #152
Bayou Midnight #188
*From Glowing Embers #249
*Smoke Screen #261
*Rainbow Fire #273
*Out of the Ashes #285
Runaway #337
The Way Back Home #341
Fugitive #357
Desert Shadows #401
Twilight Shadows #409
From a Distance #456
Somewhere Out There #498

* Tales of the Pacific Series

Silhouette Books

Birds, Bees and Babies 1990
"Labor Dispute"

Silhouette Romance

Brendan's Song #372
Sweet Georgia Gal #393
Gilding the Lily #401
Sweet Sea Spirit #413
Angel and the Saint #429
Sweet Mockingbird's Call #441
Good Time Man #453
Sweet Mountain Magic #466
Sweet Homecoming #489
Aloha Always #520
Outback Nights #536
Island Glory #675

Silhouette Special Edition

All the Right Reasons #433
A Classic Encounter #456
All Those Years Ago #684
One Perfect Rose #750

EMILIE RICHARDS

believes that opposites attract, and her marriage is vivid proof. "When we met," the author says, "the *only* thing my husband and I could agree on was that we were very much in love. Fortunately, we haven't changed our minds about that in all the years we've been together."

The couple live in Ohio with their four children. Emilie has put her master's degree in family development to good use—raising her own brood, working for Head Start, counseling in a mental-health clinic and serving in VISTA.

Though her first book was written in snatches with an infant on her lap, Emilie now writes five hours a day and "rejoices in the opportunity to create, to grow and to have such a good time."

Chapter 1

Mackenzie Conroy wasn't frightened—which was bloody stupid. Even the most seasoned Territory stockmen had enough respect for the great Never-Never to be frightened when the bull dust blew so thick there was no way to tell where the ground ended and the sky began.

But Mackenzie wasn't. She was riding Bounder, a horse she had broken herself when Dilly Dan, the station horse trainer, went east on holiday. Bounder and she had an understanding. She played along with his little jokes, his abrupt halts in the middle of a comfortable gallop, his penchant for jumping left when he was supposed to jump right, his beatific brumby-smile just before he gave her arm or shoulder a friendly nip. But there were no big jokes with Bounder. If she really needed him, he was there. They were mates.

And about now, she needed a mate.

There were willi-willies blowing. She'd seen one swirling on the horizon before the dust had gotten so thick the horizon was a sweet memory. Theoretically, she had a special fondness for willi-willies. Waluwara's Aboriginal population liked to say that she had been fashioned from one. Her hair was the red of the dust whirlwinds madly cavorting and sucking up everything in their paths. And from the time she had come to live at Waluwara, an orphaned toddler suddenly thrust into the care of a young, rough-hewn station boss and his men, she had set Waluwara whirling with her questions and her antics.

So she understood and respected willi-willies. She just didn't have any real desire to be caught in the center of one. Neither, from all signs, did Bounder.

"We've been through this before," she reminded him with a pat on his dust-smothered neck. The dust should have flown in all directions, but where could it go? Dust to dust? She didn't like that image.

"Let's keep moving. I know we're not more than an hour's ride from a boundary hut."

Beneath her she felt Bounder picking his way carefully across the plain. They were nowhere near a road, so there would be no help from that quarter. And even if they had been closer, the chances for help would have been small at best. The roads on this side of the run hadn't been graded for months. "Corrugated" was too good a word for their condition. Most of the station vehicles were in the same lamentable state as the grader. Driven along roads as rutted and worn as the one closest to her, any of them would collapse into one more heap of rusting scrap metal.

Besides, the boss, her uncle Clint Conroy, knew better than to send help until it was clear by the number of days that passed without hearing from her that she was in serious trouble. He'd tried sending help once when she was fifteen and camping alone in the hill country. Absorbed in her adventure, she'd lost track of the days, and he'd lost track of his faith in her. After that they'd come to an understanding that from that moment on she would take charge of herself, but if there was ever any real sign that she couldn't, she would be packed off to Adelaide or Darwin and a different kind of life.

Threat of that was enough to make her the most self-sufficient ringer on the station.

Bounder plodded steadily through the storm. Dust storms of this magnitude were rare, but never entirely unexpected. There were only two seasons in Australia's Northern Territory, the Wet and the Dry. With luck the Wet would arrive in another six weeks or so, in October, although the best of the rains would come later. But the previous year there hadn't been any rain until January, and then it had been the driest Wet Mackenzie could remember. Waluwara's grasslands had turned to straw and its water holes to mud flats under the sun's unrelieved onslaught. Inevitably a sizable portion of the station's cattle had succumbed to thirst and starvation.

The dust particles flaying her skin through her shirt and moleskin trousers were a result of last year's weather, too. What vegetation that was left on this part of the run couldn't hold the soil in place. The saltbush and the wildflowers weren't dead. If a good Wet came the plains would bloom, the grass would thrive, and the creeks and billabongs would fill to quench even the driest cattle's thirst.

If a good Wet evaded them again, more than cattle would perish. The station would perish, too.

Mackenzie was good at pushing away trouble until she could deal with it, so she pushed away that thought and concentrated on her own immediate survival. There *was* an old boundary rider's hut an hour's ride away, but that was in good weather. With the storm and the miscalculations she was bound to make with all landmarks obscured, she and Bounder probably wouldn't reach the hut for another two hours, maybe three.

It was already late afternoon, although only her watch could testify to that. Since the sun was blocked by the storm, the sky was nearly dark. In three hours there would be no light at all. She had her swag, and she had plenty of tucker. But she really didn't want to make camp in the middle of a dust storm. A bit of shelter would be much appreciated.

"Get on with it," she encouraged Bounder. "If you move any slower, you'll root and sprout leaves."

He moved even slower; then he stopped.

She kicked and wished she'd worn spurs. She had an old pair, highly prized, that had been forged many years before from one piece of spring steel by a blacksmith on the Wave Hill Station. Sometimes she wore them for good luck. She bloody well needed them today.

"Get on with you, Bounder!"

He dug his hooves deeper in the sand and humped his back in warning.

"Come on, mate. I'm not asking you go flat chat. Just keep moving."

He didn't.

She knew when to coax, and she knew when to listen. Now she listened, pulling her hat brim lower and her scarf higher over her nose so that even less of her face was exposed. She heard nothing but the restless moaning of the wind.

The problem could be a mickey bull, one of the unbranded, clean-skin bullocks that roamed the station in search of trouble. No matter how hard the men struggled to muster these mavericks, there were always more, waiting to impregnate registered stock with their renegade genes, waiting to gore any unsuspecting ringer.

She shut her eyes and listened with her other senses, the ones there were no names for—not English names, anyway. The Aborigines had names for such things, melodic, fluid words she had learned as a child. The elders in the village south of the homestead would understand exactly what she was doing.

At first nothing seemed unusual—if a raging outback dust storm could be considered the norm. Then she felt the source of Bounder's obstinacy. The hair lifted on the back of her arms, and her throat grew even drier.

"Hullo out there!" she shouted.

She tasted dust and heard no response.

"Where are you, exactly? Do you need help?"

Bounder swayed uneasily under her, but his hooves dug deeper.

"Good on ya," she murmured to calm the horse. "You were right. I wasn't paying attention."

She was sure there was someone nearby. It wasn't as simple as hearing a cough or smelling an unwashed body. Then she would have been able to track the mysterious human immediately. As it was, she had only intuition to guide her. She couldn't see more than four horse lengths in any direction.

She considered whether to give Bounder his head. He might go immediately to the source of their mutual concern. But if he sensed danger he might also start off in the opposite direction. She couldn't be sure.

In the end, she dismounted, looping the reins over the branches of a clump of scrub in case Bounder had plans of his own. Since she had intended to be gone for most of a week, she had a rifle, but she didn't remove it from the saddle. She wasn't unprotected. Like all the station stockmen, she had a knife tucked securely in a braided kangaroo hide pouch on her similarly braided belt. Her pouch was particularly intricate, a small vanity for a woman whom vanity had almost completely bypassed.

"Hullo!" she shouted again. There was still no answer. She began to circle the horse, widening her path until Bounder was lost in a haze of dust. She wasn't worried. She could still sense his presence, and if she got too far away, she could persuade him to snort or neigh just by giving a piercing whistle.

Three more shouts produced nothing. Three everwidening circles produced nothing.

Then one glance through a sudden gap in the dust produced a distant glimpse of a man facedown on the ground.

A man who was as naked as the day his mother had given birth to him.

"Bloody hell!" Mackenzie thrust her hands in the pockets of her moleskins and stared. "Double bloody hell!"

She didn't want to start forward. She wasn't squeamish. How could she be and do the things a ringer did? There was no part of an animal she wasn't face-to-face familiar with. Unfortunately, beef didn't arrive at the butcher shops because it had been sweetly persuaded to lie down and die for the cause.

She had seen men and women die, too. Sometimes the Flying Doctor Service had been called for too late; sometimes death just stole over the station's elderly like a longed-for dream. Once, out in the bush, she had found two skeletons in a hillside cave, locked in each other's arms as if death itself could not separate them. But never had she come across a body like this one. A body so recently dead as not to have been preyed on by dingoes or crows.

A body perhaps not dead at all?

Not yet.

That thought was the push she needed. The dust had thickened again, blown on a Johnny-One-Note gust of wind. She headed for Bounder; then, holding his reins, she started off in the direction where she knew the body to be.

It took her longer to find it than she had expected. Her skills were honed, but the bull dust played a better game of poker than she did. Fifteen minutes of bluffing went by, then twenty, before she caught sight of the man again. Still facedown. Still not moving.

Still not dressed.

Leading Bounder, she reached the stranger's side. Kneeling in the dust beside him, she was struck with a rapid series of impressions.

First: there wasn't a suspicious mark on his body. No blood, no bullet holes.

Second: his skin must have been quite pale, because now he was badly sunburned, despite being in the middle of a dust storm in an Australian winter.

Last: he was one magnificent male creature.

She stripped off her leather gloves to feel for a pulse at the base of his throat. As she touched him, she forced herself to speak.

"I'm going to feel right silly asking this if you're dead, but can you hear me?"

There was no response. Not a groan, not a twitch.

She slid her fingers a millimeter, still searching for an elusive heartbeat. "Your skin feels warm, but then it should, considering the burn you've got. If you're alive, you'll be wishing you weren't tomorrow."

His skin was not only warm, it was smooth and supple. If he was dead, he was the most tactilely appealing corpse she could imagine. Her fingertips slid another millimeter. "You picked a right perfect spot for doing a perish, stranger, but I wish you had picked somewhere else."

Her fingertips were callused, not the best receptors to sensation, but the next time they slid lower, she felt something move beneath them. A throb? She held her breath and waited for another. Minutes seemed to go by before she felt it. She pressed harder and moved again. This time his pulse was evident. Irregular and frightening, but definitely beating.

"So you're not dead." She sat back on her heels. "Yet."

What did she do next? She was in the middle of a dust storm, the nearest shelter at least an hour's ride away. And what could that shelter provide except respite from the sun and the dust? If she was lucky there might be a cache of medical supplies, but that was doubtful. The boundary rider's hut hadn't been used for anything more than afternoon shade in years. Where once it might have contained emergency supplies and even a primitive telephone hooked up to the homestead, now she would be lucky just to find it standing.

She rose and took her canteen from the saddle. Then, once again kneeling beside the man, she began the process of turning him over.

She was strong, but he was large, at least half again as heavy as she was. Dead weight was a fitting description, but with the knowledge that it would be even more fitting if she didn't get some water into him, she summoned one burst of strength and rolled him onto his back.

Impression layered impression. He was sunburned topside, too, and strangely enough, he was as burned on his arms and face—which should have had a protective tan—as he was on his torso. There were no obvious wounds here, either. But other things *were* perfectly obvious.

He was truly a sight to behold, a man like no other she had ever seen. He had dust-encrusted hair that was probably blond, a broad brow, high cheekbones, a straight nose and perfectly chiseled lips. His shoulders were wide, his hips narrow, and his chest was frosted with golden hair. His age was difficult to guess through the dust and the burn, but she assigned him thirty years with a bit of give-and-take.

And then there was the rest of him.

Her eyes strayed to the place any woman's would stray when presented with a defenseless naked man. She examined him with interest. Raised among men, she still had never seen one so thoroughly unclad. Although usually they treated her like one of them, the Waluwara stockmen were all quite respectful of her privacy when she camped with them. And even the greenest jackeroo discovered immediately that taking liberties with the boss's niece was the surest way to get sent packing. Consequently, Mackenzie's experience with men was both extensive and sadly lacking.

With little to compare him to, her instincts still told her that this man, dust and burn notwithstanding, had everything it took to please a woman. And possibly more.

He groaned. She knelt and bent over him immediately, hoping to take advantage of this small sign of consciousness. "Can you hear me?"

He didn't answer, but she hadn't really expected him to. She uncapped her canteen and bent lower. With one arm she cradled his head, while with the other she drizzled drops of water on his parted lips. At first he didn't respond, but when the water droplets rolled inside his mouth he swallowed convulsively.

Cheered, she increased the flow of water, and he swallowed again.

She had given him nearly two cups before she lowered his head to the ground and sat back on her heels once more to consider what to do next. She had water with her, and there was a bore not more than a kilometer from the hut to secure more if it was needed. Finding water, and getting him to drink it, were not going to be difficult. But there were enough additional problems that she didn't feel much relief.

She had to get him to shelter, and she had to get him medical help. And she had to do it before the sun went down, the temperature dropped and she completely lost her way. And before she could do any of those things, she had to figure out how to move him.

From somewhere in the distance she heard the howl of a dingo. She wanted to echo his sentiments. "Not having a party today, are we?" she muttered.

Bounder whinnied anxiously. "What about you, mate?" she asked the horse to calm him. "Got any ideas?"

Bounder edged closer. If she had been in scrubbier country, there would have been mulga or cottonwood to construct a stretcher of sorts to drag behind the horse. She'd seen enough American cowboy and Indian movies to rig such a thing, and making do with nothing was the name of the game in the outback. But making do with nothing actually required something. In this case, a tree. And there were none in sight.

She considered trying to lift the man into her saddle and discarded it immediately as impossible. She would never get him to his feet.

Bounder edged closer and nuzzled her. "No time for games." She tried to shove him away, although she wasn't really afraid he was going to trample the stranger. "No tricks," she said. "Not now."

Tricks. The word edged out all her other thoughts. Tricks.

"Bounder." She stood and rubbed the gelding's nose. "Good on ya," she said soothingly. "You want to be on your way, don't you, mate?"

She remembered a clear autumn night five years ago when she had led Bounder, docile as a lamb, to the front veranda of the homestead, where the boss sat in a straight-back chair watching her with his unflinching gaze.

"They said it couldn't be done," she had told him.

"I'm of a mind they were right," he had answered.

"So watch and learn something, doubting Thomas." She'd mounted Bounder as easily as she mounted any other truly broken horse on the run and kicked him in the sides. He had taken off like the wind. She'd wheeled him in a large circle, then gradually narrowed it until they were standing in front of the boss once more.

"Kneel, Bounder," she'd said. "Kneel."

And just as if he was performing in the circus, Bounder had gone down on his front legs as she swept off her hat in a graceful arc and bowed to her uncle.

Clint Conroy had faked a yawn, but his eyes had sparkled. "So you learned to break a bad brumby," he'd said. "Any real ringer can do it."

And she had known that she had just been given his finest compliment.

Now she wondered if Bounder remembered that night, too. The bow had been purely for show. Icing on the cake. The boss had known it, she had known it, and surely Bounder, with his brumby intelligence, had known it, too. But had that intelligence, in which she had such faith, retained the trick? The veranda performance had been years ago. She had asked Bounder to perform since then, but not for a year at least.

She patted him on the nose again, then fished in her tucker bag for a wedge of dried apple. She held it in front of him for just a moment. "Yours," she promised. "If you're a good mate."

He was a good mate. After she moved him as close to the stranger as she dared, she mounted him. "Kneel, Bounder," she commanded. "Kneel. Let's give it a go!"

And Bounder knelt.

Chapter 2

The boundary rider's hut was corrugated iron and fiber-board, much patched before it had been abandoned for lack of use. Night had fallen hard by the time Mackenzie stumbled through low sand hills toward the entrance. She had led Bounder the entire distance, tumbling to the ground more than once in the gradually thickening storm. But as much the worse for wear as she was, she knew the stranger was the one who deserved sympathy.

With Bounder's unflinching cooperation she had strung the man across her saddle, head dangling from one side, feet from the other. The struggle to do so had not been one of her finest moments, and not until Bounder had risen to his feet and the man remained firmly across the saddle had she been certain her plan had worked.

She had winced when she realized how the worn leather rubbed against his sunburned skin, and winced for a longer moment when she noted where the saddle and the most fascinating part of him collided. But there had been nothing to be done about either except pad and cover him as best she could with a blanket and hope he didn't regain consciousness on the horse.

He hadn't. Once she thought she had heard a moan, but when she reached his head and spoke to him, there had been no response. She had stopped repeatedly to wipe his face and squeeze water on his lips, but there had been no flicker of life. She knew he wasn't dead, but how alive he was remained to be seen.

At what passed for a door to the hut she stopped and looped Bounder's reins over a post. With her light she did a cursory inspection of the interior. Snakes were always a concern, but her search turned up nothing suspicious.

Nor did it turn up any bang-up news. There was nothing in sight that was going to make her job of caring for the man much easier. There was a bed, bush style, in the corner, which she hadn't remembered. Some enterprising rider had sunk four metal pipes deep into the ground and added two side rails over which he had crisscrossed strips of greenhide. As the hide had dried and tightened it had made a firm foundation for a bushie's swag. She guessed the rider had been a peculiarly fastidious man who didn't like snakes crawling under the covers to sleep with him. A man after her own heart.

There was a fireplace in one corner—or something a generous soul might call a fireplace—with a cast iron Dutch oven beside it and a blackened billy. And there were a storage cabinet and a three-legged table in the other. The floor was slick and hard, made of sand stolen from a termites' nest and sprinkled with water until it was glassy smooth.

Relatives of the white ants who had donated the floor had obviously chewed through what wood there was in the walls until dust filtered through a multitude of cracks. Each time there was an especially good gust of wind, the iron sheets flapped and clanged.

By no stretch of the imagination was this the homestead, but it was better than a campsite, and with luck Mackenzie could keep it warm enough to save the stranger from the misery of freezing, too.

Outside again, she commanded a fatigued Bounder to kneel. She squatted and braced herself under the stranger's shoulder, looping his arm around her neck. Then she leaned forward, pulling him with her. Three good steady pulls and he had been dragged from the horse to a blanket she had spread beside them. She rested before attempting the next part of her task, dragging him, blanket and all, inside the hut.

With much tugging and cursing she got him far enough inside to shield him from the worst of the storm. She knelt beside him and turned him to his back to give him more water, holding his head as she had before. Was the reflex to swallow even weaker now? She tried to remember if he had swallowed with more enthusiasm before. The water drizzled slowly into his mouth until she was sure he would choke; then, gratefully, she watched the muscles in his throat contract.

When he had drunk all he would, she left him while she cared for Bounder. She unsaddled, then hobbled, the horse in a ramshackle paddock with a small lean-to at the side of the hut, a space with little to offer except shelter. But there was some dried up vegetation for Bounder to feed on and a bucket that she half-filled with water from her own supply. She rewarded him with the remainder of her dried apples and left him for the night.

Inside, she stared at the stranger as she stepped around him, debating whether to try to get him on the bed or just to roll out her swag by the fireplace. The swag by the fire won. She was too tired and probably too weak to wrestle him onto the bed, and there was always the possibility he might fall off during the night, anyway.

With practiced hands she unfastened the swag and spread it a comfortable distance from the fireplace. Since she'd planned to be gone from the homestead for most of a week, she had brought extra supplies. Inside the canvas swag cover were a second blanket, insect netting, several changes of clothing and personal items—one of which, soap, was going to be greatly appreciated tomorrow.

The temperature was already dropping, and she knew her next priority was to make a fire. The man's sunburn would be a torment, even if the room was toasty warm. But the lower the temperature dropped, the worse he would feel when—and if—he awoke.

There was a woodpile behind the hut. She scanned it with her light before she picked carefully through the scrub that would keep them warm that night. Inside again, she started the fire easily and with relief watched smoke move reassuringly up the heap of stone and pipe that served as a chimney. Lighting the fire was taking a chance. A random spark could ignite what was left of the fiberboard walls, but there were a dozen easy exits. Any wall or portion thereof could be knocked out with only a moment's effort. Besides, she knew just how to make a fire that wouldn't rage or smoke. A bushman's fire.

Since the fire would attract moths or worse, she hung her netting over the doorway before she began the task of moving the stranger toward the fire. By the time she had dragged him to the swag, every muscle in her body felt deflated. She was disgustingly female and helpless. Never mind that she *had* moved him, a feat many men wouldn't have contemplated. She had done it, but at a cost. Trembling and weak-kneed, she was only glad that none of the station hands were there to witness her collapse to the floor in exhaustion.

Lying beside the stranger, she considered her next duties. She had discovered him and gotten him to shelter. She had given him enough water to keep him alive, and she had started a fire to keep him warm. There were still food and caring for his burns to attend to.

She tried to imagine rising to do either. She was too exhausted to be hungry herself. She had to search her memory to calculate when she had last eaten. Twelve hours had passed, or maybe more. She wasn't really certain, and she was too tired to lift her wrist to check her watch. If she had been alone she would have slept a little, then rummaged through her tucker bag and eaten a chunk of damper and a handful of dried beef. There might even be raisins to round it out. She couldn't remember.

But the stranger couldn't chew damper, that mainstay of bush cooking. Mackenzie made hers from self-rising flour, but even so, it grew hard as a rock after a day or two in the dry air. Good for the teeth, maybe, but not good for a man who lacked the strength to chew.

He needed broth. Thin, protein-laden broth like Edwina Wallace, the homestead housekeeper, made when someone was sick. Broth made from beef and vegetables and fed to him drop by drop the way she had fed him the water.

Mackenzie almost convinced herself that food wasn't important. Dehydration was the real problem in a case like this, wasn't it? If she could keep him filled with water, he had a chance at recovery. Soup was...

Necessary.

She dragged herself upright again and went to the fireplace. The Dutch oven was dusty, but the last cook who had used it had been conscientious enough to clean it and wipe it with fat to keep it from rusting. She used some of their precious water supply to give it a cursory wash, then set the oven just inside the fireplace to warm. In the meantime she cleaned the billy, poured water inside it and strung it over a horizontal rod across the fireplace to boil.

The stranger slept on—if his state could be called sleep—as she dragged herself back and forth across the hut. When the coals had burned down, she filled the oven half full of water and simmered a handful of salted beef with a dash of dried onions and some wild greens she had picked in a fit of fancy before the storm began. The storage cabinet had yielded a few nice surprises to top off her own supplies. A tin of tomatoes and another of beets went into the soup, too. The stranger would get the broth, and she would eat the solids. It seemed an equitable arrangement.

The concoction that emerged after some culling and mixing wouldn't have won any culinary prizes, but it smelled passing fair. She left it to simmer a little longer while she contemplated the man lying on her swag. While her back had been turned to him, he had shifted positions. The change was minimal, but definitely a change. One of his arms lay on the dirt floor. His head was at a new, more crooked angle. She was glad he had moved. Thoughts of spinal cord injuries and paralysis had plagued her. But what could she have done? Left him to the dust and the dingoes while she traveled to the homestead for a backboard and a stretcher?

She poured a little hot water from the billy in the fireplace into the billy she always carried with her and mixed it with cooler water until it was a pleasant temperature. Then she took a towel from her swag and dunked half of it in the water to clean the stranger's face.

"You're giving me a scare," she murmured as she began to gently wash his forehead. "I don't want to lose you now. I reckon I'll be miffed if this has all been a waste of time."

The firelight cast a golden glow into a room that needed even more to give it the appearance of comfort. But the stranger's face was illuminated clearly enough for her to see his eyelids twitch as she spoke to him.

Encouraged, she continued. "How long were you out there?" She wrung out the towel and started on his cheeks. "A day? Two?" As she wiped, she realized the stubble coming to life under her towel was the equivalent of several days' growth of beard—maybe four, at most, if he was one of those men who didn't have to shave often.

"Where in the bloody hell did you come from?" she asked.

That question was the most interesting, the one she'd contemplated as she'd stumbled through the dust storm. She didn't know every stockman in the Territory. Distances were so vast and populations so small that strangers could live on neighboring cattle runs and never see each others' faces.

Additionally, there was a steady parade of men through the outback. Station hands and stockmen often came and went. It was a lonely life, and those who found it appealing were usually wanderers at heart. They changed locations like they changed horses, with a brief stab of sentiment that was soon blotted out by their thirst for something new. The days when hundreds of swagmen, drovers and stockmen went from Brisbane to Perth working a season or two before they moved on were nearly finished. But there were remnants of those men left.

This man could be one of them.

Mackenzie studied the stranger's face. He was utterly unfamiliar. She wrung the cloth again and started on his chin. Even sunburned, slack and unshaven, the face was magnificent, male and proud and strong. She had never seen him before, but there was something that tugged at her when she looked at him. Not just his good looks, not just his easily studied anatomy, not just the things that any woman would be drawn to. Something more. Something that nibbled at the edges of her mind.

"What kind of man loses his clothes in the middle of a dust storm? Are you bats, maybe? Did someone strip you and leave you out there to die?"

His eyelids twitched again. She realized she was holding a naked man in her arms in a deserted hut two days' ride from what passed for civilization. Strangely, she hadn't yet thought about dressing him. Nothing of hers would fit, of course, but there was a pile of rags in the storage cabinet. It was conceivable she could put an outfit together out of it.

She tried to imagine ill-fitting clothes chafing his sunburn. She tried to imagine him coming to without any clothes. One image was as bad as the other.

"Can't think which you'd prefer," she said. "But I'd prefer to do as little as possible." She washed his neck, feeling for his pulse as she did. It seemed stronger, although she couldn't imagine why. Perhaps from the water she'd given him, perhaps because the temperature was cooler.

She lowered his head to the floor and gave his chest and arms a quick wash, although the water was turning gritty and rust-colored. There was more of him that needed washing, too. She peered at the juncture of his thighs with interest. Now wouldn't it be nice if the stranger woke up while she was cleaning his privates? Hard to explain, that.

And hard to explain if they were the only part of him she *didn't* clean. Surely he'd notice if the rest of him was clean as fresh air and one part of him an inch thick in bull dust. Wouldn't she look the shy young miss then?

She compromised and left him dust-covered from the waist down.

When it was obvious she had done all she could with his torso, she gently blotted him dry with the other end of the towel and left him to the flickering light of the fire.

The soup was bubbling merrily when she removed the top of the Dutch oven with a stick. She scooped out a cupful of broth with her tin cup and set it to one side to cool. Her mouth began to water, and she gave in to the temptation to taste her creation. Her eyes closed in bliss after the fourth taste. Edwina would have been proud.

"You're a lucky man," she said as she approached the stranger with his dinner. "I wouldn't share this with just anybody."

She propped his head on her lap in the position that was beginning to feel normal. Had his eyelids flickered again? She decided to keep talking, although she felt ridiculous. She took a spoonful of broth and guided it to his lips. Then, drop by drop, she let it dribble into his mouth.

"My name's Mackenzie Conroy," she said, "though everybody calls me Mac. I don't make a habit of rescuing strangers, usually leave them for the eagles to carry off, but you were a bit too fetching for that. Besides, I hate to see a man buried slowly in dust. Reckon it wouldn't be a pretty sight if I ever rode that way again."

Spurred on as he swallowed, she continued. "You're on Waluwara Station, though maybe you know that already. Afraid you're out where the crows fly backward now. It's not a big run, one of the smaller around here, with some of the worst and the best land. This is just about desert country you wandered into. Nothing much to see. If you were out for a holiday, you came to the wrong end of the run."

He was swallowing regularly, and his eyelids were flickering, as if his unopened eyes were trying to follow sound.

"Let's see, what else do you want to know? More about me? Nothing much to tell there. I'm twenty-four, and I've lived here most of my life. My uncle manages Waluwara. Someone in our family has for almost a hundred years. The owner's a Brit, lives in Hong Kong now, though, a man name of Sebastian St. Carroll. When his father was alive he used to come out from London and see the place sometimes to determine what was needed and how he could make improvements. But not old Sebastian. He just takes whatever's left over at the end of the year, if anything is, and disposes of it. The place is falling apart around us."

She realized that the broth was half gone. "Good on ya," she said. "You can still tuck into soup, can't you? At this rate you'll be able to walk back to the homestead under your own steam."

She fell silent as she fed him the remainder and wondered if she should try for a second cup. She decided against it. Better to wait and be sure he tolerated this cup, first. From the looks of him, he wasn't near to starving.

Unrepentant, her gaze flicked over him again. No, he wasn't going to starve, although there wasn't anything padding his frame that could be called fat. He was trim. No beer belly on this bloke. His body was sheathed in muscle, not the kind city men got in gyms, but the kind that came from living an active, outdoor life.

Except that if that were true, he would also be brown from the outback sun, not burned to a crisp.

"You're an odd one, that you are. But I reckon I don't have anything to worry about from you. Even if you're a raving loony, you won't have the strength to do anything to me. Besides, you'll need me to get you back to civilization, if you can call the homestead anything like civilization."

He grimaced in response to her voice and seemed to be trying to open his eyes. She held her breath and watched the struggle. Then, as if to save his strength for future battles, he relaxed into complete unconsciousness once more.

"Well, perhaps it's better you stay down for a while," she said. "Maybe you won't feel so crook when you finally come to. I wouldn't want to wake up either if I had a burn like yours."

She eased him back to the swag, padding the ground beneath his head with a wool jumper. Then she covered him loosely with a blanket.

The rest of her chores loomed in front of her. Eat. Bank the fire for the night. Wash. Make a bed for herself with what was left from her swag. Sleep.

Only the last was appealing. She did the others in as cursory a fashion as possible. Tomorrow she would ride to the bore and get enough water for a real wash. But tonight she did her face, hands and teeth and congratulated herself on being even that fastidious. Then, after one last peek at Bounder, she crawled onto the bushman's bed, pulled a blanket around her and fell instantly asleep.

Lights, and colors. Just out of reach. Why?
You must concentrate all your energy. See what happens if you do? Ah, you've always been too impatient, little one. You would go to anything before you would make it come to you. That is never wise.
Motion. Sensation. The sensation of air rushing past him, sensation he had never experienced.
So what if the experience is new? If only the things we were certain of were good, then nothing would be good, because we were created knowing nothing, were we not?
Yearning, a terrible, terrible yearning. Reaching out. For what?
Of all the children, you are the one who always demands more. This is good and bad. You'll never have everything you seek, but in the seeking you'll have more than the others. You don't understand me? I'm afraid, little one, that someday, someday you'll understand too well.
The stranger attempted to reach out, but nothing about him worked as it should. He cried out and nobody answered. After his effort, warmth seemed to merge with his very being. Warmth? Was that what this sensation was called? Sensation? Was that the word for the fire spreading throughout him?
He cried out again, and again no one answered.
Lights. And colors. Just out of reach.
Why?

Chapter 3

Mackenzie awoke at dawn. She had intended to be up through the night checking on her guest, but the storm and the rescue had robbed all her reservoirs of strength. Trained to sleep with one ear cocked when she was in the bush, she had slept, instead, like a person with no senses. The hut could have burned down around her, the wind could have sent it spinning to California, and she would never have awakened.

With the first light, however, she pried open her eyelids to get her bearings. If possible the hut looked worse than it had the night before: dust and rust and welcoming gaps in the walls and roof for bush flies and snakes.

"Well, we're not in San Diego." She shut her eyes again. "The devil's own job."

There was a sound from the floor. She sat up. Was the stranger awake, too? Or, Lord help her, was he dead and the sound nothing more than her imagination?

"You awake, stranger?" she asked. Something, superstitions about ghosts, perhaps, or maybe just good sense about the living, kept her from leaping to his side.

She heard the noise again. It was a rustling, nothing more. She was leaning over the side of the bed before she had time to think. The sound was familiar. Curling and twisting along the hearth was the long brown body of a mulga snake. She had the feeling that the snake was the squatter and she and the stranger were his unwelcome visitors—or breakfast.

Without making a sound she reached for her rifle, gauging how safely she could shoot in an iron box without killing herself or the stranger. The stranger was in the greater danger from a ricocheting bullet, since he and the snake were at eye level. But he was also in the most danger from the snake, and the snake *was* dangerous, perhaps not as deadly as the taipan, Australia's reigning champ, but dangerous enough to kill a man in the bush if he couldn't get help quickly.

And this man couldn't.

She aimed and gauged where the bullet would go once it severed the snake's head from its body. The news wasn't good, and as the snake slithered closer to the stranger, it didn't get better. She moved, silently, slowly, to improve her angle.

The snake moved, too.

Mackenzie aimed and asked herself if she were the stranger, would she rather die quickly from a misfire or slowly from snake venom. He had a better chance with the bullet. It might go straight through the snake, then continue to plow through the iron wall behind it. It might plow into some forgiving part of his body. Or it might plow into a vital organ. She considered the choices, and they weren't to her liking.

She raised the rifle and stared through the sight, waiting and praying that the snake would move away, just far enough away to make the shot a clean one.

Before her narrowed eyes the stranger sat up. Her aim faltered. The bloke had no timing, that was a cert. Dead to the world for the better part of a day and a night, and now he was sitting up like it was time to boil the billy and have his morning tea.

"Stay right where you are," she said.

Both the man and the snake froze, as if Mackenzie had completely taken them by surprise.

"I'm going to shoot. When I shout, duck and cover your head."

As if he hadn't heard her, the man leaned forward, stretching his hand toward the mulga snake and completely blocking Mackenzie's line of sight. He began to croon. The snake watched as he waved his arm slowly back and forth.

Mackenzie jumped to the floor and skirted them both. For a moment she had a chance at a clear shot; then the stranger moved his arm again, turning his back to her. The snake didn't move at all.

"Are you trying to die?" She continued her attempt to aim but knew how slim her chances were of getting a shot off now. Not until after the stranger had been struck, that was.

The hut filled with a strange music. She didn't understand the words the stranger was crooning, and the notes were not from any scale she had learned during two hateful years of piano lessons. But the snake seemed fascinated. It rose as if to strike, but instead it began to dance. Slowly, back and forth, it became a drab brown ballerina swaying to the stranger's music.

He moved his hand to the right; the snake moved right, too. Left and the snake gracefully followed. The stranger stretched forward, and the snake leaned to meet him. As Mackenzie watched in horror, they met in midair, brushing cheek to fang before they parted.

The music stopped, and the snake dropped to the ground. Then, almost as if it hated to take its leave, it slowly coiled and stretched its way across the floor and left by a gap near the fireplace.

Mackenzie didn't realize she had collapsed beside the stranger until he turned to survey her. Even in the state of near emergency, her gaze flicked down. He was still covered with the blanket to his waist.

"Did it strike?" she asked.

He stared at her. His expression was strained, his eyes wild. "Strike?"

"Are you hurt? Did it sink its fangs into you? Did it bloody well give you the kiss of death?"

He continued to stare. "Death from a kiss?"

"Did the snake bite you?" she asked, as if asking a child. She stretched out her hand, much as he had stretched his to the snake, and touched his cheek. He flinched, but his skin was unmarred except by sunburn. "I guess not," she said, when he didn't answer. "You're a right lucky bloke, you know."

"Am I?" His voice was taut, the deepest string on a bass fiddle just before it snapped.

"Where're you from? India? A snake charmer, maybe? That blooming snake's related to a cobra, you know!"

He didn't answer. He just continued to stare.

"I know I'm not much to look at about now," she said. "But the way you're staring has me worried. I'm not exactly a no-hoper, am I?"

"No-hoper?"

"Ugly. Stupid."

"Ugly?"

"Lord, you're the no-hoper. I reckon the sun boiled your brain yesterday."

For the first time since he had looked at her, his gaze flicked away. He took in the hut. Mackenzie was fascinated. She had the most peculiar feeling that in those few seconds he had learned everything about his surroundings.

When he looked back at her, his expression was still strained and his eyes were even wilder. "Tell me about... yesterday."

She did. In as few sentences as possible. She wanted answers from him.

"So that's how I found you," she concluded, "and that's where you were. Now it's your turn. Who are you, and what were you doing out there?"

"You say I was facedown... in a storm?"

"Dust storm." She could see he couldn't comprehend what that meant. "The ground meets the sky," she said. "Blows from hell to heaven and back again. You were somewhere in between."

"And this place we're in?"

"Waluwara. A cattle station." She could see no glimmer of recognition in his eyes. "We raise cattle. Cows, understand? We cart them off to market, where they're ground up for your American hamburgers. At least, that's where most of them go."

"Ground up?"

"We kill them first, Yank."

He didn't seem to like that idea. "Yank?"

"Yeah. You are a Yank, aren't you? You're not from here, that's a dead bird."

"Not from Waluwara?"

"Not from Australia."

"Australia?"

She was getting tired of the exchange. He was absolutely breathtaking to look at, but not much to talk to. A little confusion was understandable. He had lost a day, maybe more, of his life. But every word she said seemed to be new to him.

"Australia is a continent, the only one that's a whole country by itself. Unless you just dropped out of the sky, then you arrived here by plane or boat with a passport and a visa. And you came from somewhere. America, I'm betting."

"Why do you think so?"

"Because of your accent."

He appeared to consider that.

"Not that it's like any I've heard, exactly," she added.

"No?"

"Haven't ever heard of a Yank who asked so many questions."

He looked around the hut again. "Have you ever heard of one who didn't have any answers?"

"*Never* heard of that."

He rose, then seemed surprised that he'd done so. Mackenzie's eyes widened. He was standing in front of her, as naked as a newborn babe, and he didn't even seem to notice. As she stared, he hobbled slowly to the doorway to gaze out past the insect netting.

One part of Mackenzie's brain worked fine; the other ground to a halt when he stood. On the ground, unconscious, he had been extraordinary, a perfectly splendid example of what the human male could hope to attain with a few more centuries of good nutrition and skillful blending of genes.

Standing, moving, he was all the things she had never realized she'd wasted a thought on. She felt like a baby with its first lolly. She wasn't really sure what to do with this prize, but she wasn't about to give it back.

The working side of her brain noted the way he tested the ground with the soles of his feet. How his face contorted, in pain, or puzzlement, at the sensation. Without another thought she leaped to her feet and grabbed his blanket. Then she joined him at the door, averting her gaze.

"You forgot this!"

"What?"

She thrust it closer to him. "You're not wearing clothes."

The blanket remained in her hands for what seemed eternity. Then she felt it tugged from her. After a decent interval she looked at him. He had knotted it at his waist. "Better?" he asked.

"What do you think?"

"Apparently... I don't. At least, not very well."

"I haven't even asked how you feel."

He looked as if he found the question odd. He didn't smile, and the expression in his eyes, the look of a beast backed into a corner, didn't change. "How am I supposed to?"

"I can't answer that. You're the only one who knows."

His mouth twisted into a line. "Then why don't I remember?"

As she watched, he seemed to grow pale beneath his burn. She touched his arm. "Maybe you'd better sit awhile, until you're more clearheaded."

"I don't like it when you touch me."

She jerked her hand away. "Well, I'll try to remember that."

"I like the idea of it," he said. "But when you do..." He seemed to be futilely searching for an explanation.

"Sit down on the bed." She gestured to the blanket where she had slept, careful not to touch him. "Better yet, lie down."

"Something happens," he continued, as if she hadn't interrupted. "It's strange, unpleasant...."

"You don't have to go into blooming detail. I'm not about to throw myself at you!"

"Like something eating at me."

She stared, realizing what he was trying to tell her. "Look, stranger, that's called pain. You were exposed to the sun for a while, most likely. You've got a bad sunburn. Nothing that won't go away in a few days. But you'll be uncomfortable till then. Especially when anything or anybody touches you."

"Pain." He nodded, but with no apparent satisfaction. "I know that word."

"Apparently not well, you don't."

"Have you felt it, too?"

"Too right. Every living person's felt pain. I reckon getting born's about as painful as it gets."

"You remember getting born?"

"Of course not. Neither do you."

Something almost like relief crossed his face. "Good. One thing I don't have to try to bring back."

She had the uncomfortable feeling that he was leading toward something she didn't want to hear. She watched him cross the room and take a seat on the bed as she had suggested. He did look pale. And shaken.

"Don't collapse on me again," she warned. "I really don't want to drag you anywhere else. Just take it easy until you're feeling a hundred percent. Then we can worry about giving you some exercise, like a trip back to the homestead."

He nodded. As she watched he fingered the blanket, as if identifying all its characteristics with his fingertips. Why, she wondered, did everything seem so new to him?

"You never did say who you were and why you were out in the desert, without provisions . . . or clothes."

"I never said, because I don't know."

There it was. The thing she had least wanted to hear. "You don't know, or you don't want to say?"

"Why wouldn't I want to say?"

"Why wouldn't you know?" She started toward him, her arms folded across her chest. "I've heard of amnesia. Even here in the back of beyond we watch telly. Had a satellite dish at the homestead until it went crook. But we still get videos. I've seen stories about people who can't remember who they are. I've even met some. But the ones I've met remembered. They just didn't want to tell about it, because if they did, they were afraid the law might remember, too."

"The law?"

"What are you running from, bushranger? *Who* are you running from? You reckon I haven't heard enough stories to make yours look silly? You think the Territory's overflowing with men who left steady jobs and happy families to come out here and swat flies? Some did, too right, but there's lots of men with stories they don't want to tell. Only they don't pretend they can't remember! You can tell me you don't want to talk about who you are, but don't pretend you can't remember."

"Then there's nothing to tell."

She stood beside him. She didn't know why, but she wanted to hear him admit the truth. "If you're in trouble, maybe I can help. My uncle is the station boss. He won't care where you've come from or what you've done. He gives a fresh chance to every man who asks. But you'll have to be fair with him. If you're in trouble, you'll have to tell him, so he'll be looking out for you."

"I am in trouble."

She relaxed a little. "That's more like it."

He looked up from the blanket and narrowed his eyes as he stared at her. "I can't remember who I am. If that's not trouble, I don't remember what the word means."

She stared back and saw he was telling the truth, or doing a perfect imitation. Her eyes closed against her will, and she sank to the bed beside him. "Bloody hell."

"You mentioned hell before. I'm not sure it sounds like a place I want to see."

"Lots of people would say you're there right now."

His voice grew even tighter. "I think I may have been somewhere worse."

"Where?"

He shrugged, then winced, as if the movement had reminded him of his sunburn.

She abandoned questions about his past. The present was difficult enough. "I don't have anything to really treat your burn with. But some cool water will help temporarily. If you feel well enough, you can bathe while I'm gone."

"While you're gone?"

"I'm going to ride out to the bore...." She saw a lack of comprehension on his face. "There's water under the ground if you bore deep enough to find it. That's what a bore is. There's one not too far from here. I want to get there and back before the wind starts to blow again."

"Another storm?"

"Same one. Just taking a smoko now, I'd bet."

"Smoko?"

"Maybe you did drop out of the sky. Smoko's a rest. A break. Time for tea and a smoke." She shook her head in frustration. "Cigarette." She pantomimed smoking for him.

"They're not good for you."

"Tell that to the men on this run." She leaned over to search the floor for her boots. "I don't smoke. Makes me crook." She raised her head, then shook it in frustration. "Sick. Crook is sick, Yank."

"Crook." There was nothing relaxed or companionable about the smile that twisted his face. "Like the man lying facedown in a dust storm in the middle of nowhere was crook?"

"Just like that." She pulled on her socks, then her elastic-sided boots. "Listen, I don't know what you and that snake were doing. I don't even care to know. But we've got more snakes than people in Australia, and not many of them should be played with. Some will kill you before you can scream for help. Some take a little longer. Some get you one cell at a time. See a snake and kill it.''

She looked around. "There." She pointed to a board standing against a wall, perhaps to hold it up. "Use that and beat any snake you see over the head until it doesn't wiggle anymore. Think you can do that?''

"No."

"Then hope you really are a snake charmer."

He didn't respond.

"See that pot over there?" She pointed to the fireplace. "We call that a billy. There's water in it for washing, but first drink as much as you can. I'll leave you some bread— we call it damper when we make it out in the open. And raisins. If the damper's too hard for you to chew, soak it first. I'd boil the billy for tea, but I don't want to take the time until I get back, and I don't want you fooling with the fire. Reckon I'd like to find the hut standing."

She stood. He still looked pale, and for a moment she reconsidered. Would he wander off while she was gone? Or would she come back and find him unconscious again? Unfortunately, the matter was out of her hands. She didn't have enough water to last two people and a horse another day. She had to get to the bore.

"After you wash, look through the clothes in there." She gestured to the cabinet. "There should be something you can wear until we get to the homestead."

"How far is the . . . homestead?"

"Two days ride under good conditions. But we can't leave until the storm's over. And it may blow another day or two."

"Then we'll be staying here?"

"We'll have to."

"Does the homestead look like this?"

"No." She examined him for signs of disorientation and found none. He was naked, sunburned and confused about his own identity. But discounting those problems, he seemed well enough. Perhaps it really was safe to leave him for a little while. "I don't suppose you remember a name, do you?"

"Whose name?"

"Your own, preferably."

He squinted, staring at nothing. She could swear he was searching for something, some hint, some promise within himself. She held her breath as he did.

"I don't remember any names. Except Mackenzie."

"At least you recall the last half hour or so. That's a start." She took the damper and raisins out of her bag and put them on her tin plate. Then she pulled out a cup to leave for him, too. She took the supplies to the storage cabinet and set them on top.

"Just eat a bit, see how you do, then eat a bit more. Water's more important than food. Don't forget to drink your fill before you use what's left to wash." She considered him for one last moment before she turned away. "And it's strictly bush dunny out here, if you feel the urge."

"Urge?"

"To relieve yourself. Just go out away from the hut. Not far enough to get lost," she added. "Scoop out a hole. Bush dunny."

"Bush dunny."

"No worries while I'm gone. We'll be right enough here until I can get you to the homestead. Just don't overdo. Rest for the ride home."

Mackenzie gathered what she needed, breaking off a piece of damper for breakfast to eat along the way. She knew the stranger was watching her. He had a way of looking straight through everything in his line of vision, which most people would find unnerving. But she had been raised by men who were as unflinching as the outback wind. She figured that this one was just trying to piece his world back together.

She stood and strode to the door. "If you want my help, be here when I get back. If you're not here, I'm not going to look for you."

"Tell me somewhere I could go."

She flashed him a comforting smile and waited for one in return. When it was clear he wouldn't, or couldn't, respond, she disappeared into the daylight.

The stranger wasn't sure what was most confusing. There were pressures inside him, building in ways he didn't understand. There was the pain...yes, that was what the woman had called it, pain that seemed to define him somehow. *He* stopped where the pain began.

He held out his hand and examined it. Then he touched himself as an experiment. The pain increased, but that was certainly where *he* ended. Why did that seem strange to him? The pain seemed to wrap him, somehow, to set him apart from the air around him. That much he had figured out.

He understood skin, only not quite this way. And that was where the confusion lay. There was so much he didn't understand, the least of which was his own identity. He wasn't even sure he really understood "identity."

Panic filled him, but he succeeded in pushing it away. He attempted to take stock of what he did understand. He was in a place called Australia, and there was a smaller place there called Waluwara. He was in Waluwara, too. And in this Waluwara was an even smaller place, a structure of some sort, the most primitive of structures, if he were to be exact.

In this structure were four poles with something incredibly foul strung across them. And he was sitting on it.

He grimaced and stepped to the floor, examining what Mackenzie had called the bed. He had an instant impression of an animal dying. He touched the hide strips and recognized them for what they were. Disgust and dismay coursed through him.

You are never to cause harm to another. You will have that desire, sometimes. We have not grown beyond that, little one. But you must never harm another living entity.

His dismay increased. The voice was the same one he had heard in his dreams. Was it this thing that Mackenzie had called memory? And if it was, why didn't it relieve him?

Why did it cause a feeling of dread? Of desperation? Why, when he heard the voice, did he want to reach for something that wasn't in the hut? Perhaps something that wasn't in Waluwara, or even Australia?

He roamed the room looking for more answers. He had never been here before. Of this he was sure. He was almost as sure that he had never been anywhere like it.

The pressures inside him continued to build. He stopped at the cabinet and considered the food Mackenzie had left for him. Food was familiar, and he knew what to do with it. He lifted the damper to his mouth and bit off a piece.

Sensations exploded through every cell of his body. Surely he had never eaten anything this good before, or why, despite everything else, would he suddenly want to weep with joy? He chewed slowly, so the mouthful would last as long as possible. Reluctantly he bit off a second piece, sure that it couldn't be as good as the first. But it was. Every bit as good. And as if to double his pleasure, the damper seemed to subdue some of the pressure that had been building inside him.

He finished the whole piece, slowly, blissfully. When it was gone he pressed his fingers to the plate to pick up every crumb. Then he started on the raisins and understood what bliss really was.

Some of the feeling inside him, the pressure, was gone now. Another sort remained. He remembered Mackenzie's words about a bush dunny. He moved to the door, dragging the blanket she had insisted he wrap around him, and stood looking outside.

The sunlight caused his eyes pain. Instinctively he raised his hand to shade them. The world he saw was a barren wasteland. Nothing more than tall ripples of earth disturbed the horizon for an unknown distance.

Just as surely as he knew that he had never been inside the hut before, he knew that he had never lived in this place before. Never even seen it, at least not until just before he had been found. Something—this thing Mackenzie called a memory, perhaps?—pricked at him. Soft swirls of earth rose and fell to the ground as gusts of wind blew. But he remembered how this world had looked when the wind hadn't been so hesitant. Hell meets heaven, Mackenzie had described it. He thought he understood now what she had meant.

He had walked through the dust-bearing wind, and he had learned that it was best to walk with it to his back. But the walking had only taken him in circles because the wind had blown in spinning gusts.

And he had fallen.

You won't always succeed, little one. Sometimes you will fall, and you'll have to raise yourself high to try again. You're one of those unfortunate who doesn't want to fall, but one of the fortunate who will raise himself higher each time he does.

He put his hands over his ears, but the voice was still audible inside his head. He couldn't stop the soft, gurgling syllables, softer and more fluid than anything Mackenzie had said to him. Yet he understood these memory words as he had understood hers.

When the voice stopped he shut his eyes for a moment, trying to recover. When the voice didn't return he ventured outside. The air was warm against his skin, not a pleasant sensation. He looked above him at the sun and knew that today its rays were to be avoided.

Not terribly far from the hut he taught himself the meaning of a bush dunny, and one more pressure was relieved.

Inside again, he poured water from the billy and drank his fill. Then he prepared to wash. Without the blanket he examined himself. His body was both familiar and unfamiliar. What he could see was not unexpected. But there was the feeling that there was more—or less—to him than there had once been.

Illusion and reality? Body and spirit? Concepts flitted through his head, only to be discarded. Perhaps he was nothing more than a man without his memory, a man who would not be whole until he could remember that crucial thing called his identity.

He dipped his fingers into the billy and found there was little water left. He touched himself and watched the water that had clung to his fingers drizzle over his skin. It left a cool, pleasant feeling wherever it trailed. And after it found a home and remained there for a while, it turned to vapor and merged with the air.

The world he had awakened to was not one he knew. The body he inhabited was not entirely familiar. But there were strange, maybe even wonderful things here. Food and water and the supremely pleasant experience of satisfying bodily needs.

Calmer now, he thought of the woman. Mackenzie. He considered her for a moment. She was not familiar; yet she was. Perhaps it was only that he had known other women who had similar bodies or faces. She called him a stranger, but she didn't feel like a stranger to him.

Was she beautiful? The word gave him pause. He understood its meaning, but not how to define it for himself. He supposed that if there were other women in Australia they would share characteristics with this one. Arms, legs, breasts, hips.

But she was more than a combination of body parts. Perhaps other women had hair the color of the sun now inching its way above the horizon, hair a bright blaze of fire against pale, lightly freckled skin. Eyes the warm brown of the earth. Lips that smiled easily. Perhaps other women had these, too, along with the soft curves of breast and hip and a small waist cinched in the same hide that laced the bed.

He frowned at that. Did she know where that hide came from? If so, there was something he didn't understand. How could she endure it? Just one more thing he didn't understand among many.

He envisioned Mackenzie, but not as she had last appeared to him. She was sitting astride an animal . . . a horse, his vocabulary told him. She was riding toward the bore. Her long hair escaped the…braid—yes, that was a name for woven hair—and flew behind her as she rode, flowing against the wind like the horse's tail. She sat on the horse's back as easily as he had sat upon the bed. She enjoyed the ride, found pleasure in it.

The vision halted abruptly. He wondered why he couldn't see her anymore. He had found pleasure in the picture. *She* was pleasurable to look at, perhaps even pleasurable to be near. The pleasure seemed new to him.

There are heights you won't reach for aeons, experiences you won't know until you've convinced yourself they don't exist. Just when you think there is little more that you can learn, you will learn how little you really knew.

The gurgling voice—the memory—no longer disconcerted him as much. Strangely, now he found a certain comfort in its cadences. He wondered what else would come to him. And when.

In the meantime, he would see what he could discover without his memory. Perhaps, as the voice had reminded him, there was more to learn than he had ever imagined.

He had a last, fleeting vision of Mackenzie. Then he lay down on the swag and covered himself. In a moment, completely exhausted, he gave himself to dreams.

Chapter 4

Mackenzie took longer to reach the bore than she had expected. She hadn't been on this end of the run for some time, and distances were always farther than they seemed in desert country. But even though she had planned for that, the sun was too high when she finally sighted the telltale clump of trees.

One of her reasons for venturing to this end of the station had been to check the bores dotting the border, to see if they had been pugged up with mud by thirsty stock or silted in by dust storms. The job would have been a simple one by air, but although Waluwara owned two single-engine planes, both needed extensive—and *expensive*—repair. There was so little cash budgeted for such extravagance, it was unlikely either would fly again.

Mackenzie cursed Sebastian St. Carroll as she rode toward the bore. Waluwara was foundering badly because St. Carroll refused to commit funds for upkeep.

There was only one reason Waluwara continued to exist, and that was Clint Conroy. Despite offers from prospering stations, offers of salaries three times his present one and funds enough to run a station properly, the boss had stayed on at Waluwara. There had been a Conroy managing Waluwara for one hundred years. The St. Carrolls and others like them, others with no roots in Australia's soil, had always maintained control of Waluwara's leases, but the Conroys had lived here, died here, poured their sweat and blood into the land and alternately watched it prosper or shrivel.

There was another loyalty keeping Clint Conroy at Waluwara. There was an Aboriginal village on the station, one as old as time, yet modernized and progressive by all standards. Although a large percentage of Territory land was owned outright by the Aborigines, this tract was not. Officially it was part of Waluwara, although in every way that mattered it was part of the Dreamtime, part of the distant past and future of the country.

Clint Conroy knew that if he left as station manager, the next manager might not have the same feeling for the station's native people that he did. Paternalism or worse might creep into a system that was now based entirely on mutual respect. The boss's feelings ran too deeply to permit this. His friendships were too strong, his esteem for the village residents too great.

Clint Conroy would stay at Waluwara until drought and lack of funds turned what had once been a thriving cattle station into a ruin.

At the trees, Mackenzie dismounted and left Bounder to drink and graze. The bore was an old one, the first to have been tried on the property. There had been hopes that an artesian basin would be found under the earth here, but even though a steady supply of water had flowed from this spot for decades, the water supply was a small one.

With the help of a windmill pump, water flowed into a large earth tank facing north and south, as was customary to avoid the worst sunshine. It was narrow and long, and bauhinia trees had been planted along its border to deter evaporation. Encouraged by occasional overflow, vegetation covered the ground surrounding it.

Mackenzie wished the stranger could have come with her to this spot. The bore was a tiny oasis in country that badly needed one. Cool and green, it was a favorite resting place for birds; as she had approached, a flock of pink galahs had taken to the skies in a show of outback flash.

She wondered if the stranger had seen any birds in the States to rival the galahs. She wondered if she was right to even assume the United States was his home.

What did she really know about the stranger? Nothing. Abso-bloody-lutely nothing. He was handsome, gorgeously constructed, and he could express himself well enough when he understood what he was expected to say. He had been found in a dust storm, but seemed to have no knowledge of Australia or why he was there, and no memories of his past.

And he could charm snakes. She wondered if she had imagined the scene with the mulga snake. She had been distraught, worried about whether to shoot or not, then, once having decided to, busy trying to take aim. Had he really charmed the snake, mesmerized it with music and hand movements, or had she just been too upset to see the obvious? Perhaps the snake, its progress blocked, had simply chosen retreat. If so, the stranger wasn't a snake charmer. He was simply bloody lucky.

But what did any of that add up to? Snake charmer or not, the man said he didn't even know his name. She couldn't imagine forgetting hers. It was entwined with her sense of self, as much a part of her as her hair or her eyes. How could he forget who he was? Had he suffered a blow to the head? She'd made a cursory inspection for injuries as she'd washed him last night. She had felt no bumps, seen no bruises. Had the sun baked away his memories? When he had recovered from the physical strain of his ordeal, would his memory return?

She wondered if the memories would include a woman. Doubtless, unless he was one of those loners who chose to go beyond the black stump just to avoid entanglements. There were men like that at the station, men who liked Waluwara precisely because it offered no refinements, including contact with the world. Here some of the old-time pleasures could still be found, droving and taking to the bush for weeks at a time, riding boundary fences and counting calves on horseback.

Raising cattle might be a job for computers, high tech communication equipment and helicopters in this age, but not at Waluwara. Perhaps the stranger had heard just that. Perhaps he had come to get away from someone. Perhaps even a woman.

What kind of woman would he prefer?

The question took her completely by surprise. She began to fill her iron water canteens while Bounder grazed. What did it matter what kind of woman the stranger preferred? Once they arrived at the homestead, she would probably never see him again. He was only briefly passing through her life.

But even if she saw him every day for the next ten years, what would it matter? She lived her life by three simple rules. Stay free. Stay free. And stay free. As surely as a nun chose celibacy in order to serve God, she, Mackenzie Conroy, had chosen it to serve her own god. Freedom.

Nothing and no one would ever tie her down. She was the last of a dying breed, a pioneer, an explorer. She might be tenuously tied to a tract of land called Waluwara. She might be tied by respect and affection to the people who lived on that tract. But those ties only allowed her the greatest freedom a man or woman could know. The broad, endless plains. The thrill of oneness with a land that would never be tamed. The chance to live close to nature and far from civilization. Nothing and no one would ever interfere with her desire for those things. Living as she did was a need so basic that she would die if it was ever taken from her.

When she had fastened the canteens to Bounder's saddle, she took down her billy and filled it with water to wash. She stripped to nothing and scrubbed every inch of herself with the herbal soap that was one of her few feminine weaknesses. Several billyfuls later she had washed her hair, too. Properly rinsed, it fell below her shoulder blades, but even as she combed the tangles from it, it dried to springy tendrils in the heat.

Arrayed in clean clothes, she washed the ones she had just removed and laid them on the ground. By the time she collected them in a few minutes, she knew they would be dry.

The wind was building again. She watched dust swirling in the direction she had come from. Bounder seemed to sense it, too, edging closer to her in warning.

"I know, mate. We'd better go back. Looks like we're in for an afternoon like yesterday's. I just hope we don't find more strangers to rescue."

She slathered all her exposed skin with sunscreen. She had tried and failed as an adolescent to get a real stockman's tan. Now she protected herself at all times, despite the stockmen's teasing that she was afraid her skin would turn to leather and no man would ever want her. Massing her hair under her hat, she jammed it tight on her head. Then she finished her chores and mounted Bounder for the trip to the hut.

The dust was growing thick by the time she arrived. She had stopped to cover herself with a parka in hopes of keeping her clothes cleaner, but she still felt dirty when she dismounted. The bath at the bore had been nothing more than a small luxury. She had known it wasn't going to do her for long.

Inside the hut her eyes adjusted slowly to the relative shade. Her gaze passed around the room before she found the stranger asleep—she hoped—on her swag near the fireplace.

"Stranger?"

There was no answer. She imagined all sorts of things, the snake returning for another song, or a concussion she hadn't diagnosed, before she called to him again.

"Stranger?"

He jerked himself upright and looked around. She noted quickly, and with some anger, that he still wasn't dressed. His eyes were wild, but he sat so still that she was reminded of a statue she had seen in a Sydney museum as a young girl. A naked Greek god of delectable proportions. She had been embarrassed for weeks and secretly, oh, so secretly, thrilled.

He stared at her as if he had never seen her before.

She raised her hands to her hips. "Bloody hell. Don't tell me we're starting all over again."

Some of his panic seemed to ease. Gradually his pupils narrowed and his fists unclenched. Finally his shoulders drooped. "Hello, Mackenzie."

She relaxed. "Good on ya. I was afraid you didn't remember me, either."

He still seemed confused, though not quite as panicked. "I must have fallen . . . asleep."

"By the look of you, that's what I'd say, too. Before you bathed and dressed." She stressed the last word.

"I couldn't bathe. I drank all the water."

"All of it?" She felt a stab of remorse. "I didn't get enough down you yesterday, then. I should have tried harder."

"No. I just liked the way it felt when I drank it."

She frowned. He had such an odd way of expressing himself. "And you ate?"

"It was . . . delicious."

"Now I know for sure you're crook." She squatted and sat back on her heels to rummage through the bags for more tucker. "But since you like the food so well, it's time for more. Ever eaten salted beef?"

When he didn't answer she looked up. "Well?"

"Beef is . . . cow."

"More likely bullock around here. Any cow worth her salt doesn't *get* cooked and salted. She drops calves until she's just about too old and tough for anything except—"

He waved aside the rest of her answer. "Why do you eat animals?"

"Why not? What would we do with them if we didn't?"

He didn't answer.

"Australian beef's some of the best in the world. Not as fat as the beef you Yanks raise. Nothing much for it to get fat on." She found what she was looking for and held out a strip for him. "Here. Take this and see what I mean, though it won't hold up to a steak fresh off the barbie."

"No."

She shrugged and bit off the end. "Your loss."

"It was living once."

"That it was." She chewed thoughtfully. "Reckon it was glad to have had that experience, too. Unless the Dry went too long and finding water was a job. But Waluwara's not a bad place to spend a beast's life. Our mob's pretty wild. We don't muster them with helicopters and frighten them half to death. More than a bullock or two on the run will never even see a human face. If I were a cow, this would be the place I'd want to spend my life. Not on some fancy feedlot in Victoria."

"You like the animals."

"I do that."

"Yet you eat them. Wear their skin on your feet and at your waist."

"They live and they die. Just like we do."

"Nobody eats you, do they?"

He actually seemed to want to know. It was another in a long series of strange questions. "The crows and the dingoes would fight over me if they had the chance. And why would I care? I wouldn't be there to watch."

He grew still, as if he were looking deeply inside himself again. Then he seemed to find a satisfying answer. "I've never eaten meat."

"Afraid that's not entirely true. I fed you broth last night made with some of this beef." She watched his expression change to—what? Horror? Strong distaste? "I won't do it again. But I'm not sorry. You needed something, and that was the best I had to offer."

He looked away from her. "I haven't thanked you for taking care of me."

She shrugged. "I've got the last of the damper here. You can have that for now. I'm getting right low on supplies. I'd go out and hunt a roo—do you know what a roo is?"

He shook his head.

"A kangaroo. I can make a stew that would set your mouth to watering...." She paused. "But I won't. I'll bake us some more damper. And there's a tin or two of tomatoes left in the cabinet. We'll boil the billy and have tomatoes and toast for tea."

He seemed to be getting ready to stand, perhaps to help. She waved him down. "Stranger, you're going to have to wash and dress. This is a bit cozy even for me, and I've been raised by men. You can't stay in here like that."

She turned her back to him and went to the cabinet to sort through the rags she had seen there last night. Then it had been too dark to tell much. Now she could see that the supply was mostly just that, rags to use for chores. But there was a pair of men's undershorts and another pair of much patched denim jeans that might fit. At the bottom of the pile she found a large shirt of dubious origin with one button still in place. At least the clothes looked clean enough.

"These will do. I'll bring water in, and you can pour enough for a good scrub. Then try these on, and if they don't fit, wear them anyway."

She went outside for a canteen that she'd placed in the shade of the hut. She presented it to him with a bar of soap. "Rule of the bush. Do the best you can with the least. That water didn't fall from the sky. At least, not in this millennium."

There was a natural dignity in his answer. "I'll remember."

She thought about the measured, careful way he had answered all her questions and comments. She wouldn't want to be in his situation, yet he was handling it with a certain grace. He wasn't happy; his eyes still searched restlessly for answers. But despite every reason to, he hadn't given in to panic or temper. She tried to push away her admiration. There was already entirely too much to admire about the stranger.

"I had an idea while I was riding back here. You're not going to be ready to ride to the homestead for a while, and the dust's still blowing too hard, anyway. We don't have much tucker, especially if you're going to be finickity about eating meat. What we need is a fire. If I can wait for a break in the storm and send up enough smoke, maybe somebody will see it and come after us. A regular rescue."

"Rescue?"

"My uncle can borrow a plane or have somebody with a helicopter fly over and pick us up. We just have to let him know." She started toward the door. "I'll go out and see what I can find to make smoke with before the dust gets any worse. You bathe and dress. I'll be back."

Since one glance showed that he appeared to be ready to follow her orders, she faced the door. "When I get back, we're going to give you a name. Reckon since I've seen every inch of you, stranger's hardly true, is it?"

"You don't seem like a stranger."

She didn't know what to say to that. Without turning, she waved before stepping into the sunshine.

Mackenzie couldn't believe her luck. Less than two kilometers from the hut, on what had once been a fairly adequate road for the station vehicles, she found the remains of a tire. Farther down the road, but not much, she found another.

Both had obviously been discarded after a good shredding by the corrugated roads, the very reason she was on horseback instead of in a truck or Jeep. Despite Bounder's reluctance to help her transport the tires, she persuaded him, and they returned to the hut to find the stranger dressed and standing in the doorway.

She reined Bounder to a halt in front of him. "Well, I'm glad to see you gave dressing a bash."

Supremely male, he leaned against the doorway and folded his arms. Something vital closed in her throat.

"Is that what I did?" he asked.

She nodded, experimented with breathing and discovered she still remembered how. "You did a right good job of it, too."

"You weren't sure I'd know how, were you?"

She tried to figure out why he was as attractive in clothes as he had been out of them. She decided it was because he was standing. More than that, there was a certain assurance to his stance, an "I belong in this place" signal in the way he cocked his head and gripped the ground with his feet.

"Are you feeling better?"

"Since I'm not sure exactly how I'm supposed to feel, that's hard to answer."

"You're not supposed to hurt. I bet you still do. Especially... dressed."

He did hurt, but the experience was becoming familiar. "Bathing helped."

"I'm sorry I don't have a more permanent solution."

"Those belong on a car, don't they?" He gestured to the tires.

She dismounted and began to untie them. "More likely an ute, what you Americans call a pickup truck. They'll make a right smoky fire, though we aren't going to like the smell. I'll set it away from the hut, but if the wind blows in our direction, we'll get the full effect anyway."

He watched the way her body flowed and contracted as she stooped and stood, bent and straightened. He liked to watch her. Her movements were connected to responses in his own body. He wasn't sure of much, but that much he was sure of already. "If the wind blows?"

"It doesn't always. Sometimes it's so still here you can hear your own heartbeat."

"Let me help."

She waved him away. "Don't need it." She piled the tires on the ground. There was no hurry to get them into position. The way the dust was blowing, smoke wouldn't be any use to them now. "Let's get out of the worst of this and fix something to eat."

She made a stop for more wood for the fireplace, then followed him inside. "I'd make a fire outside, so as not to heat up the hut, but with the wind and the dust, there's no point."

"Can you tell me the date?"

"Um... the eighteenth of August... No, the nineteenth." She shrugged. "Maybe even the twentieth."

"August. Summer. That explains the heat."

"It's not summer here. You're in the southern hemisphere now. It's the end of winter."

"Winter."

"Did it snow where you came from?"

He tried to imagine snow. He had a mental picture of the word. Something cold and white, falling from the sky. But he had no sense that he had ever seen it fall or felt it melt against his skin.

"I don't know," he said. "I don't know where I came from."

Mackenzie dropped an armload of scrub into the fireplace and began to arrange it to make a cooking fire. "Maybe we ought to start somewhere else. Do you have any memories? Anything at all?"

He wondered if telling her about the voice inside his head would make it go away. "I hear words in a different language. A..." He tried to think of an appropriate name. "A man speaking to me."

"A man? A friend? Relative?"

He shrugged. "It's as if he's giving me advice. Only not me as I am now."

"Maybe you at some time in the past. Maybe you're just remembering something from your childhood." Mackenzie struck a match and watched the fire catch. "Does he call you anything?"

"Yes."

She looked up. He tried to form "little one" the way the voice in his memory had, but the sound that emerged was nothing like it. He shook his head in frustration, and his stomach knotted. "That's not right."

"I should hope not." She tried to imitate the sounds he had made. She sounded better when she was gargling Edwina's favorite sore throat remedy.

"Maybe you'd better just give me a name," he said.

She sat back on her heels and watched the fire. "A different language, huh? I wonder what language it is. When you sang to the mulga snake, I didn't recognize a word you said. Maybe we should try names from other countries."

"Hoping I'll recognize one?"

She turned her head to watch him. "That would be nice, wouldn't it? You're blond and blue-eyed, like a strapping Norwegian Viking. How about Eric?" She waited for him to respond. When he didn't, she went on. "Swen? Hans? Gunnar?"

He shook his head.

"Olaf?" She shrugged. "That about does it for Scandinavia."

"It could be any of those."

"Well, there's German. How about Claus? Karl? Ludwig? There are probably a million more I can't think of right now. Wilhelm? No?"

She rose and went to start on the damper. She removed a bag of flour and took it to the fireplace. She cleaned the billy while she thought of more names. "Let's forget blond, blue-eyed and foreign for a minute and just do simple English names. Matthew? Mark? Luke? John?"

"Those sound familiar."

"You've read the Bible, I bet."

"That sounds familiar, too."

Using the billy as a bowl, she mixed flour and water until she had a thick dough. "Tom, Dick, Harry? There are probably thousands of names. Millions."

"Is Mackenzie an Australian name?"

"It was my grandmother's maiden name. She was from Scotland. But I told you, everybody calls me Mac."

"I don't."

An interesting sensation tingled through her. No, the stranger didn't call her Mac. He thought of her as someone different. Mackenzie. For some reason she liked that. "Conroy, my last name, is Irish."

"What are some other Scotland names?"

"Scottish names? Angus? Leslie? Malcolm? The Irish ones are more popular in Australia right now. Sean, Brendan...Kevin, Patrick."

"Patrick."

She turned. Something about the way he'd said the name made her think they'd discovered something. "Does that sound familiar?"

He was staring into space. She wondered what he saw when he did that.

The name was familiar, but he had no idea why. "Yes and no," he said at last.

"Well, that's better than anything else, isn't it?"

"It could be."

"Patrick. Not as fitting as Swen or Eric, maybe, but not bad, really. Shall we call you Patrick, then? Just for now?"

"Patrick." He tried to let his tongue make the decision.

"Paddy, for short?"

"Patrick . . . is already too short."

"I'm sure there's a last name to go with it that doubles the length."

"I'll answer to Patrick." He turned to face her. "But I was beginning to like Stranger, at least the way you say it. Strine-ger." He imitated her accent perfectly.

"You sound every bit as funny to me."

He didn't like the distance between them. He had already found that the closer he stood to her, the more familiar she seemed. He narrowed the space between them. "Tell me what you're doing."

She realized just how tall he was. Squatting below him made her feel at a distinct disadvantage. "Damper can be just as simple as flour and water, but this has leavening. Not yeast, because that would take too long, and I'm always on the move when I'm away from the homestead. I add water and mix it." She held the quart pot up for him to see. "Then I'll bake it when the oven gets hot. See how I have it in the coals? I'll add the damper when it's hot enough and stack coals on top. Meantime we'll boil the other billy for tea."

He tried to remember if he had ever had tea. He couldn't associate any food with a characteristic taste. That seemed strange, even to him.

"In cases where people forget . . . who they are . . ." he began.

"If you're going to ask my opinion about amnesia, I don't have one. It's not every day it happens, you know. You're the first bloke I've met who might really have it."

"Might?"

"You could still be bluffing. Like I said before, maybe you have some secret you don't want me to know, so you're pretending to forget everything. Or maybe you just have kangaroos in your top paddock.''

"Kangaroos? Like the ones you were going to hunt?''

"You might be bats. Crazy,'' she explained, when it was clear he still didn't understand. "But if you are, you're right well-behaved about it.''

If he was crazy, it seemed a positive thing to be decent about it. "Am I? Good.''

"As for the other, like I said, I don't know anything about amnesia, except what I've seen on telly. But it's probably like anything. Quite likely there are different kinds, depending on how you get it. In stories, memory always comes back at the worst times. Like when the girl is going to marry her real love, she finds that's she already married to a real bounder. Or when the man's about to join the police, he finds out he's a convict escaped from the lockup. That sort of thing.''

Behind the offhand way she related her information, he sensed a certain wariness. "If there could be a question about whether I'm trustworthy, why are you helping me?''

"I can take care of myself.'' She set the damper aside and reached for the extra billy. "Try anything and you'll find out.''

"I don't doubt you.''

"Don't you? See? Now we know you've got good sense.''

He was confused. "Why would I think anything else?''

She filled the billy and considered the question. "Because I'm female,'' she said at last. "And there's not a man alive who doesn't think he's better than I am because of it. Not until I've proved otherwise.''

"I must really have forgotten everything.''

She stood. She was a tall woman, but she was half a head shorter than he was. "When your memory comes back, look deep inside yourself. You'll find heaps of prejudice.''

He felt a surge of something he couldn't quite name. Understanding? Tenderness? "You're sure?''

"As sure as I am of *my* name.''

"What if I don't?''

"Then we'll put you in a museum and charge admission."

He touched her cheek. The movement seemed perfectly natural to him, but obviously he'd startled her. She flinched, but she didn't move away.

He closed his eyes. Yes, this was better. He'd had the feeling that he ought to be able to understand her thoughts. Some of them had been obvious to him, but most of them were a jumble. Now, though, with his skin touching hers, he could define both thought and feeling more clearly.

"You haven't had an easy time of it," he said. "You really have had to prove yourself, and you've done a good job of it. But you wish it had been different. You wish someone would understand your feelings and give you what you need."

Suddenly the connection was broken. He opened his eyes, surprised that she had jerked away from him. "Did I hurt you?" he asked.

"Cheap theatrics! With your snake charming and your mind reading, I'm beginning to think you're from the bloody carnival!"

He watched her. As before, some of her thoughts were still clear, but he couldn't shake the feeling that he ought to understand more of them. "Theatrics?"

"Pretending to know what I'm thinking. Pretending to yammer with snakes. You're a fraud, a regular con man!"

"Don't you know what I'm thinking?"

"That's a blooming stupid question!"

Confusion and the resurgence of panic began to wash through him. "Give me a blooming stupid answer."

"No, I don't know what you're thinking! I can guess from your expression or the things you do, but I can't know for sure. I couldn't crawl up inside your head even if I wanted to!"

He tried to piece together what she was saying. "Even *if* you wanted to?"

"Why would I care what you think? Why do you care what I think? Thinking is private."

"I'm sorry. I didn't mean to—"

"Not that you got it right, anyway! The carnival probably sacked you because you don't know what you're talking about."

He stared at her, blue eyes into warm earth brown. "You're not telling the truth. Why?"

"I don't need anything from anybody. Never have. Never will. And I don't need a two-bob mind reader!"

She was denying what was obvious to him, but her spoken message was louder than any thoughts he could read. Now his confusion brimmed over, followed closely by sadness that he'd hurt her. "I'm sorry. I didn't mean to hurt you."

"Hurt? You didn't hurt me! You made me mad."

"I don't see a difference."

"Then you've forgotten something basic!"

He didn't think he'd forgotten this. He thought that perhaps what he had forgotten was that telling the truth, like reading minds, wasn't always appreciated. "Thanks for helping me remember," he said, hoping that his words would make some of her pain go away.

She turned her back to him, and he noted that more of her thoughts were shadowed now. "You are a strange one, Patrick," she said at last.

"No stranger than you are to me, Mackenzie."

"No more conversation. We're both hungry. I'll get the damper cooking."

He moved away, sure that she wanted him to, although he was sorry to break even that tenuous contact with her.

He wondered what else he would learn about Mackenzie in the next days.

He wondered what else he would learn about himself.

Chapter 5

Mackenzie knew that the stranger—no...Patrick—wasn't asleep. He was restless, and the canvas swag cover crackled as he turned from side to side.

She was restless, too. The day had lasted forever. There had been nothing to do in the little hut except cook, eat, cook and eat again. The forced inactivity had reminded her of the rare illnesses of childhood, when she had been forced to lie in bed and count cracks in her ceiling.

She had kept conversation minimal by not initiating any herself. Apparently Patrick had needed silence, too, and he had obliged her. There had been no opportunity for a signal fire. The dust had swirled throughout the afternoon and evening. The wind continued its keening now, and even though it was dark outside, she could sense dust sifting through the cracks in the wall. Dust storms could go on for weeks. She wasn't sure what she would do if this one continued that long.

"Can't you sleep, either?" she asked, when Patrick turned over again.

"No."

"I'm used to activity. I didn't do anything today to make me tired."

"I don't know what I'm used to."

She admired the lack of self-pity in his voice. He might feel many things, but he didn't feel sorry for himself.

"Are you warm enough?" she asked. "I could put more wood on the fire."

"Too warm."

"The sunburn." Mackenzie could sympathize. She sat up, glad for something to do.

"I've got an idea that might help a bit." She got up and went to the storage cabinet. In her inventory, she'd noted a tobacco tin filled with soda, left over from some ringer's damper-making days. She hadn't needed it herself, but she hadn't thought of it as a remedy for Patrick's sunburn until now.

She held up the tin for him to see. "There's soda in here. We can mix this with water and spread it on the places that hurt worst. It might soothe the burn enough for you to get some sleep."

He was quiet for a moment. "That's a primitive approach, isn't it?"

"In case you haven't made note of it, this is a primitive place."

"I'd like to try it, if you think it will help."

"What do you usually do for a sunburn?" she asked.

Without much hope he asked himself the question, as he had unsuccessfully asked himself others since awakening in the hut. What had he done for a sunburn? What had he called himself? Where had he lived and what had he done there? Why did everything seem so new, so untried? Why?

This time, without warning, the silence was broken. A door cracked open inside his mind, and suddenly he could hear a thousand voices screaming a thousand answers.

Nausea filled him, and he felt as if he were falling through space, an unwilling prisoner of the discordant symphony. Pain like none he had ever known filled his head. He covered his ears, but the voices screamed on. For a moment he feared he would explode. Then, with an excruciating surge of willpower, he slammed the door shut again.

"Patrick?" Mackenzie crossed the room and knelt beside him. She touched his face. Despite the burn, he was icy cold. "Are you all right?"

When he didn't answer, she framed his face with her hands and turned it to examine him. Rarely had she seen the kind of agony that stared back at her. "What's wrong, Paddy?" she asked. "Are you feeling worse?"

As she waited for an answer, his skin seemed to warm to her touch. Finally, after what seemed like minutes, he took a deep breath. She could feel a shudder pass through him.

"Are you all right?" she repeated.

"Shall we try the soda now?"

"Are you all right?"

He didn't know what it meant to be all right. He didn't know anything, except that he couldn't face the voices again. Not now, and maybe not ever. "Yes."

"Did you remember something?"

He paused, trying to imagine how he could communicate what had happened to him. There was no way. "No."

Mackenzie was the last person in the world to push anyone into a revelation. A man or a woman had a right to his or her own thoughts and feelings. "Take off your shirt while I mix it."

She crossed the room and busied herself mixing water and soda in a cup until she had the right consistency. She kept her back turned to Patrick so that he could have a bit of privacy. She didn't know what had happened to him, but she knew that, whatever it was, he needed time to pull himself together.

More than ever she wished she could get him to the homestead. So far his recovery had been good. But he had obviously undergone a huge shock. Heatstroke, serious sunburn, memory loss. Any one of these problems needed better care than she could give in a rudimentary hut in the middle of a dust storm. It was entirely possible that Patrick could relapse. What she had witnessed might even have been the start of something worse to come.

"All set?" she asked.

"Yes."

She turned and reminded herself that she had seen him this way from the moment she had found him lying in swirls of dust. Still, her mouth went dry. In the flickering firelight Patrick was undeniably gorgeous. Broad shoulders, muscular chest, the proud, strong face of a Viking warrior. There was nothing about this man that was ordinary.

She heard herself volunteering to dab on the soda. She heard him accept. There was no real reason she should be the one to do it. He could reach most places on his body. Perhaps she had volunteered because he still seemed shaken.

And perhaps the reason had been a more selfish one.

"This might hurt a bit," she warned, as she went to the closet for a rag. She chose a scrap of flannel and washed it at the fireplace before approaching him with the cup.

"I think it already hurts a lot."

"You think?"

He didn't smile; in fact, she realized that he had never smiled at all. "I'm beginning to have some sense of the relativity of pain."

"The relativity of pain." She shook her head. "You've such an odd way of saying what you mean."

"So you've informed me."

"Well, I'm afraid when I'm finished with you, you'll have a better idea of the relativity of pain."

"You'll cause pain to lessen pain." He appeared to consider that as she settled herself on the bed behind him so that she could reach his shoulders. "How do I know if you've really helped the pain at all, or if it's just that when you've finished causing it, I've been fooled into feeling better?"

"You bloody well must teach a class in philosophy at university somewhere. That's who you are."

"If I carved people into sculptures for a living, you couldn't make it sound any worse."

"I'm not much of one for education."

"Why not?"

She wasn't about to tell him the real reason. "Reckon I just wasn't the right sort for it. Get prepared. I'm going to start on your shoulders."

She touched him tentatively. When he didn't jump, she began to swirl the rag in circles.

"But you did well in classes," he said.

Instantly she jerked her hand away. "I told you before, I don't like anyone pretending to read my mind!"

"So you did." He stiffened. This time when she touched him, he winced, and as if she could feel it, she decreased the pressure against his skin. "Did you do well in classes?" he asked.

"Sometimes."

He tried to tell himself he couldn't know her answers before she gave them. Obviously there was something wrong with sensing her thoughts. Obviously there was something wrong with *him* for wanting to.

"Relax," she said. "I'm not going to hurt you any more than this."

"How do you know I'm worried you'll hurt me?"

"It just makes sense."

"Then shouldn't it make sense to me that you'd be good in school? You're intelligent."

"How would you know?"

That confused him, and he searched hard for an answer. "From things you've said and done," he said.

"Oh." She still wasn't satisfied that he had just been adding up facts, but she was ready to drop the subject.

She worked in silence, but her thoughts clamored for recognition. One part of her brain reminded her of all the stranger's quirks and problems; the other part cherished every movement her hands made, every pass over his skin, every muscle that rippled under her fingers. She had washed him when he was unconscious, and even though he hadn't responded, the experience had been tantalizing. Now, as his flesh reacted to everything she did, the experience was... better.

She swirled the rag over the back of his neck. In the firelight his hair was outback sunshine, a pure, untainted gold.

The backs of her fingers brushed against the shortest hairs at his nape, and they clung momentarily, as if begging her to stop and explore that different sensory delight.

"My uncle used to have an aviary," she said. Her hand halted in its path. Why had she told him that?

"A place to keep birds."

"At least your vocabulary hasn't suffered."

"What about the aviary?"

"Nothing."

"Something must have reminded you of it."

She couldn't fault him for figuring that out. She sighed. "When I was old enough to reach the latch on the cage, I opened it one day and let all the birds go free."

"And your uncle was furious."

That, too, should have been apparent to almost anyone, whether they knew Clint Conroy or not. "Yes. But he understood."

"Freedom is important to both of you."

She told herself he wasn't reading her mind. Mind reading was impossible. "I suppose you can tell that from the way we live."

He supposed he could. "Yes." He felt her hands move across his skin again. Faster this time, as if she was determined to get the job finished as quickly as possible. He mourned for the slower pace. He suspected there was as much healing in her hands as in the solution on the rag. "Anything that threatens freedom frightens you."

"Nothing frightens me."

He wasn't going to accuse her of lying. Certainly she must know her own failings better than anyone. "But staying free is important," he said.

"Nothing is going to take away my freedom."

"And that's why you've never shared yourself with a man."

"That's it!" Mackenzie jumped to her feet. For a moment she'd been a hairbreadth from shoving him across the room. But she had realized, just as she was about to try, how much a shove would hurt him. "Finish this up yourself!"

He closed his eyes. He felt completely drained. Why was everything so difficult? "Apparently that's not what you were leading up to telling me."

"You've got—"

"A bloody nerve," he finished for her. "I don't, Mackenzie. Not really. What I've got is a bloody lack of understanding of what I'm supposed to say and what I'm not!"

She was a thoroughbred racing down the final stretch only to discover that the crowds had gone home, the other horses had turned back to the stables, and the finish line had washed away. With a harsh sigh she sat down again and started soothing a path down his spine. "You're guessing I'm such a no-hoper I've never had a man?"

"You think I'd answer that? I haven't lost *all* my good sense."

"No answer will go worse for you."

"I think there have been dozens of men who've wanted you." He paused to see how that had affected her. Encouraged by her silence and an indescribable feeling that she was pleased, he went on. "You're truly lovely, even under the dust."

"Who do you remember well enough to compare me to?"

A door was slammed and locked in his mind. He could unlock it, peek inside and see what women's faces emerged. But nausea gripped him at the thought. The cacophony of voices he had unleashed the last time could have driven him mad. Whatever answers lived behind that door, he could not release them now. Not now, and perhaps not ever.

But even without those doors unlocked, one face danced through his mind. For just a moment Patrick saw the image of a woman. Her hair was light and her eyes a new-leaf green. She was willowy and graceful, with a face that reflected every thought and feeling. In that moment he compared her to Mackenzie and knew that both were extraordinarily beautiful.

"I've lost my memory, but not my ability to see what's in front of me," he said.

"A dinky-di bit of flattery, that."

"Flattery? That's like a lie, isn't it?"

"A friendly lie."

He sat quietly as she finished his back. Without words between them, he could simply enjoy the feel of what she was doing to him. And what she was doing was remarkable. His skin hurt, and even as she touched it, the hurt continued. But the feel of her hands against his flesh, even with the rag intervening, was also a great comfort.

And more. Her touch both cooled and warmed him. The paradox was baffling, yet his body was living proof it existed. He didn't want the pain to continue, but he wanted the movement of her hands to continue forever.

"I'm finished with your back. Shall I do your chest? Or would you rather?"

"I'd like you to." Something shifted between them, a subtle change in the air. He knew she needed an explanation of some sort. He chose one of the many that presented themselves. "You can reach places I'd have trouble with."

"Right-o." Mackenzie got up to mix more solution; then she moved around to kneel in front of him. He sat cross-legged, like a Hindu guru, or was it a Buddhist monk? Whichever, he seemed perfectly at home, as if he could sit that way, utterly motionless, forever.

"Small consolation, I suppose," she said, "but the sunburn's not as bad as it was yesterday. It's fading in spots."

He wondered how he would feel when it disappeared. Would he still feel each movement, perceive his boundaries in the same way? "What will happen when we get to your home?" he asked.

"What do you want to happen?"

"I don't know."

"I should think you'd want your memory back, first thing."

"What if my memories aren't good ones?"

"Do you feel they might not be?"

He considered. He could feel the cloth, cool and provocative, moving along his right shoulder. He fixed his gaze on Mackenzie's face. Her lips were pursed, as if she was doing something that required great precision.

He wanted to try her lips against his. The thought came out of nowhere, yet it seemed the most natural one in the world.

A kiss. His lips against hers. That was what the action was called. He tried to imagine what it would feel like; he wondered if he knew.

"Patrick?"

He remembered her question. "I don't know," he said. "Are your memories good or bad?"

"Good, mostly."

"But there are bad ones, too?"

She listened carefully to his inflection. Yes, he had asked a question. He wasn't pretending to know...probably. "I remember my mother dying," she said.

Something twisted inside him. He swallowed, but it wouldn't go away. He felt a surge of such sorrow that he could hardly breathe.

"She was young, and she always smelled like violets. I didn't know that until later, you see. Not until I smelled violets at a flower stall in Sydney on a school outing. Then I realized." Mackenzie wondered why she was telling Patrick this. It was the hut, she supposed, and the damnable wailing wind. It mimicked the sound of mourning. She could almost hear her own childish sobbing in each ghostly shriek and moan.

"You were very sad when she died."

"Very." She wet her rag again and stared past him at the wall, which was buckling under the wind's assault. "But then I came to Waluwara. There's been nothing to be sad about here."

She wasn't telling the whole truth, but already Patrick had learned enough not to point that out. "My memories will be the same, I suppose," he said. "Sad ones. Better ones."

"Since you're human, too, that's bound to be the way it is."

"Will this be a good or a bad memory for you?"

She brought her gaze, and her attention, to him. "This?"

"This. Our time here."

She frowned. "I don't know. It's not over yet, is it?"

"You are my first memory."

"Pardon?"

"My first memory. I have no memories except of you."

Try as she might, she could not lower her eyes. His were blue, a straight-up-to-the-heavens blue that threatened to suck her into awareness, even into an eternity, that she wasn't ready for.

"*I* have other memories," she said.

He bent his head forward. Until the briefest moment before he kissed her, she could still see his eyes. Then they closed. Hers closed, too, and she felt his lips against hers.

The kiss was both a surprise and a certainty. She could not move away. She was as trapped by him as if he had wrapped her in bands of steel. She couldn't breathe, she couldn't think. She could only yearn and, in her yearning, press her lips harder against his.

She had been kissed before, but never had she felt this unity with a man. Somewhere between his lips and hers, she had lost a piece of herself.

Unnerved, but unable to resist, she turned her head a little to savor the sensation. His lips parted, and she sighed against them. His hand settled on her hair, and his fingers wove through it to caress the back of her neck. His lips took up the same rhythm, pulsing in time to her heartbeat until she was convinced he had somehow become a part of her and knew her body as he knew his own.

He was the first to draw away. She stared at him and found his eyes were still every bit as depthless and unshadowed.

She thought of a thousand important things to say and said none of them. "Well, you haven't forgotten everything." She moved away, carefully placing the rag inside the cup before she held it out to him. "I reckon you'd better finish this without me."

"I would have remembered that."

"You're trying to tell me a kiss was new to a man who looks like you?" She laughed, only forcing it a little.

"For you, too."

"Sorry, but no."

"Yes."

"You're a case, Patrick. You'll have one go-in after another if you insist on telling everybody what they're thinking."

"Can you tell what I'm thinking?"

She screened her mind of all intuition, but in the flash before she did, she had an impression of confusion, of yearning as powerful as her own had been, of desire for more of the same.

"No. And I don't want to know." She thrust the cup into his hand. "I'm going to bed. You want something to do, you can worry about the wind. Find out what *it's* thinking, why don't you? Because if it doesn't stop blowing soon, you'll have a raving loony on your hands."

"It will die down by tomorrow."

"What?"

"The wind. It will get worse, then better. By...dawn it will almost be still outside."

"How do you know?"

He watched her settle herself in bed. "You didn't?"

She stared at him. For a moment something just short of fear shot through her. Who was this man? A better question yet, why had *she* been fated to find him? He towered above her, part innocent child, part Greek god or Viking warrior, part sideshow magician, part—a large part—man.

"Go to sleep," she said at last.

He stared down at her. He didn't want to sleep. He wasn't sure what he wanted, but it wasn't sleep. "Thank you for helping me. My sunburn feels better."

"I'm getting out of here tomorrow!" She turned over so she couldn't see him anymore.

"Good night."

She didn't answer. She stared at the iron flapping under the restless fingers of the wind. From the looks of it, despite her words, she wouldn't be going anywhere tomorrow. She shut her eyes and hoped that Patrick was going to be proved right. Then she changed her mind. She could put up with another day at the hut better than she could put up with a new discovery about her guest. Patrick was strange enough. If he could predict the future as well as read minds and charm snakes, he would truly be a force to be reckoned with.

She thought about the kiss. Just her bloody luck, he was already a force to be reckoned with.

Since there was no longer any wind, the thick black smoke of Mackenzie's signal fire billowed straight up to the sky. Dawn had arrived as calmly as Patrick had predicted. The fire had already been burning for two hours, fueled by the last of the scrub piled beside the hut.

Mackenzie was glad she and Patrick had dragged the tires a good distance away, because the smell of the burning rubber was hideous. If no one came to get them by early afternoon, she had already decided that she and Patrick would start for the homestead and travel until nightfall. There was no guarantee that another dust storm wouldn't catch them— no guarantee except Patrick's personal assurance, which she refused to accept—but the combination of the smell of the tires and the prospect of another night in the hut was enough to make her reckless.

"When the sun gets to that spot—" she pointed to the sky "—we'll start back."

"Your horse is too tired and hungry to carry two." Patrick leaned over the side of the shelter where Bounder was hobbled and watched him eat the tufts of dried grass that Mackenzie had found for him.

Twice Mackenzie had warned Patrick to stay out of Bounder's reach. Bounder was nobody's dear little pony. But she wasn't going to warn Patrick again. Bounder would take care of that in his own time.

"He won't have to," she said. "I'll walk and you'll ride. You're still weak, and well you should be."

"No."

"I won't argue. That's what we'll do. The trip back will be slow, since we'll have to go from bore to bore. It might take three, even four days. But there's always the chance someone will come looking for me."

"A good chance?"

She smiled ruefully. "I stirred up rather a large fuss the last time someone did. They'll think twice before they set out. Unless they see the smoke, that is. The Aborigines use smoke to send messages across great distances. If anyone sees this, they'll know it's a signal. We don't even need to use a code."

"Is there a code?"

"There's a whole language. I know a little." Actually, she knew a lot. But that wasn't something one bragged about. It had been a gift from her Aboriginal friends, just as teaching her to track had been a gift, and helping her to look deeply inside herself to her own instincts had been a gift, too.

"The Aborigines. Australia's native people?"

"That's right. They were here for maybe forty thousand years before Europeans caught sight of the continent. There's a village of several hundred on the run, and most of our stockmen and station hands belong to the tribe."

"Then this is their land?"

"Technically? No. In the ways that matter? Yes."

Bounder finished the grass and looked around for more. Clearly disgruntled, he started toward Patrick to see what he was offering. Patrick held out his hand.

Mackenzie bit back her warning. Patrick did as he pleased. There was no point in wasting her breath.

He crooned something to the horse, and Bounder's ears perked up. The horse stood still and listened.

"A blooming miracle," Mackenzie whispered.

Patrick curved his fingers toward the fence, and the horse followed the motion. In a moment he was standing in front of Patrick, and Patrick was rubbing his nose.

"He's a beauty," he said.

"You know horses?"

"I have no idea."

Mackenzie waited for some sign that Bounder had tired of being domesticated and was ready to assert himself. It didn't come. "You know horses," she said. "By rights, he should have nipped a finger or two by now."

Patrick brushed flies away from the horse's eyes. Bounder didn't flinch. "He was a wild horse before you tamed him?"

"How do you know that?"

Patrick considered. "Just under the surface he's full of spirit."

"Oh." Mackenzie relaxed a little. It didn't take extrasensory perception to see that. "We call our wild horses brumbies. You couldn't guess how many there are out here in the bush. They're descendants of thoroughbreds, turned out to fend for themselves when the land was just being settled. Most pastoralists despise them. They eat the food our cattle need, pug up the water holes, unsettle the mobs."

"What happens to them?"

"The lucky ones are left free or brought in for training."

He didn't ask what happened to the unlucky ones. It was much too clear.

"There's no money in it," Mackenzie said. "But every year the Waluwara stockmen take a week or two to catch the most likely brumbies we can find. We train them and sell them for riding stock after a year. It's nothing more than sentiment. Too much 'Man From Snowy River.'"

"What's that?"

"A poem about wild horses, wild places and times that are gone now."

"You wish they weren't gone."

"The world is fair teeming with people and things they've invented to make it a better place. But in my mind, it's not a better place for all that."

"Is this wild enough for you?" Patrick gestured to the seemingly endless plains surrounding them.

"I'd like to see new wild places." Mackenzie didn't know what it was about Patrick that made her expose so many of her secrets, but whatever it was, she was exposing herself again. And she continued. "There's challenge here, and I like that. But there must be places like the outback, places I haven't seen yet, that still need to be explored."

"Have you tried to find them?"

"No. I'm needed here. But maybe someday I'll take a holiday to Africa or the Asian jungles." She gestured to the plains as he had. "Maybe I'll even get to see the Amazon rain forest before they cut down all the trees and make it an outback, too."

Bounder came to attention under Patrick's stroking hand. At the same instant, Patrick came to attention, too. "Do you hear that?"

Mackenzie listened. With the luck she'd had so far, she was prepared to hear the wind rising. Instead there was something different in the air, something just out of reach. She held her breath. There was no sound, nothing more than a sense that the atmosphere was somehow disturbed. Then, from a great distance she heard the unmistakable hum of an engine.

"Don't get in a flap," she warned. "Small planes are right common out here. Someone might be flying over on his way to somewhere else."

Patrick didn't answer, and Mackenzie fell silent again. The hum grew louder until she knew it wasn't a light plane at all. Now the sound was unmistakable.

"It's a helicopter," she said. "And there's no reason it would be flying this way except to look for us!"

She took off running, removing her hat as she did to wave it at the still-empty sky.

Patrick watched her hair fall free, hair as brilliant as the rising sun. Her slender, womanly body almost leaped for joy. He continued stroking Bounder, but it was Mackenzie he watched, Mackenzie he wanted to touch.

Their days at the hut alone together were finished. Somewhere he had a life to get back to.

He didn't want to leave.

The best things are always the most difficult. You must give up the things you understand and love in order to find greater happiness. Letting go is the first step toward possession.

The voice from his memory troubled him. The words troubled him more. He wondered if he had ever wanted to possess anything in his past the same way that, in this moment, he wanted to possess Mackenzie.

"Letting go is the first step toward possession," he repeated out loud.

He had no choice except to wait and see.

Chapter 6

The evening sky was a deep, brilliant gold, with a subtle purple band rising steadily from the horizon. A small flock of sulphur-crested cockatoos descended with the darkness into a cluster of ghost gum trees at the edge of the garden ringing the homestead. Mackenzie sipped bottled lemonade on the front veranda and watched the sunset, Waluwara's most reliable form of entertainment.

When she heard footsteps on the porch, she knew immediately whom they belonged to. "I assume you'll want an explanation."

Clint Conroy took his place beside her. He had already showered and dressed for the evening meal, a ritual he always insisted on even when he was alone. He wore dark trousers and a plain white shirt. His dark hair was uncovered; his hat, a battered, wide-brimmed felt like Mackenzie's own, had been left inside.

Mackenzie felt a moment of pride as she waited for his answer. At forty-three he was a good-looking man, tanned and fit, with a stockman's permanent squint that only added to his attractions. Australia's dry climate set well on its men, honing them to their basic essence, just like life in the bush.

The boss's face stated clearly that here, inside this man, inside this life, there was no room for pretension.

"I assume you have an explanation," he said.

She recounted the last days, trying to put as much information into as few words as possible. The boss would want to know all the subtleties, but later, and only if they were necessary. She didn't tell him about the snake, or about what, at the time, had seemed like remarkable gifts in a man who couldn't remember his own name. Here, back in civilization—or this beloved version of it—she had come to doubt her own perceptions. Nothing Patrick had said or done in their days together couldn't be explained. She had been too sensitive, concerned for his health and their mutual situation.

"We left Bounder to come in by himself. I hope he does," she finished.

"You had a bit of luck. If Harry hadn't seen the smoke you'd be camping out again tonight."

"I wouldn't have minded, but the stranger needed to see a doctor."

"Harry said your signal was easily visible."

"Harry taught me to light signal fires."

"There's not enough money in this station to pay him for what he does."

Harry David was the boss stockman, an Aborigine who was as at home on a horse as he was in the house in the village that he shared with his parents, wife and four children. He and Clint had grown up together, attended the station school together, fought, laughed and gotten drunk together. They were as alike as they were different, mates who had saved each other's lives so many times that neither bothered to keep count.

"I would have gotten the stranger back here if I'd had to," Mackenzie said. "But this was easier."

"It would have been easier if Harry hadn't had to beg for a chopper."

Mackenzie heard the bitterness in her uncle's voice. She understood it only too well. Waluwara needed its own helicopter, as well as planes that worked. "I'd have settled for a road and an ute with four good tires."

"I haven't seen the man yet."

Clint had been out on the other end of the run when she and Patrick had landed at the station airstrip. She was surprised he had returned so soon. "I wasn't expecting you home tonight," she said. "What brought you back?"

"You'd been out in the storm too long."

She digested that but declined to make a fuss. This once it was nice to have had someone worried about her.

As they talked, the sky deepened to a darker gold. Mackenzie looked out over the garden, nearly dormant now, but not brown, because Edwina kept it just wet enough to save it during the worst of the Dry. "I didn't mention the most important thing about our guest."

"That is?"

"He doesn't remember anything. Not even his own name."

Clint took out tobacco and papers to roll a cigarette. Tradition died hard at Waluwara. He smoked a while before he answered.

"Is he lying?"

"I don't know. I don't think so."

"But you found no evidence of injuries?"

"Not a bloody one."

Clint cleared his throat. Mackenzie knew she'd been chastised for her language. "What sort of bloke is he?"

That was hardest of all to explain. Mackenzie cleared her throat, too. "A bit odd," she said at last.

"Odd?"

"Nice enough, mind you. But, well…strange. Odd. He's forgotten so many things. He remembers words, but not always what to say in a conversation." She stopped when it became clear she wasn't making sense.

"I should think if his memory's gone, that would account for it."

"Maybe."

"Harry called the Flying Doctor Service?"

"He did. They said they'd have someone out today if it was an emergency, but it looked to me as if Patrick needed good food and rest more than he needed a doctor. Edwina looked him over and thought the same."

"Patrick?"

"The name seemed a bit familiar to him. It was better than calling him Stranger."

"Much better."

Mackenzie turned at the sound of Patrick's voice. The man stepping onto the veranda was hardly the battered, burned creature she had rescued from dust, sun and dehydration. He had showered and shaved. Edwina, a serene, capable woman who took everything in her stride, had found clothes for him much like the ones her uncle wore. The white shirt emphasized the breadth of his shoulders and the sunburn that was, even now, beginning to darken to a tan. The khaki trousers fit snugly against his narrow hips and thighs and traced the muscular length of his legs. Her gaze lingered too long. When she looked up, she saw that her uncle was aware of her interest.

"Patrick," she said. "I was just telling my uncle about you."

Clint turned to greet their guest. His eyes betrayed nothing, but Mackenzie knew that his impression of Patrick would be formed in a matter of seconds. He extended his hand and Patrick shook it. "Clint Conroy," he said.

Patrick nodded. "Thank you for your hospitality."

"Mac was just telling me a little about your ordeal."

"I'm afraid there's only a little to tell. It begins when she found me."

"So she says."

Patrick joined them at the railing. After the helicopter ride he hadn't had more than a glimpse of the homestead before the housekeeper had hustled him to a room, given him a quick once-over and insisted he get into bed after his shower. He hadn't even been allowed out for a meal. The same woman had brought food to him on a tray.

The house was white, one long, sprawling story set several feet above the ground on stone pillars. The veranda railing and the fence surrounding the garden were graceful, almost fanciful sweeps of iron smothered in places by thick vines.

His mind sorted through an array of words until he came to the correct one. "Oasis." He looked at Mackenzie and wasn't sure if he had found the word for her or for the house and surrounding gardens. She was wearing a dress the same color as the leaves of the silver trees at the garden's edge, but her arms and legs were bare. She had clipped her hair back from her face with gold barrettes, and surrounded by that wild blazing cloud, her features were perfectly framed, dainty and elfin and . . . worried.

"When I saw the house from the air," he said, "I thought it was a mirage."

"This time of year it seems so," Clint said. "But when the Wet comes and the creeks and billabongs fill, everything for miles is lush and green."

"So wet you'll wish it were dry again," Mackenzie said. Immediately she wondered about her words. She had sounded as if she expected the stranger to stay until the Wet came. The truth was that he would probably be leaving as soon as the doctor had seen him.

"You're not Australian, so you might not understand our seasons," Clint said.

"I'm not Australian. You're sure?"

"Too right."

"I think he's a Yank," Mackenzie said.

"Likely," Clint agreed. "Do you want to find out?" he asked Patrick. "Or would you rather we not give it a bash?"

For a moment Patrick thought of the voices that screamed behind a locked door in his mind. Inside him somewhere were all the answers he needed. But he wasn't sure he could survive learning them.

He didn't know how to communicate that to Mackenzie and her uncle. Perhaps the best thing was to let them help him. If he discovered one answer at a time, perhaps he would learn enough to tame the voices until all the answers had been set free.

"What do you know about memory loss?" he asked Clint. "I don't know...or remember anything."

"Little, I'm afraid. I know it can come from an injury to the brain. Or sometimes the mind just forgets what it finds too painful to remember."

"I think someone left Patrick to die," Mackenzie said. "He had no food, no water, no clothes—"

"No clothes?" Clint turned his gaze to his niece. "No...trousers?"

"Not a stitch."

Clint turned back to Patrick. Patrick's eyes gleamed a little brighter, and he shrugged. "Not my choice, I'm sure."

"Well."

"Why would anyone leave him in that state unless they wanted him to die?" Mackenzie asked.

"Perhaps he had provisions. Perhaps he got lost, left his horse or his car. He was dehydrated, delirious with thirst and suffering from the heat, perhaps he tore off his...clothes."

"We flew right over the area where I'd found him," Mackenzie said. "There was nothing there."

"Can you tell Harry where he was?"

"Of course."

"Then I'll send him out with another man tomorrow to see what they can find."

"They won't find anything. The storm will have covered all tracks."

There was a noise behind them, the sound of a woman clearing her throat. "Dinner's on the table."

Patrick watched the look the housekeeper, Edwina, exchanged with Mackenzie's uncle. She was in her thirties, small, with golden brown hair and skin the soft brown of a mourning dove's breast. There was an elegance in the way she carried herself, royalty garbed in a blue housedress and starched white apron.

He understood much from the look that passed between them. More, he guessed, than anyone was supposed to understand. There was love in that look, love, repression, yearning. He could have discovered more, but he'd learned from his encounters with Mackenzie that this was already too much. He looked away and forced himself to think of something else.

"Patrick doesn't eat meat," Mackenzie told her uncle. "That's one thing we discovered."

"There'll be plenty he can eat," Edwina said. "I've never starved a guest."

"I apologize for the extra trouble," Patrick said. "And I want to thank you for finding me these." He pointed to his shoes, canvas sneakers that had once been someone's tennis shoes in the days when there had been a usable court behind the homestead.

"You won't wear leather, either?" Mackenzie asked. "You woke up in the wrong sort of place, Paddy. You should have found your way to the next run. They raise canvas there. Thousands of acres of it. It's a show to watch them harvest shoes and belts. Tents, too."

She was rewarded with a smile that almost snatched the oxygen from her lungs. He could smile. Yes, he could. "I haven't forgotten everything," he said. "Not quite."

She smiled, too, a response to his that she could not have denied in a million years. "I'm glad to see it."

She turned to share her smile with her uncle and saw he was not amused. He offered her his arm. It was a courtly gesture, pure gentleman squatter asserting his position as lord of the countryside. She took it rather than make a fuss. The boss's message was clear. Until further notice, anything as intimate as smiling with Patrick was prohibited.

The dining room was long and wide, with sheer curtains that garbed the tall open windows and billowed enticingly with every puff of breeze. Mackenzie chose not to notice the walls that needed paint, the carefully patched linen tablecloth, the chips in the Wedgwood china that had been her grandmother's most prized possession. The graciously appointed dining room and the formal evening meal might be a strange tradition in a place where drought, death and poverty lurked at the doorstep, but it was a tradition her uncle had fought hard to preserve. She would do no less.

She sat at her uncle's right and Patrick at his left. The conversation was polite as the meal was served. Edwina had obviously gone out of her way to prepare a special dinner. In addition to the ever-present beef, there were more vegetables than usual, some fresh from the kitchen garden that was faithfully tended by Edwina's brother, Ned. There was also a loaf of her homemade bread and Waluwara's own butter to go with it.

Mackenzie watched Patrick eat. He made no attempt to disguise his pleasure. She suspected that his opinion about her own cooking skills had just undergone an adjustment.

"Patrick eats like someone who's never tasted food before," Mackenzie said. "I think I could have served him saltbush and sand at the hut and he would have tucked right into it."

"Nothing like a little starvation to make a man appreciate simple things." Clint squinted at their guest. "How do you feel?"

"How can a man know how he feels if he can't remember how he used to feel?" Mackenzie asked.

Clint turned his steely-eyed gaze to her. She smiled. "Sorry."

"I feel fine," Patrick said. "Hungry, I suppose. When I eat I feel even better."

Clint looked down at his plate. Mackenzie could almost see his thoughts. "He'll take a bit of getting used to," she said.

"*You're* taking a bit of getting used to," Clint told her.

"Sorry. It's just I've gotten adjusted to the situation. You haven't."

She expected her uncle to launch into more questions, questions Patrick wouldn't be able to answer. Instead he began a report about what was happening on the section of the station he had just come back from. They discussed the conditions he had seen, and what to do about them, as they ate the meal. Patrick seemed to listen attentively as he finished seconds, then thirds.

"Save room for dessert," Mackenzie warned him. "You won't want to miss it."

"It couldn't be better than this."

"Better than boiled carrots? I think so."

"We've a number of Yanks in the outback," Clint said, leaning back in his chair to sip tea while Edwina cleared the table. His eyes followed her as he spoke. "Most of them are connected with your military. You have bases here. Did you know that?"

"Bases?" Patrick considered. "No."

"A man might want to leave the service. Might even want to sell secrets he'd learned there."

"If I have any secrets for sale, they're secret to me, too."

"Patrick, a spy?" Mackenzie said. "What? Do you think he was taking a shortcut to Beijing and got lost on the way?"

Her uncle's expression was answer enough.

Dessert was custard served with tiny peaches Edwina had picked and preserved herself.

Mackenzie watched Patrick eat—when she was sure she wasn't being observed. There was something almost mesmerizing in the expression on his face. Despite his situation, the simplest things obviously gave him pleasure. She thought of the kiss they had shared last night. She had avoided thinking of it all day, but now the memory asserted itself.

She was young and in some ways, perhaps, untried. But she was far from foolish. Last night she had been powerless to deny her attraction to this man, this stranger who didn't even have a real name. The attraction was still there, and denying it wouldn't make it disappear. Like all the other aspects of her life, she was going to have to face it squarely and decide what to do about it.

Except this time, like no other, she suspected a simple decision wasn't going to suffice. Not quite.

Her uncle coughed, and for a moment she thought she'd been caught in the act of staring. Color rose to her cheeks, a unique and thoroughly unpleasant experience. Her uncle coughed again, and she faced him.

He wasn't trying to get her attention. He coughed again, and his hands went to his throat. His face had turned a dark red. He was choking.

Mackenzie leaped to her feet and positioned herself behind him. Circling him with her arms, she covered one of her hands with the other and shoved her fists against his diaphragm. Once, twice.

He continued to choke.

"Get Edwina!" she shouted to Patrick.

She didn't look up to see if he responded. She held her breath and used all her strength to try unsuccessfully again. The chair was in the way. She was afraid she wasn't applying enough pressure to his diaphragm because of it. Now Clint's skin seemed to be turning blue.

"Stand up, Uncle Clint," she demanded. "Now!"

The words were hardly out of her mouth before she had been tossed against the wall. Patrick jerked her uncle from the chair and, with one arm across Clint's midriff and another at the side of his head, began to pummel and twist him simultaneously.

"What are you doing?" Momentarily dazed from the force of Patrick's shove, she shook her head. Then she started unsteadily toward them.

Clint's body jerked, and something flew across the room. He gasped once, twice, before he began to breathe normally again.

"What in the bloody hell did you do to him?" Mackenzie demanded.

Patrick seemed as stunned as she was. "He couldn't breathe."

"Of course he couldn't breathe! Do you think he turns red and blue for entertainment? What did you do?"

"He saved . . . my life," Clint answered.

Still shaken, Mackenzie ducked her head to search the floor for the culprit. She took longer than she needed, waiting until she was under better control before she spoke. "A peach pit." She didn't look at either of the men as she disposed of it.

"It was lodged in his throat," Patrick said.

"I had that part figured out, thank you," she said.

Clint sat down and reached unsteadily for his cup. He played with the handle but didn't lift the cup to his mouth. "For a minute there...I thought I'd be pushing up daisies during the Wet this year."

Mackenzie took her place again, too, and with the residue of manners still left to her, signaled for Patrick to do the same. "That wasn't the right sort of maneuver," she said. "Do you know what you did?"

Patrick looked directly at her. He didn't smile. "Yes. I got him breathing again."

Mackenzie knew more than her share of first aid, and nothing Patrick had done could be found in any book she had ever read. But what did that matter? She had the grace to feel ashamed of her own behavior.

"Well, I couldn't get him breathing," she said. "I'm sorry. You're right. Whatever you did, thank you for doing it."

Neither Clint nor Patrick uttered another word for the rest of the meal, and Mackenzie couldn't think of anything to break the silence. When it was time to leave the table, she rose and the men stood, too.

"You have everything you need for the night?" she asked Patrick.

"Yes, thank you."

She wanted to say more, but what could she say? Patrick had revealed another new and, in its own way, odd part of himself. In the revelation, he had saved the life of the human being she loved most in the world.

"Edwina gave you some ointment for your sunburn?" she asked, knowing that the housekeeper had.

"Yes. I'll take care of using it."

"Right-o."

"Have a smoke with me out on the veranda?" Clint asked Patrick.

"No. But I'll keep you company."

Mackenzie watched the two men exit. She was glad not to be asked to join in this male ritual. The puzzle of Patrick the Stranger was too complicated to be solved that night. With a certain amount of gratitude she gave the problem over to her uncle.

"Out here in the bush we have a name for a man who saves another's life."

"Friend?"

"Mate." Clint rolled and lit his cigarette. Moments later he blew spirals of smoke into the inky black of the outback night. "You might not understand it, since you're not from here."

"Maybe not."

"This country isn't like yours. When a man wanted to settle new land in America, he packed up his family, or just himself, and headed off into the wilderness. He could be fair certain there'd be game for food and plenty of water, trees to build a cabin. There were a million problems he might have, but the basic things were his for the taking."

Patrick gazed out into the darkness and thought he understood. "But not here."

Clint shook his head. He smoked awhile before he continued. "You have your myths, we have ours. You Yanks think of yourselves as rugged individualists because you could make it alone if you wanted. We knew we couldn't make it alone out here, right from the start. So we have mates, partners, you might say. We depend on each other for our lives. A mate does something for you, you do something for him."

"You don't have to do anything for me."

"I'd almost decided to, anyway, before you had to start me breathing again." Clint turned enough to look at Patrick. "You're welcome here until you want to leave. There'll be something on the run for you to work at, if you stay."

"You don't know anything about me."

Clint turned back to the night. "I know all about you."

"Oh?"

"For the most part you're telling the truth about your memory. You don't remember much, and what you do remember confuses you, so most likely you try to deny it. I think your memory will come back eventually. You need time and quiet to rediscover who you are. I can give you both. You're not afraid, even though you don't understand what's happened to you. You're a man of courage, also a man with certain talents, if your demonstration at dinner was any clue."

"I surprise myself."

Clint gave a dry chuckle. "I don't know what you are or were running from, Patrick, but you can rest here before you have to run again."

"Thank you."

"There's only one thing."

"Mackenzie?"

Clint nodded, not surprised that Patrick had guessed. "Has she told you anything about herself?"

"Not much."

"She came here when she was four, after her mother died. She's only been away from the station a few times since. She finished secondary school in Adelaide and did another year in Sydney. I thought she needed to experience city life, but school was an agony, and she hated the city."

"School was an agony?"

"Bored her no end. And she hated being penned up after having all this." He gestured into the darkness. "Do you find that hard to understand?"

"I don't know."

"This is no place for her, but the city is no place for her, either. You've heard of the man without a country?" He looked at Patrick. "I suppose if you have, you don't remember. Anyway, Mac is a woman without a place. She needs young people and challenge she won't find here. But she needs more challenge than she found in Adelaide or Sydney. So it comes down to a young woman who's looking for something, only she doesn't know what."

"And you're afraid I might take advantage of that?"

"How do I know—how do *you* know—there's not a wife and three little Patricks waiting for you somewhere across the oceans? Or right here in Oz, for that matter."

Patrick knew there was more to Clint's concerns than that. But he had also learned to keep such knowledge to himself. "And if there isn't?"

"We won't know that for a while. Perhaps never."

"You would be sad to lose her."

"I would be sad to lose her to the wrong man." Clint carefully extinguished his cigarette butt before he dropped it into the bushes. "I lost her mother, my sister, that way."

"Mackenzie's father?"

"Was a ruddy bastard. He got Mary Kate pregnant, then left her to have the baby by herself. She was too proud to ask for my help. So she disappeared without telling anyone why. I never saw her again. I didn't even know about Mac until one day she was standing at my front door with a social worker."

Patrick heard anger. More important, he heard a warning. He and Clint might be mates, and Clint might be willing to do what he could for Patrick in return for saving his life. But there were limits to his hospitality, and one of them was named Mackenzie.

"When does a girl become a woman in Australia?" Patrick asked.

"That's a strange question."

"Is it?"

"She becomes a woman when she grows up."

"And how do you measure that? Years? Biology?"

"Both." Clint faced him. "Why?"

"Maybe I've forgotten everything, and maybe I haven't. Tell me if I'm wrong. Isn't Mackenzie a woman now?"

Clint's gaze didn't flicker. He stared into Patrick's eyes and noted the way they seemed to beckon him toward some higher understanding. He felt both unsettled and moved by what he saw. "God help you if you hurt her," he said at last. "Because it will take God and an army of angels to stand between us if you do."

"Why would I hurt her?"

"Because you're a man, and sometimes it's easier to hurt a woman than not to."

Patrick stayed on the veranda after Clint had gone inside. The lush darkness was broken only by lights in the men's quarters to the side of the homestead, the silence only by a distant dog's intermittent barking. Patrick noticed neither. Clint's parting words were still as loud and mysterious to him as the voice he sometimes heard in his memory.

Chapter 7

"Even if you've ridden before, you've probably never used a saddle like this one." Mackenzie held up a saddle for Patrick to admire before she slung it over the blanket she had already settled on the back of Gimme, a fat, gentle mare who owed her easy life to the children in the village, who used her as their mount when they were learning to ride.

"This is an Australian stock saddle, different from your Western saddle. No horn." She smacked the front of the saddle. "This Johnny strap's just for mounting. Don't try to hang on to it when you're riding, or you'll probably fall off."

"Maybe I'll fall off anyway."

She heard good spirits and not a trace of fear. If Patrick was still tormented by his personal demons, he was learning not to show it. "The doctor will have my head if you do. I doubt he'd approve of anything as strenuous as riding yet."

"He told me to do anything I felt up to."

Mackenzie fastened the saddle in place. The doctor had flown in yesterday afternoon to examine Patrick. He'd had nothing but positive words about Patrick's physical state.

Extraordinary, he'd called it. Other than the residue of sunburn and exposure, there had been no trace of anything wrong with him.

Except that Patrick still didn't know who he was.

"He told you to rest," Mackenzie said.

"And not to worry about anything. How can I worry if I'm riding around the station with you?"

Patrick didn't look like a man who was worried. He looked, in fact, just like one of the station hands. Garbed in a blue plaid shirt, white moleskins and a jaunty, wide-brimmed hat, he could have passed for an experienced stockman. Only the traditional braided leather hatband and belt were missing. At least he seemed resigned to sitting in a leather saddle.

"Well, it feels right peculiar to be teaching you to ride, when for all we know you might be a blooming Olympics champ." Mackenzie stepped to one side and gestured for Patrick to mount. "I'll hold her while you get on, then I can adjust your stirrups."

Patrick swung himself up with little effort. The experience didn't seem familiar, but he'd seen enough people on horseback yesterday, while he'd waited for the doctor, to have an idea what was expected of him. He took the reins and held the horse steady as Mackenzie adjusted the stirrup leathers.

"You sit well," she said. "Maybe you have done this before." She stepped back and cocked her head. "How does that feel?"

He didn't know how it was supposed to feel. But he could tell that the horse accepted him on her back. She was resigned to this ordeal, weary, even, of teaching riders the fundamentals. But she was willing, particularly if he didn't make any unreasonable demands. He leaned over her neck and tried to croon to her in the language of his dreams. Although the words that emerged were frustratingly incorrect, she seemed to appreciate the effort. Her ears flipped forward as if in thanks.

He sat up straight again. "We're ready." He met Mackenzie's eyes; they were wary.

"Lean over a horse's neck like that and you're just ask-ing to be thrown. She doesn't know what you're doing. She just feels your weight shifting."

"She understood."

"Are you going to let me teach you, or are you going to try to teach me?"

"Why don't we just see how I do? Then we'll know who should teach who."

She would have been incensed if the words had come from anyone but Patrick. But there had been no attempt to put her in her place; he had been perfectly serious. She mut-tered under her breath as she went to get her mount. From behind her she heard Patrick crooning to Gimme again, but she resisted the impulse to look over her shoulder. Patrick would have to learn by himself, and if he ended up on the ground because of it, then so be it.

Sunfisher was a black gelding the boss had about de-cided to sell south for pet food. His thoroughbred ancestry had never been in question. What was in question was his ability to accept his place. In stockmen slang, a sun fisher was a bucking horse who could leave the ground in one di-rection and land heading the opposite way. That nasty habit was the least of Sunfisher's problems. He was high-spirited and contrary, determined not to earn his keep. There was no spot for a horse like him on a station that had to get not only a good day's work but a day and a half from every living occupant, just to survive.

Mackenzie had been the only thing to stand between Clint Conroy and Sunfisher's trip south. She had fallen for him on sight and worked with Dilly Dan from that day forward to make him into a useful mount. But neither she nor Dilly Dan, one of the best horse breakers in the Territory, had made the necessary adjustments in Sunfisher's behavior.

She saddled him now with a wary eye. He was known for docility until the instant he knew his rider's attention had wavered. Then he was hell on the hoof, a bucking, twisting demon who could send the best riders on the station soar-ing through the air in a matter of seconds. She had taken her own spills off his back, and once, while she had been saddling him, he had dropped to the ground and tried to roll on her.

Today he stood still, plotting, she supposed, what mischief he would work when she was settled on his back. For just a moment she considered taking out a different horse, but Sunfisher's days were numbered unless his behavior improved. It was up to her to see that that happened, and quickly.

In the saddle, she turned him toward Gimme. Patrick still sat comfortably on her back, and the mare looked perfectly content. Mackenzie coached Sunfisher closer, but not too close. "We'll have to stay a distance apart," she warned Patrick. "Sunfisher's known for his bad manners. It would be just like him to kick Gimme or nip her if he gets the chance."

"I can see that."

"Then you're a horseman for certain." She fought Sunfisher for control of the reins and won, but the battle lines had been drawn. "Shall we move on?"

"I'm looking forward to it."

Mackenzie started off. Patrick rode beside her, but not close enough to provoke Sunfisher.

"I don't even know what to tell you," she said. "Maybe you're a station owner or a station owner's son yourself."

"With an American accent?"

"Maybe you're from Texas."

"Well, start with the differences between here and Texas."

"Everything we have here is bigger than your ranches. Much bigger. Only the profit's smaller."

"That doesn't sound fair."

"Waluwara's nearly as big as your Rhode Island." Mackenzie gestured to the buildings beside the homestead. "And there are towns in Australia that are smaller than the homestead. We have to provide everything for ourselves. Can't jump in the car and go for milk or bread. That's the store." She pointed to a small unpretentious building. "There's a little of everything in there. Too little. Edwina and I go to Brisbane once a year and buy all our supplies."

"What's that structure between the store and the homestead?"

"The cool house. That's spinifex packed between the walls. We keep it wet, and as the water evaporates, it cools the inside so it's fifteen, maybe even twenty degrees cooler inside than out. That's all the first settlers had to keep meat cool with. So that's why salted beef was so popular. Every stockman had his own recipe for brine."

She continued the tour as they ambled on. Patrick listened to the information, but he heard more, much more. She was fiercely proud of the station and the life her ancestors had carved from nothing. But she was frustrated, and more. The "more" was hard to detect. He didn't have a word for it. He would understand more clearly if he could touch her, but he remembered how upset she had been when she accused him of reading her mind. He was learning to respond only to words spoken out loud. He had even experienced some success filtering out the other messages that seemed so clear but were obviously not meant to be heard.

They passed the remainder of the buildings, stockmen's quarters, an office, a men's dining room, and continued past stockyards built of steel tubes, the most modern structure in sight.

"We're trying to upgrade the cattle," Mackenzie said. "We've got Brahman bulls and a few Santa Gertrudis. Someday the whole mob will show their influence." She glanced at Patrick. They hadn't come far, but she was determined that he not overdo this first ride.

He looked as at ease in the saddle as if he had been in it since birth.

"Maybe you really are from Texas," she said.

"A carrot ranch, maybe."

She couldn't help herself. She grinned. He smiled, and the sunshine suddenly seemed brighter.

Sunfisher took advantage of Mackenzie's one moment off guard to crab walk in Gimme's direction, make a sharp turn and snap a quick kick at the mare's flank with his hind hooves. Mackenzie jerked the reins and gouged his side with her heel, but not before the damage was done. Gimme, like a child who has been unfairly teased on the school playground, charged the gelding to teach him some manners.

The next seconds passed so quickly that afterward Mackenzie had only a ragged impression of them. Gimme's ears flat against her head, teeth bared in a hideous grin. Patrick low against the horse's neck, his reins forgotten. Sunfisher twisting and twirling beneath her. Gimme moving closer. Then, sunshine, the trilling of a butcher-bird in the bloodwood trees just ahead of them, and two completely docile horses waiting for the ride to continue.

"Are you all right?" Mackenzie asked.

"Fine."

"I thought you were a goner for certain. Sunfisher would have liked nothing better than to trample you into the dust if you'd fallen."

"Gimme was just pointing out that she wasn't going to take any abuse."

"You dropped your reins."

"I can control her better with my hands and voice."

She noticed that his hands were still pressed along the mare's neck. "She's trained to obey certain signals."

Patrick straightened. "And she knows to obey certain others."

Mackenzie could hardly argue, since whatever Patrick had done had been a success. "Sunfisher's going to end up in a pet food sack."

Patrick looked pained. "He's not a bad animal. He just doesn't want to be here."

"Here?"

"In captivity."

"Are you trying to tell me you read animal minds, too?"

He looked beyond her, to endless stretches of earth fanning out into a sea of brown grasses. "So do you. He moves a certain way and you know what he's about to do."

"I don't pretend to know his motivation."

"You know it. You're fond of him because he's like you. He doesn't want to be fettered. He wants freedom, a chance to determine his own destiny."

"Bloody hell, Patrick. He's a horse!"

He turned his gaze to her. He seemed to be looking into the distance again, as if searching her eyes for something as elusive as the horizon. "Don't try to tell me you don't understand what I'm saying. You understand more than you pretend to."

"What's that supposed to mean?"

"You have fine instincts, but they make you uncomfortable."

"Oh, so Sunfisher's mind isn't the only one you're reading today."

He didn't smile. "Is the ride over?"

She took off her hat and waved it, to brush away flies and gain control of her temper. "It doesn't have to be. It's up to you."

"I'd like to go a little farther."

A little farther was an hour's ride across dry creek beds and along dirt tracks that only seldom saw wheels. Mackenzie pointed out paddocks, seemingly limitless areas that had been fenced and set aside for controlled grazing. She named birds for him, a rogue kookaburra laughing from a cluster of trees at the edge of the paddock, a pair of wedge-tail eagles circling overhead.

There were more birds as they neared a large water hole, hooded parrots, rosellas and the ever-present galahs. There were cattle scattered across the landscape in docile, heat-drugged clusters. And there were trees here, eucalyptus, bloodwood and a variety of scrub nestled beside an underground spring that seeped along the grasslands to form a wide, shallow pond.

"This will turn dry soon, if the Wet is too late coming. I've been here when it's nearly desert." Mackenzie dismounted at the water's edge to let Sunfisher drink his fill. She watched Patrick dismount as if he had done it a million times.

She showed him how to hobble Gimme, demonstrating on Sunfisher. He spoke to the horse as he did. She knew an apology when she heard it, no matter what the language.

She took her supplies off Gimme's saddle and gave the mare a friendly slap on the rump. "I brought sandwiches and fruit. And we can boil the billy."

"Why did you hit her?"

"I didn't hurt her. It's a signal. Now she knows she's free to wander and graze a little while we rest."

His eyes smiled as surely as his lips didn't. "You're sure she understands?"

"Of course she does. Look at her."

This time his lips smiled, but she pretended to ignore the meaning behind it. Yes, she understood and communicated with horses, too. So what of it?

She busied herself finding sticks for a small fire. In a few minutes the billy was heating. When she turned to see what Patrick was doing, she discovered that he had taken the extra blanket from her saddle and spread it on the lush grass at the water's edge. As she watched, he unpacked the tucker bag.

She had only meant to stop for a short rest, but it looked as if Patrick was planning something more elaborate. She couldn't fault him; she was certain he was tired. And trousers, saddle and horse rubbing against his sunburned legs couldn't be pleasant.

She took off her hat and sailed it to the blanket's edge, following closely behind. Flopping on her back, staring through the leaves of a gum tree, she could see only slices of the sky. The sun wasn't yet overhead, but the view through the leaves was a clear, brilliant blue.

"I'd give nearly anything to see a cloud," she said. "Can you tell me what it's like to live where it rains regularly? Or do you remember?"

He let his mind drift, careful at the same time not to open the door that led to a thousand voices. He thought of rain. Clear, cool rain and the sound of something... Thunder. He let himself peer through the shimmering silver curtain of water to see trees, majestic and green-leafed, swaying in the storm. There was a woman swaying there, too, her hair like moonlight, her slender body twirling in the raindrops.

"It's different," he said.

She waited for more, but he was silent, tight-lipped and pensive. "Well, at least we know you weren't a poet or a journalist," she said at last.

"I thought I was a mind reader or a philosophy professor."

"Did you remember rain?"

"I think so." He put a sandwich on a plate and set it beside her.

"But that's good, isn't it?"

"I don't know what's good or bad."

"Score one more for the philosophy professor." Reluctantly she sat up. "The doctor told the boss your memory will come back on its own, perhaps a bit at a time, perhaps all at once. In his view, there's nothing to be done about speeding up the process. So I guess I shouldn't keep asking you to try."

"You're curious about me."

"I imagine *you're* curious about you."

He took a bite of his sandwich, and the taste exploded through him. He still couldn't imagine forgetting something as pleasing, as powerful, as taste. Yet every bite seemed new to him.

"I'm curious about you," he said. "You've told me just a little. How about telling me more?"

Without answering, she went to check on the water. She was uneasy about the way he was watching her as she bent over the billy to add loose tea and a gum leaf she had picked for extra flavor. She wasn't quite certain why he was interested in her, and that uncertainty troubled her.

When she returned with the billy, she poured them each a cup before she spoke. "There's nothing to tell, really. I never knew the man who fathered me, never even knew who he was. I told you that I only remember a little about my mother. I have snaps of her that belonged to Uncle Clint. She had red hair, too, but a lighter, copper color. Her eyes were green. I don't really look like her."

"Where did you live while she was alive?"

"Near Adelaide. She worked as a housekeeper on a small sheep property in the hills. It belonged to an old man and his sister. I remember I had my own pet lamb, but I don't remember much else. Then one morning my mother couldn't get out of bed. I went to find the old man, but by the time he got her to hospital, Mother was too ill to respond. They said she died of pneumonia. Now I wonder if she died of heartbreak."

"Heartbreak?"

"She was a quiet woman, even with me. I don't remember that she had any friends. She kept to herself. I think she was ashamed, or perhaps she just mourned the man who'd left her with a baby she hadn't counted on."

"How fragile . . . we are."

"Yes, aren't we? Flimsy, delicate wildflowers to be flattened by the first gust of wind. Except that not all of us are quite that willing to go down."

"It's hard to imagine she would have been, either, if she grew up here."

"I know. Waluwara nearly always kills you or puts starch in your spine. Anyway, the old man and the South Australian authorities traced my mother's family, and I was brought here. They let me bring my lamb, and by the time that bugger died, he was the toughest old piece of mutton ever to run through Waluwara's paddocks. I got tough, too. The men here raised me, and later Edwina and a governess or two did what they could to soften that. Most of the time Edwina helped me with my lessons when Uncle Clint wasn't here to do it. I had classes over two-way radio and with the Aborigine children until I was too old. Then I went to school down south, and finally took one year in Sydney."

"And you disliked school."

"I told you that part."

"Because you were bored."

She didn't answer.

"Because school was too easy?"

She laughed, with no humor. "If you remember school, your memory probably goes like this. The teacher gives you a paper with fifty questions on it. If you're a good student, you sit there and quietly answer all fifty. If you're a smart student, you realize after five that you know how to answer them all, and don't need to practice on the other forty-five. But if you don't answer them, you become a bad student.''

"And you were a bad student?"

"I tried not to be. I liked the books I was given to read to keep me quiet. I'd read them in a few hours, but then I'd be scolded for continuing on without the good students, who might be taking three or four weeks to read and study the same book."

"What did you do about it?"

She finished her sandwich before she spoke. "I came back to Waluwara. I was allowed to read what I wanted here, as swiftly as I chose."

"And you've read a lot?"

"You can give our library a go while you're here."

"A library?"

"Uncle Clint is a reader, too. Books are his only weakness."

"Knowledge can't be a weakness."

She stretched out and turned on her stomach to see him better. "Nothing's quite that simple. There are things we'd all be better off not knowing."

He joined her in stretching out. She watched him unfold his legs and turn to his side. The sun glinted off his golden hair. "What would I be better off not knowing?" he asked.

"Well, considering how little you know now, that's a fair cow to answer."

He smiled. She smiled back, lazy and content and something else—something she wasn't certain she wanted to name. "Answer it anyway," he said. "You must have had something in mind."

"Well, the universe is full of secrets. We don't know why we're here. We can't even make a guess. And every time we do guess, we start in bashing somebody else because we're so certain we have the only good answer."

"I think you were talking about something more personal."

"Do you?"

He touched her hair. One moment his hand had been at his side, the next it was stroking a long red curl as if it suddenly had a mind of its own. He understood enough about this woman to know that his touch wouldn't be appreciated, yet his impulse had been stronger than his knowledge.

He pulled his hand away when he realized what he'd done. "I think I understand what you were just saying."

She didn't move, but she wasn't smiling now. She was watchful. "Oh?"

"I knew I shouldn't touch you, but I did, anyway. And knowing you didn't like it took some of the pleasure away. I would have been happier not knowing either of those things."

She released a long breath. "Maybe, but maybe you need to know a little more. I'm not like most of the women you've met."

She waved her hand in frustration when he started to interrupt. "I know you don't remember any women, but you can be sure there are some. And when you remember them, you'll realize what I'm saying is true. Most women want to find a mate, someone they can settle down with, make a home with, have children with. Most men want the same, only it's better hidden. But I don't want that, Patrick. I want my freedom. I want to be out here, in the sun and the wind, not behind a stove or a desk."

"Touching your hair leads to all that?"

She knew he was teasing her. She smiled again, but reluctantly. "Don't you remember what touching a woman's hair can lead to?"

"No. Tell me."

She wasn't quite so certain he was teasing now. "Making love," she said matter-of-factly.

"Making." He tilted his head in thought. "You mean creating? Taking the barest fragment of an idea and molding something new from it. Is that right?"

"Bloody hell, Patrick."

"Then love. That's the closest bond two people can have, a feeling so strong that when it's shared, it changes everything around it. Isn't it?" He touched her hair again, this time less tentatively. "So if I touch your hair this way, eventually you and I will create the most perfect bond that people can establish. How can that be wrong?''

"I hope your memory comes back soon.''

He twined the curl around his fingers, and she thought of a fish being reeled in for the kill. "This making love," he said. "Isn't it a pleasure?"

Her eyes were fixed on his, and they didn't waver. "So they say.''

"Then why would you resist?''

"Because I don't want that perfect bond, or whatever it was you called it. I don't want to have to consider someone else. Not because I'm selfish. Because I'm not. I don't want to hurt anyone. And I would hurt a man if I couldn't be what he wanted.''

"What if the man only wanted you to be what you are?''

"A ringer? A station hand? A woman who smells like horses and cattle, whose hands are as tough as the saddle she sits in every day? I don't know any men like that. Even the men I work with—who should understand, mind you—want to go home to someone soft and giving.''

"Then you're afraid that making love would turn you into something you don't want to be?''

"No. I'm more afraid it wouldn't. I might try to be those things for a man, but in the end, I could only be me.''

"Hungry for adventure, yearning for freedom.''

She was glad he understood. "There aren't many places left where a man or a woman can have those things.''

"I think there's adventure everywhere." He leaned closer, and his hand dived deeper into her hair. "And in every moment.''

"What about freedom?''

"Freedom grows inside you.''

"The philosophy professor again?''

"I don't think so. A man. Just a man." He watched her eyelids slowly close. He touched her forehead with his lips, savoring the warmth and resilience of her skin. His body was flooded with sensation so intense that for a moment he thought it was pain.

It was pleasure. He kissed her eyelids, and his hand tightened in her hair. If he had ever known this joy, he would not have forgotten it. Touching Mackenzie was a gift so monumental that, for a moment, he could only be grateful.

"Mackenzie." His voice was hoarse to his own ears. He kissed her cheek, the side of her nose and, finally, her lips. They were soft and giving, the things she had said that a man wanted from a woman. He wanted them, and he kissed her harder to test their softness. He could feel the warmth of her breath mingle with his own to ignite the pressures building inside him. She hadn't touched him anywhere, but he could almost feel her hands on his body, in places covered with clothing, places where sensation seemed to pool and heat.

She murmured something, neither an invitation nor a protest, but she turned to her side, and he pulled her closer. She was still inches from him, but he could feel the soft contours of her body as if they were melting into the planes of his. Her lips parted, and so did his. His tongue touched hers and found a new taste that shot wild, dark excitement through him.

He had forgotten this pleasure, but he hadn't forgotten how to seek more. He touched her neck with his fingertips as he kissed her, stroking the smooth expanse of skin again and again before he moved to her shoulder. Her arm lifted to pull him closer, and he discovered the softness of her breast.

"No." The arm that had pulled him closer pushed against his chest. "That's enough." Mackenzie sat up.

He was breathing hard. "I don't think so."

"It's enough for me. Too much." She ran her fingers through her hair and told herself her hands weren't trembling. "Find your memory with someone else, why don't you? I've a life here, and I don't want it changed."

"How much adventure and freedom can there be at Waluwara if anything new frightens you?"

She knelt and began to gather up what was left of their meal. "There was nothing new about being kissed, Patrick. Don't flatter yourself into believing you're the first man who's gotten that far.''

"I'm not."

She glanced at him. He looked too shaken and too pleased by it to suit her. "I've kissed other men."

"I know."

"What do you mean you know?"

"What do you want me to mean?"

She closed her eyes. "Wipe that look of utter satisfaction off your face, will you?"

"I'm not utterly satisfied." He touched her cheek, and her eyes opened reluctantly. "Neither are you."

She wanted to deny it, but it seemed useless. Her gaze dropped to his lips, and she remembered exactly how they had felt.

"We'd better get back." She forced her gaze from him and found Gimme a short distance away. Sunfisher was nowhere in sight.

She looked around and couldn't spot him. "That's odd." She got to her feet and shaded her eyes with her hand. "Sunfisher's gone."

"No." Patrick stood, too. "There."

She looked in the direction he was pointing and saw the horse, a too distant blot against the horizon. "The hobble broke! I didn't check the hide well enough. Bloody hell, we'll never get him back now!"

"Do you want him back?"

"I'm not of a mood to walk to the homestead!"

Hands on her shoulders, he turned her to face him. "Do you want him back? Do you want him to have a chance out here on his own? Or do you want to keep trying to train him?"

"He's half brumby, half broke. He won't have a chance out here as dry as it is. He'll stay away from the water holes near the homestead and won't know how to find the others."

"He might."

She swallowed something like a lump in her throat. "Damn him, anyway! Maybe he'll survive a while, but he'll be one of the first they catch at the next muster, if he lives that long. Off he'll be shipped. I had a chance with him, and I ruined it with my own carelessness.''

"You're not going to try to catch him?"

"It would be useless."

He could feel her sorrow, just as earlier he had felt her passion. He put his arm around her shoulder, but she pulled away. "Gimme can carry us both, but we'd better start now before the worst heat," she said.

"I'll get Sunfisher for you."

She stared at him as if he had lost his mind. "What are you talking about?"

He started forward. "I'll get him."

"You get within calling distance and he'll take off like a rocket. He can jump these fences, even if the cattle can't."

He didn't pause. "But I won't be making anything worse if I try."

She considered going after him. Despite outward appearances, Patrick was not completely recovered. She was certain the ride had tired him, even if he wasn't aware of it. Distances were deceptive in open country, and Sunfisher was farther away than he appeared.

She didn't go. A part of her wanted to see Patrick fail. He was so certain he understood everything, even if he couldn't remember his own name. He was certain of himself, certain of her, certain of a horse no one had been able to properly break. She wanted him to be proven wrong.

About the horse, or about her? She couldn't push the question away, as unpleasant as it was.

The cattle grazing in the area lifted their heads as Patrick drew nearer to Sunfisher. She hadn't warned him about them. Waluwara cattle were a wild lot. Even those in this relatively civilized paddock could be startled with the wave of a hat or a shout. She wished she could warn him now, but running forward to do it or shouting would surely cause the exact trouble she wanted him to avoid.

She stood still instead and watched him draw closer to Sunfisher. Patrick moved with a peculiar grace, a stealthy, purposeful gait that covered the distance in less time than she had expected. As she watched, Sunfisher caught his scent and lifted his head to peer at the man, enemy on foot, closing the distance between them.

She saw Patrick extend his hand as he moved closer. The breeze carried words, but she was too far away to understand them. Sunfisher bunched his magnificent body as if ready to charge, but Patrick drew closer, and the horse stood without moving.

"Bloody hell," she whispered.

Patrick stopped just yards from the horse's head. He didn't attempt to cover the final distance. He held out his hand. She knew he must be talking, crooning, perhaps, as he had done to the snake, but the breeze no longer carried any sound. The cattle stood as still as the horse, watching, waiting.

Sunfisher tossed his head. His whinny pierced the air between them. She waited for him to rear up, to charge Patrick or gallop toward the horizon.

He did neither. As she watched, he moved slowly toward the man, the stranger, the enemy, the untried horseman, and nuzzled his hand.

She wanted to weep.

Chapter 8

"There's blokes who got a way with 'orses, and blokes who ain't." Dilly Dan leaned on the fence at the side of the ring the station used for breaking horses and peered at the duo inside.

"You're saying he's one of those who does?" Clint Conroy watched Patrick swing himself onto Sunfisher's bare back. The horse stood as calmly as if he had been rigorously trained for show.

"I'm saying it's time for me to move east. My daughter's been after me for a year now. She's got me a little place on the coast in Queensland. Look out and see the seabirds, I can, every morning when I wake up."

Mackenzie, standing on Dilly Dan's right, protested, but the old man shook his head. "It's time I go, little girl. The Wet's coming, and every day I wake up and dread it. I want to look forward to the days that are left me."

"Dan's right," Clint said.

Patrick guided Sunfisher to the fence. The horse walked willingly toward them.

"You got Injun blood, son?" Dilly Dan asked.

Patrick leaned over Sunfisher's neck. "Could be."

"We're civilized 'ere. We use saddles and bridles in Oz."

"Sunfisher and I have an understanding."

Dilly Dan laughed, a croaking, wheezing snort that Mackenzie had heard every day of her Waluwara life.

"Does he have an understanding with anyone else?" Mackenzie asked. Patrick shifted his weight to face her. He looked both comfortable and thoroughly alert, ready to take on the world or only this one sharp-tongued woman.

"Or is he a one-rider mount?" she continued. "He won't be much good here, if that's the case."

"Well, why don't you ride him and see?" Patrick asked. He slid off Sunfisher's back. The horse stood placidly beside him.

Mackenzie knew a dare when she heard one. She slipped between timbers in the fence and approached the horse with her hand extended. He lifted his head a little to view her, then returned to his docile stance.

"Want a boost up?"

She considered. She wasn't as tall as Patrick, but she could wriggle and hump her way up on the horse's back if he stood perfectly still. Or she could, with intelligence and grace, accept Patrick's help. She had just enough vanity to go for the latter. "I'll take a boost."

He bent over and cupped his hands. She presented him with her foot, and in a moment, with the help of his powerful thrust, she was sitting squarely on Sunfisher's back.

"Now what?" she asked. "Do I have to speak his language?"

"It would help. But since you refuse..." He favored her with a brief, cocky smile. "Just squeeze him hard with your knees when you want him to stop. Guide him with your hands on his neck."

Reluctant to take any more advice or to spend any more time admiring that smile, she urged the horse forward. In a moment they were cantering smoothly around the ring. Without a saddle she felt as if she were floating. Harry and another Aborigine stockman, Johnny, stopped to watch, and she waved as she passed them. When she was tired of the spectacle, she spoke softly to Sunfisher and gripped him harder with her knees. For a moment she doubted he would stop at such a meager command, but he slowed and finally stopped in front of Patrick once again.

"What do you think?" Patrick asked her.

She didn't have a chance to answer. Dilly Dan did it for her. "I think it's a blooming miracle, that's what I think. And I think you've pinched me blooming job."

"Pinched?"

The old man took off his hat, a hopelessly battered model that had only rarely been off his head. His face was the same beat-up brown as the hat, but now it was even more wrinkled with a smile. "Nabbed it, you did. I'm not needed on the run anymore. I'll pack me things and 'ead for Cairns tomorrow. You're the new 'orse breaker. That is, if it's right with the boss 'ere."

"You really think he can do it?" Clint asked.

"Never seen a bloke that was better with 'orses, 'cept when I looked in me mirror. Never will again."

Mackenzie patted Sunfisher's neck, but her eyes were on Patrick. In the three weeks since their first ride together, he had steadily become a part of the station. After his success catching Sunfisher, Mackenzie had suggested that he work with Dilly Dan. Patrick was never going to be any help with the cattle. With his distaste for eating meat and using animal products, he certainly wasn't going to be a stockman.

But he was a top horse breaker. In two weeks he had learned everything Dilly Dan could teach him. In another, he had begun to teach the old man.

"The job's yours, if you want it," Clint said.

Mackenzie couldn't let the offer go unchallenged. "And what if he remembers who he is tomorrow and takes off for a reunion with his wife and kids in Chicago or Dallas?"

Clint gave her a long look, as if assessing why she would object. "Then we'll find someone else. And be glad he was here as long as he was. But it's time for Dan to move on. He's ready for a holiday."

"Putting me out to pasture," Dilly Dan said. "And I'm right glad of it."

Mackenzie shrugged, but she didn't feel nonchalant about this new development. At no point had she really believed that Patrick was going to stay at Waluwara. Now, at least temporarily, he would be paid to do just that. She was torn between pleasure that he was staying and unhappiness that his departure was going to be delayed. She had no doubts he would leave as soon as he regained his memory, and the longer he stayed, the more complicated her feelings became.

The two stockmen joined them. Harry smiled at Patrick; the two men had already become friends. Clint explained what had transpired, and the stockmen shook hands with Dilly Dan and wished him well.

Dilly Dan and the boss went toward the office to get the bookkeeper to settle all debts, and Johnny went to check on the generator. Mackenzie slipped through the fence to stand beside the men.

"It won't be the same without Dilly Dan," she said.

"Thought you were always ready for change," Harry said.

"Not that kind. I'll miss him. Won't you?"

"I miss him, I'll go walkabout to Cairns for a holiday."

"You hate cities."

"I like Dilly Dan." Harry turned to Patrick. "You going to come meet my family today?"

"I'm looking forward to it."

"You're going to the village?" Mackenzie asked.

"Want to come?" Harry asked her. "Tilly been asking for you."

"Has she?" Mackenzie considered. Tilly was Harry's middle daughter, a ten-year-old darling with Harry's incredible smile. "Shall I saddle Gimme and take Tilly for a ride?"

"She has lessons." He smiled at Mackenzie's frown. "Okay, but then you help with her reading."

"Done." She turned to Patrick. "Mind if I come?"

"Mind?" He lifted a brow. The rest of his answer was clear. She felt both welcomed and, somehow, threatened.

She pushed away what surely amounted to adolescent jitters. She had spent as little time as possible with Patrick in the past weeks, but she could not avoid him any longer. "Harry, you're taking the ute?" she asked.

He nodded.

"Why don't you take Patrick with you? I'll follow on horseback."

"We'll see you there."

She watched the two men stroll off together. She doubted that Patrick understood what an honor it was to have been invited to meet Harry's family. Harry was an important man in the village, just as he was on the station at large. He was friendly to everyone, but he was also a man of great dignity and pride. He did not extend true friendship to all.

She caught Gimme and Bounder, who had found his way back to the homestead after a week in the open, and was saddling them when she saw her uncle approaching. His expression was a study in contrasts. Since it was rarely possible to discern his feelings with a glance, she knew that something important had happened.

"I just got a cable," he confirmed.

"Bad news?"

"I suppose that depends."

"Who was it from?"

"St. Carroll. He's coming in two weeks. He wants to get here before the Wet."

"Bloody hell."

Clint's gaze flicked to her. He didn't smile.

"You have a better response?" she asked.

"He's bringing a team of geologists. He's had news they found a manganese deposit over at Silver Tree. He hopes they'll find one here, too, since the terrain's similar."

"Any drilling they do should be for another bore."

"There's more."

"What?"

"He's considering putting the station up for sale."

She hardly knew what to say. "But the St. Carrolls have always owned Waluwara."

"He can't maintain his leases if he doesn't make improvements, and I doubt he has the money for those. He's a gambling man, and I think he's gambled away most of his inheritance. Either he can sell shares in the station, or he can sell it outright. He has no love for the life here and no loyalty to family traditions. What he knows about cattle would fit on his thumbnail."

Clint rolled a cigarette and lit it. "I've known his thoughts on this for six months."

"Why didn't you tell me?"

"Because I hoped he would sell."

"But another owner might be worse."

"Another owner might be me." Clint smoked for a while and let his words sink in before he continued. "I've money saved."

"I know. But enough?"

"My parents made good investments, and so did theirs. I took a few chances with what they'd saved and won. I couldn't manage buying the run on my own, but there are others who would invest if I asked. I'd be the majority stockholder."

"Waluwara would belong to you." Mackenzie hugged herself. "But that would be wonderful!"

"If he finds ore, he won't sell. If he doesn't, and he spends all the money necessary to look for it, he won't have enough money to keep it."

"So everything depends on whether he's successful or not?"

"If he is, he'll take the ore, get the money and not spend a dime more than he has to on the station. He'll let it go to rack and ruin."

"He already has."

"Rack, maybe. We're still a step away from ruin."

"What can we do to keep him from finding ore?"

Clint finished his cigarette before he looked at her. His face said it all.

"Nothing?" She stared at him. "You're not going to do anything?"

"You're suggesting I do something dishonest?"

"I'm suggesting you give it a good think!"

"I raised you better than that."

Her eyes didn't waver. "You raised me to put Waluwara first. That's what you've always done. How moral is it to let Sebastian St. Carroll strip this land of everything without putting anything back into it? What will that do to the people in the village, or the people here at the homestead whose lives are this place?"

"I reckon I'll put you in charge then, Mac. You find a way to stop them. Sabotage their equipment. Arrange accidents and injuries. Lie to them."

She looked away, toward the homestead with its peeling paint and rusting iron roof. "Bloody hell."

"That's what you want, isn't it?"

"You didn't get to be the boss here for nothing, did you?"

"We don't have to make this a picnic for them, but we'll do nothing to interfere."

"Can I say a few prayers?"

"Will the Big Boss recognize your voice?"

"Maybe I'll ask Harry to intercede for me. He's on speaking terms."

"It can't hurt."

Clint turned to walk away, but Mackenzie stopped him with a hand on his arm. She wanted to reassure him, but she couldn't think of anything that would help. "She'll be right," she said at last, falling back on slang. "No worries."

He covered her hand in a rare display of affection before he started toward the homestead.

Waluwara village consisted of small, simple block homes interspersed with huge, lacy-leafed pepper trees surrounding a complex of larger one-story buildings that housed the village school, clinic and administration offices.

The clash of one people of Stone-Age weapons and New-Age respect for their environment with another people of advanced technology and a primitive understanding of the land had resulted, after centuries of discord and bloodshed, in a society that was still struggling to find common ground.

The traditions that had so long sustained the Aborigines had been irrevocably altered with European migration to Australia. Land that had once been theirs to roam and revere was claimed now by others. Entire tribes had been exterminated, including every Aborigine in Tasmania.

The result had been a rift in the social fabric of a people. Alcoholism and other forms of intoxication were serious problems. Education and employment were often interrupted by the habits of a migratory people given little incentive to change their ways. Balancing past injustices with present realities was a topic of great debate among all segments of Australian society.

The debate still raged in the Northern Territory, with extremists on every side. The debate was not raging at Waluwara. Harry David and Clint Conroy, two men with one sensibility, had pledged to work together to find a solution.

The village was part of it. Technically the land was still pastoral leasehold land, but an arrangement had been formed to allow the residents full administration and usage. Although the village proper was small, the surrounding area, hundreds of square kilometers, was considered tribal land, too. Compared to the squalid living conditions on some Territory stations, Waluwara Village was a model of what could be accomplished.

There were still problems; they were inevitable. But there was mutual respect between cultures, and a belief that compromises could be found.

As Mackenzie rode into the village, one of those compromises was evident. One of the schoolteachers, a young man who had recently come from Perth to spend the year, was finishing up the school day by taking nature lessons from his students. The children were teaching him their names for the vegetation and insect life surrounding the school. There was a policy here that the children's own talents and knowledge be respected and that their rhythms be considered in planning the school day. Balance was the watchword. At Waluwara no child was expected to sit quietly morning and afternoon memorizing facts about a world far removed from his or her own experience.

A little girl with soft dark curls tugged at the teacher's shirt and pointed toward Mackenzie. Mackenzie waited in silence as he nodded his permission. Then she dismounted and opened her arms as Tilly ran toward her.

The village children were exuberantly affectionate. The life here was good, their parents indulgent. Tilly wrapped her arms around Mackenzie's waist and gossiped with her in the tribal dialect. Mackenzie smoothed Tilly's hair and gossiped, too.

Dismissed for the day, the other children in the class came to welcome her. She lifted one to her shoulders, village-style, and, leading the horses, started toward Harry's house. The children peeled off one by one until only Tilly and Len, the little boy Mackenzie carried, were left. Then Len wriggled down to go find his mother, and Mackenzie and Tilly were left alone.

"Is school still going well?" Mackenzie asked in English.

"Fine. I like geography."

"How about addition and subtraction?"

"I like multiplication best."

"Good on ya."

"Did you bring me a book?"

"I did. You can read some of it out loud to me before I leave."

Tilly ran on ahead of Mackenzie and the horses as they neared her house. Mackenzie fastened the reins before tapping on the door frame. As always, the door stood open in welcome.

Lula, Tilly's mother, greeted her and, arm around Mackenzie's waist, ushered her inside. Tilly's baby brother, who had an appropriately dignified name but was known to all as Brother, sat on his mother's opposite hip as naturally as if he were rooted there.

The house was simply furnished. Much of the village life was lived outdoors, and it wasn't unusual for the family to sleep under the stars when the sky was clear. The sky, the earth and the stars were friends, not hostile enemies to be walled away.

Patrick and Harry were sitting at a small table drinking steaming tea. The two men couldn't have been more different in appearance, but they shared an indefinable essence. Seeing them together this way made it clearer to Mackenzie why they had already become friends.

She chatted with Lula and the men while Tilly changed into jeans. Harry was about to take Patrick on a village tour. When Tilly joined them again, both men stood. Brother held out his arms, but to Patrick, not to his father.

"May I?" Patrick asked Lula.

Lula set the baby in his arms. Brother cuddled against him as if they had been long acquainted. Patrick touched the baby's hair, then his nose.

"You look like you've never held a littley before," Mackenzie said.

"I haven't."

She wondered if he was making a guess, or if he had remembered something. "Well, you look happy you're finally having the chance."

Patrick swayed, almost as if he was experimenting. When Brother laughed, Patrick swayed again. Then he laughed, too.

The sound went straight through Mackenzie, and her breath caught in her throat. Patrick's laughter seemed to crystallize all the miracles, the rare and splendid things of the world. If he had laughed before, it hadn't been like this, spontaneous and thoroughly delighted. Whatever demons tormented him, they were forgotten for this brief moment.

"May I take him with us?" Patrick asked.

"Don't make Patrick give up his new toy," Mackenzie advised Lula. "Besides, it will give you a proper rest."

Patrick turned to her, and his eyes still showed residues of delight. She smiled at him, helpless to do anything else.

"Why don't you have one of these, Mackenzie?" he asked.

"Apparently you've forgotten it takes a mother and a father to produce a Brother."

"No. I haven't forgotten."

She could almost swear he was volunteering. She turned away so he wouldn't see the quick flash of desire that surged through her. "Tilly, are you ready?"

"Can I ride Bounder?"

"Do you really think you can handle him?"

Tilly nodded.

"Harry?" Mackenzie asked for permission.

"I think she can do it. She fall off, she pick herself back up again."

"Let's give it a go," Mackenzie said. She didn't spare Patrick another look, afraid of what she might see.

As she and Tilly rode through the village, two dogs followed at the horses' heels. They were cattle dogs, blue heelers trained to work beside the stockmen when mustering or yarding a mob. Clint and Harry prided themselves on Waluwara's contribution to blue heeler lines. These two specimens were fat and lazy, long past the age when the sight of a bullock sent them into a frenzy of activity. They trotted dutifully along beside Gimme as if pretending they were still useful.

"A regular pair of frauds," Mackenzie said. "Looking for a handout, I reckon."

"You've brought something for them?"

Mackenzie had, as always, and she smiled her answer to Tilly. "You can give them each a treat when we stop."

"Where are we going?"

"I thought we'd ride up to Two Rock Hill."

"Right-o."

They chatted as they covered nearly a kilometer. Harry had two other daughters, one thirteen, who was away at school in Alice Springs, another several years younger than Tilly. But it was Tilly who, as a baby, had attached herself to Mackenzie and claimed her as a friend. They had always had a special bond, much the kind of bond that Clint and Harry shared. They were as united by their differences as by the things they had in common.

"When I'm a woman," Tilly said, "I'm going to have my own station and raise horses."

"Are you? I thought you were going to live in the city and write books."

"I'll do both."

"At the same time?"

"Different times. Same life."

Mackenzie laughed. "Don't ever let anything or anyone stop you."

She could hear the dogs wheezing with exhaustion beside her. The sun was still high, and the air as dry as desert sand. Tilly had a stoic tolerance for discomfort, but Mackenzie knew better than to test her limits. "Let's stop over there and have some water," she said, pointing to a thicket of twisted mulga trees. "You can give the dogs their treats so they can head back home."

They guided the horses toward the thicket, where shade spread its gnarled fingers along the rock-strewn ground.

Tilly pulled Bounder to a stop before they reached the shade, but Mackenzie didn't notice. "I'll get the water, you—"

Her next words were drowned in a spasm of barking. The dogs streaked past her, as if reliving their days in the sun. From nowhere—or so it seemed—a mickey bull, one of the station's deadly rogues, came charging through the thicket to rid itself of this new irritation. Gimme, famed for complacence, rose to the occasion and leaped out of the way. Bounder leaped, too, a whirlwind of heels and tail, but Tilly, without the benefit of Mackenzie's years in the saddle, wasn't skilled enough to ride out the storm.

"Tilly!" Mackenzie succeeded in positioning Gimme between the little girl, who had fallen to the ground, and the bull, who had turned for another go at them. She whistled sharply to the dogs and charged toward the bull. The dogs, who in retirement hadn't lost their instincts, covered the ground just ahead of her.

The bull charged, too. Mackenzie would have given everything for her whip. Her chances of turning him weren't good, but there were no other options. There hadn't been time to get Tilly on her horse. She could only hope that the little girl would catch Bounder and get away while she diverted the bull.

She whistled and screeched, grabbing her hat to wave in the bull's face when he drew near enough. The waving hat was just enough of a menace to turn him. He wheeled as she passed him and started toward her once more. Mackenzie had a split second to search for Tilly. The little girl lay exactly where she had fallen.

"Get up, Tilly!" she screamed.

There was nothing else she could do, not even watch to see if Tilly obeyed. She charged the bull again, screaming and whistling in turns. The dogs charged, too, staying what seemed like only inches from the animal's heels.

At the last second the bull wheeled left. This time he lumbered away, his dignity greatly wounded. The dogs followed, one on each side, as if they had plotted their tactics for many hours. A cloud of dust followed them into the distance.

Mackenzie dismounted and ran toward the little girl, who still hadn't moved. "Tilly!" She slid to a stop at the child's side and fell to her knees.

Tilly didn't even moan. Her eyelids weren't closed, and she stared into space, at something Mackenzie couldn't see.

Mackenzie was gripped by horror. "No!" She felt for Tilly's pulse, but her hands trembled so violently she couldn't find it. "Tilly, wake up!"

Tilly didn't move. Her expressive dark eyes were blank.

Mackenzie stood and looked wildly around. She couldn't ride off and leave the child alone, but she couldn't move her, either. She had to get help. If anything could be done, it had to be done right away. Gimme stood quietly by, as if she understood that she might be needed. Mackenzie grabbed her rifle and loaded it. She aimed over the thicket of trees, shot and reloaded until she had sent a clear distress signal.

"Come on!" she shouted. "Somebody, come on!"

There was no response. Not even the birds that dwelled in that harshly beautiful place gave an answering call.

* * *

"Are there horses nearby?" Patrick asked.

Harry stopped in the middle of a sentence, in the middle of his tour of the village. "Not far."

"I've got to find Mackenzie."

Harry frowned. He looked at Patrick, then just beyond him, as if putting together what he had seen in Patrick's eyes. "We can get them now."

He took Brother from Patrick's arms and unceremoniously handed him to a woman standing nearby. Then he started off at a trot, and Patrick fell in beside him. Neither man said another word until they had left the village proper behind. At the ramshackle paddock that housed half a dozen station horses, Harry crawled through the fence with Patrick right behind him.

"There's tack there." Harry pointed to a small shed at the paddock's edge and started in that direction.

Instead of following, Patrick gave a shrill whistle and started toward a white mare whose ears had perked up at the sound. When he reached her side he grabbed the mare's mane and hoisted himself onto her back before she had a chance to consider his actions. He leaned over her neck and crooned in her ear. She danced beneath him, distrustful at first of this human who rode without a saddle. Then, as he crooned, she gathered her body and sprang toward the fence.

Patrick rode low on the mare's neck, encouraging her to move faster. He had a flash of Harry's surprised face, then nothing more as the mare sailed over the wooden railing. Patrick gripped with his knees and sat forward even farther.

Outside the paddock he guided the horse by instinct, bypassing the village, although he knew that was the way Mackenzie and Tilly had gone. He had a crystalline vision of where Mackenzie was and the best way to get there. He didn't have time to question where the vision had come from, or why he had been entrusted with it. He only knew that he couldn't ignore it.

The mare ran faster, as if she had been given a vision, too. Patrick scanned the horizon, although he knew he wasn't close enough to find what he sought. To his left, in the distance, he saw dust stirring and the silhouette of an animal, one of the station's cattle, against the horizon. He picked up the sound of dogs barking, carried on the clear afternoon air.

The sound of the dogs faded, and suddenly the air was split with gunfire somewhere in front of him. He urged the mare on as the gunfire resounded again and again. He closed his eyes and saw Mackenzie standing by a small grove of trees, stunted, arthritic trees that grew where water didn't flow. He saw her raise her rifle and pull the trigger. And on the ground at her feet . . .

"No!" He opened his eyes and scanned the horizon again. The gunfire sounded once more, closer, but still not close enough. Helplessly he rode the mare harder.

The gifts you have now are infinitely precious. But, like all of us, you are already bored by what you can do. Perhaps someday those gifts will be denied you. Then, by losing what you had, you will discover more.

He found no comfort in the voice or the philosophy. For a moment his concentration faltered. The vision of Mackenzie and Tilly faded, and all he could see was endless bleak land, broken only by low hills and . . .

A thicket of mulga trees.

"Mackenzie!"

Even from a distance he could see her turn. She raised her hand to her mouth as if to stifle a sob. He crooned to the mare, winded now, but still gamely carrying him toward his goal. The distance grew shorter, and the mare slowed. At the thicket he slid off her back and went right to Tilly's side.

"A bull came out of the thicket, one of the wild ones," Mackenzie said. "He scared Bounder, but he got out of the way. Tilly fell off. She . . . she . . . I don't know if she's breathing! I can't find a pulse. She hasn't moved or moaned. Don't move her, Patrick."

He knelt beside the child and lifted her wrist. He began to murmur to her as he laid his head on her chest. Her skin was warm from the sun.

Mackenzie knelt at Tilly's other side. "Will you stay here with her and let me ride for help?"

"No. Stay here."

He touched Tilly's neck, as Mackenzie had done.

"Is she . . . ?" She couldn't bear to say the word. One moment Tilly had been chattering about her plans for the future, the next she was lying motionless. "I closed her eyes. They were open. She wasn't . . . looking at anything. She can't be . . ."

He heard the sob in Mackenzie's voice. He shut his eyes, but the sob seemed to grow louder. Her sorrow entwined with his own. "Shh . . ." he said. "Be silent."

She bit her lip and twisted her fingers together. Patrick was completely motionless. Then, with his eyes still closed, he put his hands on each side of Tilly's head. He began to murmur again. The words flowed through him until there was a river of words. He felt the little girl resist them, but he murmured still.

"Patrick?" Mackenzie watched in horror as Patrick began to move Tilly's head from side to side. "No, Patrick. If she's injured her spine . . ."

When he didn't respond she tried to grab his hands, but she was overwhelmed with such a feeling of inertia that she could not force herself to move or speak again. The world seemed to stop spinning. There seemed to be nothing in it except one man and one child and a woman who was a million miles away from them.

She heard murmuring and watched as Patrick moved his hands to Tilly's neck, then to her shoulders. The murmuring grew louder. She recognized the words, but somehow could not fathom their meaning. Patrick's hands moved to Tilly's chest, then beneath her to her back. He straightened her contorted body as he murmured louder.

Mackenzie felt tears drain down her cheeks, but she couldn't even lift her hands to wipe them away.

"Tilly," Patrick whispered. "When you're ready."

The sun seemed to go behind a cloud, but the sky was cloudless. There was no sound, not even hoofbeats, although Mackenzie could see Harry riding like the wind toward them. The air was filled with a powerful pungent sweetness that choked her lungs. She drew in breath after breath of it as she sobbed for Tilly.

"Mac?" The little girl sat up slowly. She looked around. "You never cry," she said, almost as if she wasn't sure this was the same woman she had just been conversing with.

Mackenzie threw her arms around her before she even realized she could move again. "My God, Tilly, are you all right?" she asked.

"All right?" Tilly pushed Mackenzie away. She pointed to her father. "Why is he here?"

"That's a good question, mate," Harry said, dismounting and coming to Patrick's side. "Why am I here?"

Mackenzie started to explain, then stopped abruptly. She looked at Patrick for the first time since Tilly had sat up. He didn't meet her eyes.

"Tilly got the wind knocked out of her," she said at last, turning to Harry. "A mickey bull charged her, and she fell off Bounder."

"What kind of ringer you going to be, Tilly?" Harry chided. "Can't you ride better than that?"

The little girl hung her head, but her eyes sparkled. She had seen the worry on her father's face. "I fell good," she said. "Real good."

"She did," Mackenzie said.

"And you heard her fall?" Harry asked Patrick. "All that way you heard her fall?"

Patrick turned to him. The two men stared at each other for a long moment. Harry nodded before he turned to his daughter. "You feel good enough to ride back with me?"

"Can I?" Tilly made it clear she thought this was a special honor.

"We'll go back now. I'll catch Gimme for you. No more Bounder."

Mackenzie listened as Tilly, who was standing now, chattered away. Harry went for Gimme, who, after the crisis, had moved off in search of afternoon tea. Mackenzie touched the little girl's curls, felt the warmth of her cheeks, but she still couldn't convince herself that Tilly was there, alive and unharmed.

Finally she stood motionless beside Patrick and watched Tilly and her father mount and start toward the village. Only when they were spots on the horizon did she turn to him.

"She was dead," she said.

"Obviously not."

"Who are you?"

"I wish I knew."

She saw strain on his face, beneath his deep blue eyes and around his mouth. He looked older somehow, as if the encounter with Tilly had aged him.

"I'm afraid of you," she said. She stepped away as she said the words, although she hadn't intended to. "I'm afraid of you!" She could feel hysteria setting in, but she was as powerless to control it as she had been powerless to move when he healed Tilly. "I want you to go. I don't care what my uncle says. I want you to go!"

"I know you do." Patrick stared into the distance.

"You were speaking her language!" She covered her cheeks as she finally realized what she had heard. "You were speaking her dialect. There are probably less than three hundred people on this earth who speak it!"

"Obviously I'm one of them."

"How?" The questions tumbled one after another in her head. There was no order of importance. They clustered around one central question. "Who are you!"

"I'm a paradox," he said. "An enigma. A man with no memories, no home, no people."

"I tried to reach her, to grab your hands, and I couldn't move."

"Time passed swiftly. Only seconds elapsed before she came around. It seemed slower to you."

"Don't treat me like an infant!" Nothing was holding her back now. She covered the space she had put between them and grabbed his hands. "I thought you were going to hurt her. But you brought her back to life with these!"

"Since that's not possible, she couldn't have been dead."

She heard the utter lack of expression in his voice. Something twisted inside her. "You know more than you're telling, don't you? Are you a devil? An angel? Are you going to destroy us or help us, Patrick?" She dropped his hands and slammed hers against his chest. "Then strike me down, damn you, but I'm telling you to leave us! There's no place for angels or devils at Waluwara. We're barely hanging on to our own!"

He grasped her hands and covered them with his. Her breath was a sob in her throat, and her eyes were wild and tear-filled.

He gazed into her eyes and saw her fears, fears as boundless as his own. He tried to calm her, to calm himself. "I'm a man. I've never been an angel or a devil, and I'm not a god. What I am...I don't know. But I know what I'm not."

"You saved Tilly's life."

"I seem to have healing powers."

"What other powers do you have? You came before you could have heard the shots. How did you know I needed you?"

"I don't know." He lifted her hands to his face, rubbing them against one cheek. He needed the feel of her, even though she was stiff against him. "I often know where you are and what you're doing."

Her eyes widened. "You follow me?"

"In my mind." His hands grasped hers tighter. "Sometimes I have glimpses of others. You...you I see clearly."

"No more!"

"I can block my thoughts of you. Is that what you really want?"

"I want you to go!"

"No, you don't." He pulled her closer. There was nothing gentle about his touch. At that moment he yearned for her with a need that was completely new to him. "You don't want me to ignore you or forget you. And you don't want me to go. You know I won't bring trouble here. Whatever I am, whoever I am, I'm not evil!"

She struggled against him. "You read minds, commune with animals, have visions. You heal children, maybe even bring them back to life! You speak a language you couldn't even have heard before!"

"All those things must have explanations."

"None of which you believe!"

"And how do you know what I believe?" He dropped her hands and circled her waist so that she was fully against him. He drew sustenance from the feel of her, the only sustenance he was capable of finding. "Do you read my mind, too? You could, you know, if you chose to."

"Never!"

"You're lying. You know what I'm thinking now."

She knew only too well. Her eyes closed as his head dipped down to hers. When he took her lips with his, she knew only too well what he wanted from them and from her. She struggled, but there was no strength in it. The struggle was within herself.

"I'm afraid of you," she whispered when he kissed her cheek, her chin, the pulse at the base of her throat.

"You're afraid of us both," he said. "So am I."

"I want you to go."

"I have to stay."

She didn't ask how he knew. She didn't ask why. The fight drained out of her. She felt his hands, hungry against her skin. She felt his lips, aching for hers. And she knew that he had imprisoned her with his need for what she could give him.

He could not leave, and she could not make him go. Whoever he was, he would remain at Waluwara until his drama had been played out. And she, despite all her fears and misgivings, could do nothing but play her part, too.

Chapter 9

"I don't know whether to hope you're right or wrong." Mackenzie stood with arms folded, gazing toward a group of men who were about to sink a bore on the northeastern end of the run.

"Will it be such a personal victory for you if I've made a mistake?" Patrick asked. He touched her chin, forcing her to turn.

When she didn't—and couldn't—answer, he shook his head and moved closer to the site to watch the men begin.

Mackenzie didn't call him back, but his question nagged at her.

Patrick seemed to be able to read minds, heal injuries and envision the future. Now Patrick claimed to be able to find water under the earth.

Having been made aware of the urgent need for a new water supply on this edge of the run where thirsty cattle were dying, Patrick had ridden out with Harry one day the previous week to view the terrain. He had agreed that Clint's chosen location for a bore would eventually be successful, but only at great cost. Then he had pointed to a distant spot no one had considered and promised that water would be closer to the surface there. So much closer that the station's share of the drilling could actually be found in the budget.

Harry had convinced Clint that Patrick's choice was worth a try. With financial assistance from the Water Resources Branch of the Northern Territory government, drilling had been scheduled.

Now, two weeks after Tilly's fall, Mackenzie wondered if this would be another example of Patrick's baffling powers or a defeat that would firmly anchor him to his humanity. The station needed this new water supply. She didn't really want the bore to be a failure. But neither did she want Patrick to be a success.

"They're about to commence drilling. Are you going to stay and watch?" Clint asked, taking Patrick's place beside her.

"I don't think so. I promised Edwina I'd help her get the guest rooms ready for St. Carroll and his crew tonight."

"Afraid Patrick was wrong?"

She couldn't admit her ambivalence. She had not talked about Patrick's gifts with her uncle. What was there to say? Taken case by case, day by day, each incident could be explained. She believed in intuition. She had known people from the village, old men and women, who were so attuned to the land and its rhythms that they could predict the future. They could foresee weather changes, droughts, floods.

She had known healers, people who had a special ability, a special touch with the ill. She had known men like Dilly Dan, who seemed able to tell what an animal was thinking.

And although she had never known a dowser, she had heard of men who traveled the outback with crooked sticks or metal rods and claimed they could find water. Her uncle had never used one, but she had heard that the boss at nearby Silver Tree had been using a dowser to find water when the manganese deposit had been discovered there.

So what could she say? That she believed Patrick conversed with snakes and brought back the dead? Which of them would look crazy then?

"Nothing to say?" Clint asked.

NO COST! NO OBLIGATION TO BUY!
NO PURCHASE NECESSARY!

PLAY "LUCKY 7"
AND GET AS MANY AS FIVE FREE GIFTS...

HOW TO PLAY:

1. With a coin, carefully scratch off the silver box at the right. This makes you eligible to receive two or more free books, and possibly another gift, depending on what is revealed beneath the scratch-off area.

2. Send back this card and you'll receive brand-new Silhouette Intimate Moments® novels. These books have a cover price of $3.39 each, but they are yours to keep absolutely free.

3. There's no catch. You're under no obligation to buy anything. We charge nothing—ZERO—for your first shipment. And you don't have to make any minimum number of purchases—not even one!

4. The fact is thousands of readers enjoy receiving books by mail from the Silhouette Reader Service™ months before they're available in stores. They like the convenience of home delivery and they love our discount prices!

5. We hope that after receiving your free books you'll want to remain a subscriber. But the choice is yours—to continue or cancel, anytime at all! So why not take us up on our invitation, with no risk of any kind! You'll be glad you did!

You'll look like a million dollars when you wear this lovely necklace! Its cobra-link chain is a generous 18″ long, and the multi-faceted Austrian crystal sparkles like a diamond!

PLAY "LUCKY 7"

**Just scratch off the silver box with a coin.
Then check below to see which gifts you get.**

YES! I have scratched off the silver box. Please send me all the gifts for which I qualify. I understand I am under no obligation to purchase any books, as explained on the back and on the opposite page.

245 CIS AJDR
(U-SIL-IM-05/93)

NAME

ADDRESS   APT

CITY   STATE   ZIP

7 7 7	WORTH FOUR FREE BOOKS PLUS A FREE CRYSTAL PENDANT NECKLACE
🍒 🍒 🍒	WORTH THREE FREE BOOKS PLUS A FREE CRYSTAL PENDANT NECKLACE
🍑 🍑 🍑	WORTH THREE FREE BOOKS
🔔 🔔 🍒	WORTH TWO FREE BOOKS

THE SILHOUETTE READER SERVICE™:HERE'S HOW IT WORKS
Accepting free books puts you under no obligation to buy anything. You may keep the books and gift and return the shipping statement marked "cancel." If you do not cancel, about a month later we will send you 6 additional novels, and bill you just $2.71 each plus 25¢ delivery and applicable sales tax, if any.* That's the complete price, and—compared to cover prices of $3.39 each—quite a bargain! You may cancel at any time, but if you choose to continue, every month we'll send you 6 more books, which you may either purchase at the discount price . . . or return at our expense and cancel your subscription.

* Terms and prices subject to change without notice. Sales tax applicable in N.Y.

"I'm surprised you trusted him," Mackenzie said. "You've no proof he's doing more than guessing."

"I reckon it's a good guess. I know the terrain. There's as much chance of finding water there as there is anywhere."

"You never used a dowser before."

"I never had one living right at the station. I've taken Patrick's measure. A guess is a guess, a mistake, just that. But whether he's right or not, I know he won't cheat me."

Mackenzie's gaze followed Patrick. He was talking to the men. As she watched, he removed his hat and swept his hair off his forehead. In that brief moment the sun glinted in the golden strands and his attractions were even more potent.

She felt the impact of that attraction deep inside her, just as she always did. She avoided being alone with Patrick now, avoided it so well that they hadn't had a truly private conversation since Tilly's fall. But every time she saw him, whether at close range or from a distance, she felt a stronger pull.

"I might trust him," Clint said, "but that doesn't mean you should."

She felt just as she had as a child when Clint had caught her leaving a paddock gate unlatched. She turned to him and saw the only father she had ever known. She saw concern on his face and something more abstract. She searched for what it was before she spoke.

"You're bothered I'm grown up now, aren't you?"

He didn't answer. A muscle jumped in his jaw, but for once she didn't heed the warning.

"You're afraid I'll leave."

"Not true. You're free to go any time. There's no real life here for you."

"Then what is it?" She touched his arm. "You've raised me to have a level head. I'm as much like you as a woman can be. Why don't you trust me to make my own decisions about Patrick?"

He didn't look at her. "You haven't had the experience."

"If I haven't, it's because you made certain every man who crossed Waluwara's borders knew better than to *give* me any experience."

"Did you want to be fair game for every swagman who came along? Do you think the blokes who wander this country are the kind who would do the right thing by you?"

"Some are, and some aren't. But it's my job, not yours, to tell the difference."

"Are you saying you've learned? If you are, you might ask yourself why you've chosen a man who may have a past that will haunt you."

She wasn't going to deny her attraction to Patrick any more than she was going to explain that she had no intention of doing anything about it. The issue here was something broader.

"It's my mother, isn't it?" she asked. "You're afraid I'll turn out just like her, get myself preggie and disappear. Well, no worries, boss. I won't die and saddle you with another little Mackenzie."

He faced her. The expression in his eyes could have set fire to the brush at their feet. "Have I ever indicated that I felt saddled with you?"

"We're talking around the point. I know you love me, and you loved my mother. But I'm *not* my mother."

He searched her eyes, and little by little his expression softened. "No," he said, "you're not. She had the benefit of a mother to raise her. You were raised by men who didn't know the first thing about taking care of a child."

"Don't you think you did a fair job of it?"

He ignored the question. "There are things you don't know."

"Then maybe it's time you told me."

He seemed to be considering.

"Do I remind you of her?" she asked.

He started to reach for her, then dropped his hand. "You don't look like her. But there are other ways you resemble her. Your mother was the laughter and sunshine at the homestead when she was growing up, just as you've been. She was cherished and petted, but never spoiled. There wasn't a person who knew her who wouldn't have done anything she asked, but, of course, she was never the kind who did."

He looked over Mackenzie's shoulder to the horizon. "When she was nineteen, the son of a station manager over near the Roper River asked her to marry him. They met at a race meeting. He would come courting her in his plane, and the two of them would giggle and tease each other like children. We all thought they were a match, that they could be happy together, but Mary Kate wasn't quite ready to say yes."

"You never told me any of this. Was he my father?"

"I wish to God he had been." He looked at Mackenzie. "Your grandmother and grandfather thought Mary Kate needed a holiday, somewhere new she could go to think things over. So they sent her to stay with friends on a sheep station in New South Wales. The friends had a daughter Mary Kate's age, and the two girls got along so well they spent a week together in Sydney, too. We thought she'd had a fine time, but when Mary Kate came home, she wasn't the same. The laughter was gone, the chatter was gone. She was an echo of what she'd been."

"Do you know what happened to her?"

"One day after she came home we woke up and Mary Kate was gone forever. We never saw her again. We looked everywhere, had professionals investigate. The friends she had stayed with hadn't a clue as to what might have happened to her while she was with them. Your grandmother died a year later, from heartbreak. Your grandfather followed in six months. Then one day you appeared, and the mystery was solved."

"Not entirely."

"No. But apparently sometime in the weeks she was in New South Wales she met a man. I still have no idea who, but it's just as well. I would have killed your father if I'd learned who he was."

She struggled to suppress a shudder. "The mother I remember never laughed and rarely spoke."

"None of that would have happened if I had been more careful."

She stared at him. "Don't you think it was my mother who should have been careful?"

"She was young, but I was younger. At the time I wondered if it was right to send her to stay with strangers. I should have done more to stop it."

"Right-o. You should have found her a convent for her holiday."

"Don't make light of this. We were all at fault for putting her in danger!"

"Danger? Look around you, boss! The Territory is what danger looks like. Every day at Waluwara is a dance with death. But I'm certain you didn't wrap my mother in cotton wool when she lived on the run, and you couldn't wrap her in cotton wool when she left it. She made the mistake, not you, but if you ask me, her only mistake was skipping out on the people who loved her. I wasn't a mistake, no matter what the circumstances of my birth. The real mistake was her shame!"

She watched him inhale, a long, deep breath that he let out so slowly it was almost imperceptible. He was a master at controlling his feelings, but she knew he was struggling now.

"I am not my mother," she said. "I am me, Mackenzie Conroy. I'm going to make mistakes. Big ones. And they'll be my mistakes, thank you. But I'll never be ashamed of myself, the way Mary Kate was. And you will never be ashamed of yourself again."

"What gives you the right to talk to me this way?"

She started to answer, then she shook her head instead. "If you don't know the answer to that, we're really in a bad trot here."

He turned away from her. Mackenzie let him; she understood his need to retreat.

"Is Patrick going to be one of those mistakes?" he asked.

"I can't tell the future." She looked in the direction of the man who seemed to be able to do just that. He was squatting on the ground beside the men who'd been hired to drill. They were all dressed alike in the outback uniform of wide-brimmed hats, moleskins or jeans and cotton shirts. But Patrick stood out. He always stood out, no matter where he was or whom he was with.

"But if Patrick is a mistake," she said, "he'll be my mistake, not yours."

"I don't want you to get hurt."

"No worries, boss." Mackenzie started toward the ute that she planned to take back to the homestead. "He won't be given that choice."

As she drove away, her uncle was standing exactly where she'd left him. But she guessed that despite his parting words to her, he had moved a mile during their conversation.

She just wasn't sure where *she* was moving. Or why.

There was nothing drier than the Northern Territory just before the Wet. Although the sun was going down, the air still sucked all the moisture from human tissues until blinking and swallowing were torments. Mackenzie thought it fitting that Sebastian St. Carroll had chosen this season for his first visit to the station his family had owned for generations. She was glad he would see what life was really like for the people who labored so hard to produce the money he threw away on worthless ventures.

The station's Holden, the most presentable vehicle on the run, pulled up in front of the homestead with one passenger and Clint. Her uncle had driven to the airstrip to bring back the guests' luggage. Someone—Mackenzie would have laid a wager that the passenger was St. Carroll—had felt too important to walk from the airstrip. But the other visitors had apparently chosen to stroll the short distance to stretch their legs.

As she waited, Mackenzie ignored the urge to straighten her skirt. In deference to her uncle she had put on a stylish turquoise dress, and she even wore her grandmother's pearls. But she wasn't going to preen for the worthless peacock who was stepping out of the car alongside her uncle. Sebastian St. Carroll wasn't worthy of the effort it took to line up a seam.

She looked over to the men beside her on the veranda, key station employees, who were also waiting to meet St. Carroll. Jack, the bookkeeper, was there, along with Lawton, the business manager. Dr. Al, the resident veterinarian, had come, too, and so had Patrick, despite spending a rough day at the bore site. Missing were Harry and another stockman, Reg, who managed the yards. Both of them had cheerfully declined the invitation to supper in order to go home to the village and their own families for a more enjoyable meal.

Any one of the station employees was worth two of St. Carroll, but the men waited calmly, wearing their natural dignity along with their best city clothes. Mackenzie caught Patrick's eye. She guessed that her uncle had invited him solely because he made an impressive addition to the other station employees. Despite his lack of memory, there was no subject on which he couldn't converse intelligently. Even his questions were a cut above the ordinary. If the rest of the men were diamonds in the rough, Patrick was eight perfectly-faceted carats.

Although he didn't smile, she sensed that Patrick understood her turmoil over Sebastian St. Carroll. She narrowed her eyes, and he shrugged. She could have sworn he was telling her to behave herself.

There was no time to consider whether such a thing was possible. Her uncle's passenger stepped up to the veranda, and she extended her hand as Clint introduced him. She wasn't surprised to find she would have won her wager.

"Welcome to Waluwara, Mr. St. Carroll."

Sebastian St. Carroll was tall, dark-haired, dark-eyed and surprisingly good-looking, with a thin, aristocratic face and a toothy smile. Mackenzie had expected a face like a bandicoot.

"A pleasure, Miss Conroy." St. Carroll took her hand and held it in his for a moment. "It's quite a treat to find someone like you in this place."

She had been prepared not to like this man, this inconsiderate death adder who was draining Waluwara dry, but now such intense feelings of ill will filled her that, for an instant, she was tempted to jerk her hand from his. Unfortunately, too much rode on this, too much to let childish feelings get the better of her.

He passed on, and the others arrived from the airstrip. She murmured proper greetings to the team of geologists, engineers and metallurgists, along with the pilot St. Carroll had engaged to fly them in. She counted five men, two more than Edwina had been told to expect. She supposed a man like Sebastian St. Carroll had no particular interest in making life easier for the people who served him.

She watched as her uncle introduced the guests to the men from the station. All had been invited for a formal sit-down supper, an event that was probably going to curl St. Carroll's noble toes. The gentry and the peasants at the same table together, Australian-style. She could hardly wait.

St. Carroll left the group of men immediately after perfunctory introductions and returned to her. "Miss Conroy, may I have the pleasure of escorting you inside?"

She smiled, the only blast of cold air in the hot spring evening. "Are you certain you wouldn't prefer a rest before we have drinks? We can hold supper as long as necessary."

"I slept in the plane. I'll wash up quickly and be back to join you in a jiffy."

She could hardly wait. Leaving the station employees behind on the veranda for a smoke, everyone else started inside. Mackenzie rested her hand on St. Carroll's arm and let him lead the way into the house that technically belonged to him, although he had never set foot inside it before.

In the hallway she introduced him to Edwina, who took over, ushering him to the best guest suite. Mackenzie took the other visitors to the opposite wing and installed them there. Luckily she and Edwina, anticipating the possibility of extra guests, had prepared additional guest rooms.

In the parlor she read the expression on her uncle's face. She felt chastised. "I'm trying," she said.

"Don't try too hard."

She realized she had misinterpreted his concern. "What does that mean?"

"It means that bloke is a bit of a lady-killer."

She laughed without humor. "That bloke is a bit of a jerk."

"Stay out of his way, or he could make things complicated for you."

She didn't protest Clint's interference. This time the conversation was not about uncle protecting niece. Clint knew she wouldn't be flattered by Sebastian St. Carroll's attentions. This was station manager protecting station. Mackenzie knew the difference.

"The only place I want to be is as far from him as possible," she said.

"That might not be far enough."

"I'll handle him. And I'll do it tactfully."

"If it comes to a choice between tact and strength, use the latter." Clint turned at the sound of footsteps.

"The place is a bit run-down, wouldn't you say?" Sebastian asked. He ran his finger over the trim around the doorway. "Still, one can't expect the same standards here as in London or Hong Kong, can one?"

"One certainly can't," Mackenzie said. She paused just long enough to get hold of her temper. "But one can expect a tall, strong drink that will make even our Territory standards seem good enough by the end of the evening. What may I get you?"

"Scotch. Straight up."

"Right-o." She was glad her uncle had had the foresight to have the empty liquor cabinet stocked. She had no tolerance for alcohol whatsoever, and Clint rarely drank. But now their mission for the next weeks was to make St. Carroll as tolerable as possible. If it took strong spirits to do so, the price was a small one.

The men came in from the veranda to join them; then St. Carroll's consultants and pilot filtered in. For a little while she played publican and measured out drinks like a professional.

The last man she had to serve was Patrick. Tonight he was dressed in dark slacks, white shirt and a striped tie. His sunburn had long ago turned to tan, and the sun had bleached his hair a brighter gold. He was a beacon against the dark good looks of St. Carroll, and her defenses withered at the sight of him. "Holding up all right?" he asked.

She didn't ask how he knew what she was feeling. She sighed and pushed a drink toward him. "Fine, thanks."

"I'm scoring you."

"Scoring me?"

"One point for sarcasm. Two if it passes over St. Carroll's head. Three if St. Carroll actually believes you're trying to be friendly."

"I don't know what you're talking about."

He lifted a brow. "Don't you?"

She smiled. "Go away."

He raised the glass to his lips and took a sip. His entire face showed his shock. "What in the bloody hell is this?"

She hooted her delight, forgetting for a moment where she was and why. "Whiskey on the rocks. Irish whiskey, to match your name. Don't you like it?"

"Men drink this to feel good?" He held the glass away as if to see the contents better. "There's a word for someone who doesn't drink, isn't there?"

"Wowser. Patrick, if you're a wowser, don't pass the word around the station. You won't have a mate in sight."

He took another sip. "I'm supposed to get light-headed and lose my inhibitions?"

"Do you have any inhibitions?"

He took another sip. "I suppose we'll find out."

"Lord help us." Mackenzie was enjoying herself, but the moment passed when she saw that St. Carroll was bearing down on them. Her good spirits ebbed as he drew closer and died by the time he was standing in front of her. "Do you need another, Mr. St. Carroll?"

"Please. Call me Sebastian. We're practically friends already."

That thought flushed ice water through her veins. "Do you need another, Sebastian?"

"And may I call you Mackenzie?"

"No. Call me Mac, like everyone else."

"You're too much woman for a name like that."

She wasn't sure if she gritted her teeth or smiled; the two had been closely related for the past hour. "Still, it's my name. The one I answer to," she said. She made him another drink whether he wanted it or not and held it out to him.

"I can't remember what Clint told me you do here," Sebastian said, turning to Patrick.

"I train the horses."

"And he sees to them when they're not being ridden," Mackenzie said.

"You're not an Aussie, are you?"

Patrick sipped his drink before he answered. He found he was developing a taste for Irish whiskey, although the feeling that the room was growing steadily brighter was disconcerting. "I suppose I am. Not by birth. By inclination."

"I can't fathom anyone with an inclination like that." Sebastian smiled at Mackenzie. "Not that there aren't some perfectly lovely specimens of the breed about."

"The *breed,*" she said, "thanks you for being too, too kind."

"Of course, I haven't seen enough of the country to make any sort of judgment, have I? Only this."

"You should be here in the midst of the Wet," Mackenzie said. "I'm sure you'd appreciate Waluwara the way it is now."

"Why do you stay?" Sebastian asked. "You first, Patrick. You're from the States, correct? Why stay here when you could work somewhere more congenial?"

Patrick held out his glass for a refill. Mackenzie raised a brow, but obliged him. "If there's a more congenial place," he said, "I can't remember seeing it."

Mackenzie laughed. She wasn't going to explain his comment to Sebastian. "I stay here because it's home," she said. "And because there's a freedom and a peace that you can't find in cities."

"Apparently no one has shown you city life the way it can be."

"And apparently no one has shown you station life the way it really is. We're so pleased you've come to remedy that." She could almost hear Patrick adding points in his head. But she smiled gamely on.

Edwina entered the room and sought out Clint. Mackenzie watched them quietly converse. Edwina was one of the few people Clint treated with complete deference. In the years that she had run his home, Edwina had rounded off the edges of his harsh, uncompromising life so that when he was at the homestead he experienced the small graces of civilization. Mackenzie suspected, from the way her uncle treated Edwina, that in his own way, Clint was grateful to her for that.

When Edwina left, Clint announced that the evening meal was ready to be served. Sebastian held out his arm to Mackenzie. There was something about his manufactured charm that set her teeth on edge, something even more complex than a dislike that had been born before she ever set eyes on him. She rested her fingertips on his arm and wished him a million miles away.

At the boss's instructions, Edwina had outdone herself. With the help of two young women from the village, she started the meal with a rich cream of vegetable soup garnished with the parsley she lovingly nurtured in a small herb garden. Everyone but Sebastian vigorously tucked into it.

Sebastian pushed his bowl away as if the sight offended him and asked for another glass of wine. "You'll have to pardon me," he said, "but I really can't abide anything with so much fat in it. The Orientals have influenced me that way, I suppose. I'm afraid I require fresh vegetables and seafood. A little chicken now and then. Nothing fancy, you understand."

"It's a fair cow, isn't it," Mackenzie said pleasantly, "that none of those things are available this far into the center of the continent this time of year."

"We do keep a few chooks for eggs," Clint said. "But I'm afraid you'd lose a tooth on one if we caught and cooked it. They're range hens, as tough as leather. Even the dingoes don't favor them."

Sebastian's eyes narrowed to slits. "Well, it seems I'll have to survive on this wonderful wine while I'm here. Australian, is it?"

"From the Barossa Valley," Clint said. He answered questions that Sebastian put to him about Australia's wine country as everyone finished the soup. Sebastian started on his third glass.

After the first course Edwina served a salad of crisp, tinned vegetables that she had prepared with a sweet and sour dressing. Sebastian deigned to eat most of his.

Mackenzie watched Sebastian finish his fourth glass of wine and Patrick his second. Both men seemed perfectly steady, but there was a telltale flush creeping up their respective cheeks. A lock of Patrick's hair had fallen across his forehead, and his eyes were suspiciously bright.

Disaster struck when Sebastian waved away the prime rib one of the village women tried to set in front of him. As he did, he knocked over his water glass. "See what you've done," he said, shaking his finger at the girl. When she disappeared, unperturbed, into the kitchen, he cocked a brow at Clint. "I'm surprised you let these people serve you, Conroy."

Mackenzie saw the familiar muscle jump in her uncle's jaw, but it was Patrick, growing more flushed by the moment, who responded. "Pardon me, St. Carroll, but I'm fairly new here. Why wouldn't Mr. Conroy ask Grace and Sarah to help with the dinner?"

There was a long silence. Clearly Sebastian thought that Patrick had overstepped his bounds. "Surely you would understand," he said at last. "You Americans aren't without prejudices."

"Interesting. So it *is* prejudice we're talking about."

Mackenzie put her fork down. Patrick's tone had been perfectly pleasant, but the air was so charged that for a moment she felt as if she were yards from a mulga thicket once again, kneeling beside Tilly's motionless body.

"You misunderstand. I have no prejudices," Sebastian said. "I just know what I see. These people are still children. They have to be civilized before they can be expected to make good servants."

"Is serving you the reason they should be . . . civilized?"

"Surely you don't think they should be accountants or physicians? From the boomerang to the stethoscope is quite a leap, hey what?"

"These are people who rarely *needed* physicians before the Europeans came to this continent and infected them with killer diseases, hunted and maimed them, gave them alcohol and tobacco and poor food habits.''

"Rather like what you Americans did to your Indians."

"I hope you'll view the Aboriginal people here with an open mind," Clint said to Sebastian, obviously trying to steer the conversation away from Patrick. "Their customs and habits may be different from ours, but in the important ways, they are no less advanced."

"In many ways," Patrick said, "they're more."

"You're an outspoken chap, aren't you?" Sebastian asked Patrick. "Someday you'll have to tell me about your background. Surely someone with such strong opinions must be well educated. Certainly too educated to train horses."

"Animals have no guile, no ulterior motives, no bigotry. In some ways I find them easier to understand and admire than people."

Clint deftly turned the conversation to information on the last muster, to the price per kilo for beef on the hoof, to whether the introduction of Brahman blood into the herds was truly going to be the saving grace for Territory cattlemen. Mackenzie let the conversation flow around her. She looked at Patrick and found he was looking at her. His eyes weren't quite focused.

What on earth were you trying to do? she asked him, without saying a word out loud.

Sebastian St. Carroll is a worthless example of humanity, he answered.

For a moment she was sure the table conversation had halted abruptly. Humiliated, she pulled her gaze from Patrick's to see how his words had affected everyone, particularly the subject himself.

But there was no response. The conversation was progressing as if nothing had occurred.

And indeed, it hadn't. Horrified, Mackenzie realized that Patrick's words had sounded in her mind alone.

Patrick leaned over the railing of the paddock where the horses to be used the next morning were kept. His head spun in the most peculiar way. He was experimenting with the phenomenon, widening and narrowing his eyes to see if more or less light would affect it. The horses gliding languidly through the moon-silvered night were indistinct forms whose every movement throbbed inside his eyes and at the base of his skull. The connection was remarkable.

"I thought I might find you here."

He knew the speaker was Mackenzie, but for the life of him, he couldn't determine exactly where in the darkness she was. "I wanted some fresh air," he said. The words took time to say. A surprising amount.

"No wonder." She appeared out of nowhere to stand beside him.

"Shh ... Don't spook the horses."

"Why not? Where could they go?"

"I don't want to watch them run."

She laughed. The sound sent lightning bolts through his eye sockets.

"Pain doesn't stop at the skin," he said, hurt that she didn't seem to understand.

"A new revelation? How about another one? Blokes who drink too much get themselves in this state on a regular basis."

"Not possible." He found that "possible" was hard to say. Almost im ... possible. "Not ..."

"Paddy, you're sloshed. It's plain to see that you just can't hold your grog. Neither can I, by the way, which is why I don't drink. It's a source of great chagrin, but there it is. I'm a whacking boor after one schooner. You're almost as bad."

"A boor?" He had to turn and look at her, even though all instincts told him it was a bad idea. He could feel his eyes focus, and the experience wasn't pleasant. "Am I a boor?"

She smiled. It was truly a joy to see him at less than his best. Just a little downtrodden, he was more appealing than ever. "Not exactly."

"St. Carroll is a boor."

"At least that."

"He wants you."

She was growing more enchanted with the conversation. "How can you tell?"

"He looked at you like he wanted you served on his dinner plate."

"Did he? I didn't notice. I was too busy watching you try to run all over him."

He stood straighter and tried to speak with dignity. "I would advise giving him a wide breath."

"Berth. The word's berth."

He opened his mouth to respond and watched her frown after he did. He tried again, and her frown deepened.

"How many languages do you speak?" she asked. "I swear that one sounds like German."

His brain—he could just conjure up the image of what was supposed to be inside his head—seemed to be turning to liquid. He wondered if it would ooze out of his ears.

"Well, I came prepared," she said, when he didn't—or couldn't—find the right language to answer. "I thought I might find you in this state. Here." She lifted a vacuum bottle to the railing and tugged off the cup that was capping it. Then she filled it with hot coffee. "This is supposed to help."

He watched his hand reach for it. After a successful landing, he watched the same hand weave through the air toward his mouth. He managed most of the cup.

"There's more," she said. "I should stay here with you until you drink it all."

He was torn between gratitude and regret. His stomach tossed and trembled as the coffee found its destination. His quiet groan was in a universal language.

"I brought you something else, too, though I know this isn't the best time to give a gift." Mackenzie set the bottle on the ground and reached inside her jacket pocket. "I'm tired of watching you hike up your pants. I know you won't wear leather. I plaited you a belt out of jute. It's a vegetable product, what they use to make rope—"

"I know what it is."

"Right-o. Here." She shoved it in his direction without looking him in the eye.

He didn't know whether the gift or the coffee was clearing his head, but he felt a little steadier as he set down his cup and took the belt from her hand. It was beautifully made, wide and tightly plaited in a herringbone pattern that resembled her own leather belt. She had fastened the jute to a heavy brass buckle fashioned to look like a horseshoe.

"You made this for me?"

"No one else would want it. It's not nearly as flash as a leather one."

He stroked the length of the belt with his fingertips and tried to remember if anyone had ever given him a present. "I don't know what to say."

"No worries. I just got tired of wondering when your trousers were going to fall down." She clamped her lips together as she realized what she'd said.

He looked up, laughter in his eyes. He smiled a cockeyed, not quite controlled smile. "Won't this take all the suspense out of your life?"

"I can live without it." She looked at the stars, because she knew if she kept looking at him, she was going to laugh. "You know, you were almighty rude to St. Carroll tonight."

"Was I? I hardly remember."

"Poor bloke. Now he's going to feel like he doesn't belong here."

"He doesn't." Patrick fingered the belt as he tilted his head to look at the stars, too. "What do you see up there, Mackenzie? Are you looking for something special?"

"I remember looking up at the stars with my mother beside me. It's one of the few things I really remember about her. After she died and I came here, I used to sneak outside at night to see the sky. My uncle would find me wherever I went and carry me back to bed, but I always felt safer falling asleep if I could see the Southern Cross first. I think it was my mother's favorite constellation." She pointed. "Do you know it?"

"It's been pointed out to me."

"Did you know that the desert Aborigines say it's the footmark of the wedge-tailed eagle, Waluwara?"

"That's where the station name comes from?"

She glanced at him. He was squinting toward the sky, looking very serious now. She wasn't sure which Patrick was the most appealing, the one who lacked inhibitions or the one who was trying so hard to level his tilting world.

She looked back at the stars. "Yes, it is. Those two—" she pointed above her "—Alpha and Beta Centauri, are the eagle's throwing stick, and the coal sack, right there, is his nest."

"The stars are moving," he said.

"Your head is probably still spinning. Drink some more coffee."

"I come outside every night to see the stars, too. I can't sleep until I do."

She tried not to feel the emotional tug of his words. "You're probably from a city, and seeing stars so clearly is a new experience."

"I'm beginning to believe I'm not from anywhere."

"That's not possible."

"I don't belong here any more than St. Carroll does."

"That's not true." But even as she said the words, she knew she was lying. He didn't belong here, and, more frightening still, she couldn't imagine a place where he could belong.

"Our minds touched tonight."

She didn't look at him. "That's whiskey and wine talking."

He mimicked her voice perfectly. "Not possible. Not true. The alcohol's talking." He looked at her. "Mackenzie, you know you're just delaying the inevitable."

"Nothing's inevitable."

He reached for her and almost judged the distance correctly. His hand brushed her breast instead of her shoulder. He heard her indrawn breath. He couldn't seem to remember how to make his hand move again. Even fully clothed she was so soft. He wanted to caress her softness forever.

"Don't," she said.

"You can say that out loud and say something entirely different inside your head."

"Every man likes to pretend a woman's saying yes when she's saying no." She lifted her hand to push his away, but it had moved to her shoulder. He pulled her closer.

"No, it's something all humans do. Men, too. Right now my own mind is saying no and my body is saying yes."

"Tell your body to forget it."

"It's not listening." He touched her cheek. "What am I thinking?"

"You're preparing a defense of the religious views of Martin Buber."

"I'm thinking that a man who doesn't know who he is has no right to complicate the life of a woman who knows exactly who she is."

Her eyelids drifted shut. "That's sound thinking."

"But while I'm thinking *that,* my body insists I do *this.*" He continued stroking her cheek as he leaned forward. Her lips were warm and surprisingly giving. He heard the chorus of yes and no inside her and knew that he was not alone in his ambivalence.

His world spun, but in a way he was growing used to. Not from liquor he couldn't tolerate, not from uncertainty, but from his feelings for the woman he held. He held her tighter, and the world spun faster.

"I'm beginning to think that the place I belong is with you," he whispered.

She put her hands against his chest, but she couldn't make herself push him away. Because increasingly, despite her protests, despite weeks of avoiding him, the place where she felt at home was in his arms.

He kissed her again, and she sighed against his lips. She tasted coffee and passion and all the promise she had denied herself. He touched her breast again, and she could only repeat her sigh. Her world spun, too, and for the first time she knew the indescribable joy of being anchored safely in her lover's embrace.

"What am I going to do about you?" she whispered when he unzipped her dress to caress the bare skin of her back.

"You can't do anything. No more than I can do anything about you."

"You mean we're powerless?"

His hands glided over her skin, and the feel of her flesh was more pleasing to him than any beautiful thing he had seen in the world. His voice shook with emotion. "The power is ours together. And that's where the problems ... and the possibilities ... lie."

"One of those possibilities is tragedy. For both of us."

"When I hold you like this, I can't believe in tragedy." He felt her bend beneath his hands; he felt her body flow against him as if it had been made to fill all the empty spaces in his life. He kissed her again, and the only possibility he could believe in was that, one day soon, they would be one.

He let her go at last. She moved away, but she gazed into his eyes for a long moment. She knew, once again, what he was thinking. He watched as she hurried back to the homestead through moonlight and the soft glow of stars a million light-years away.

Chapter 10

"I should think any cow foolish enough to wander into this desert deserved to die." Sebastian lounged against the four-wheel-drive Toyota that had brought him out to the bore site and watched the men struggle with the unwieldy drilling equipment. There had been one technical problem after the other since early morning. The team sinking the bore had not begun to reach the level they had hoped to attain that day. "I can't say this seems a good use of station funds."

Mackenzie thought of a thousand relevant points to make. Diplomatically, she made none of them.

"Why are they looking for water here?" he asked, when she didn't respond.

"It's a good prospect." She pointed into the distance. "There was a water hole there until several months ago, a large one. That's why we never had a bore in the area. But the hole went dry, and now there's no water for miles."

"I should think you would have done better drilling right where the water used to be. Why didn't you?"

"We were advised this would be a better site." She purposely refrained from telling him whose advice they were following.

There was a whoosh and a screech. Then a steady, irritating chug. The equipment was working again. Mackenzie hoped it would inhibit conversation.

Clint joined them. "Well, they've got it going again," he shouted.

"How long will it take, do you suppose?" Sebastian asked.

"There's no way of telling. I've seen them find water in a day, and I've seen them take weeks."

"Weeks? Can the station really afford weeks?"

"The station can't afford to go without water. Not unless we're no longer raising cattle."

Sebastian shrugged. "I rather hope to raise manganese."

"And what would you do with the rest of the property?" Mackenzie asked. "Build a camp for tourists who want a taste of dust and flies? Give it back to the roos and the dingoes?"

If Sebastian heard her scorn, he didn't acknowledge it. He laughed. "Ah, Mackenzie, you're so protective of this...this desert. I know that about you already."

She looked away from him to signal her disinterest in his response. "Anybody could tell I love Waluwara. I'd have to love it to live here."

She didn't look at her uncle. She had been rude, and Clint had been there to witness it. But the truth was that even half a day in Sebastian's presence had taught her that he would never take anything she said seriously, anyway. Sebastian had his own agenda. He would not be swayed by logic, pleas or sarcasm. Like her uncle, she was an excellent judge of character, and Sebastian was a man who had little.

"Shall we continue the tour?" Sebastian asked Clint.

Mackenzie knew that Sebastian's pilot was waiting to fly Sebastian and his consultants over a good portion of the run that afternoon. She and her uncle had to get through the rest of the morning with Sebastian. Then they would receive a well-deserved break.

"Someone else is coming." Clint shaded his eyes.

Mackenzie shaded hers, but all she could see were plumes of dust stretching toward the cloudless sky. "One of the station vehicles?"

"One of the utes. Looks like Patrick. Drives like Patrick," Clint said.

She laughed a little. If Patrick had ever known how to drive, he had not known how to maneuver the rough tracks of an outback station. Harry had taught—or reminded—him how to brake and steer. But no one could teach a way to make this kind of driving tolerable, particularly with a hangover. "He'll smash the crown of his hat on the cab roof the way he's jolting up and down."

She watched him pull to a stop and get out. He walked like a man with a massive headache—and not just from the ride. As she'd guessed, he took off his hat and punched it back into shape as he approached. She noticed that the belt she had made for him was proudly displayed.

"No horses to train this morning?" Sebastian asked in greeting.

Patrick frowned, as if processing sound and thought were harder than usual. "I came to watch the men find water."

"You think they'll find it today?" Clint asked.

Patrick turned to Mackenzie. She smiled at the gingerly way he moved his head. "That's my guess."

"So you're a gambling man," Sebastian said.

"No."

"Then why does it matter if they find it today or next week?"

"I didn't say it mattered. I said I was here to watch."

Sebastian snorted. "Do you know something the rest of us don't?"

Patrick faced him, steeling himself to ignore the pain in every movement he made. His gaze traveled over Sebastian's face. It was a face he had seen in disturbing dreams last night, a face that showed a complete lack of human virtue. He wondered if Sebastian's vices were as apparent to everyone else.

"I do know something," he said, staring into Sebastian's dark, oddly opaque eyes. "I know they're going to find water."

"So I was correct last night. You must have a good education. Was geology your field?"

"Nothing so narrow." Patrick dismissed Sebastian with a flick of his hand and turned to Mackenzie. "Are you going to stay, too?"

"I can't." She wanted to. A day in the full sun with Patrick sounded like paradise compared to seeing the sights with Sebastian and her uncle. But Sebastian had requested her presence on the morning tour, and she was not about to antagonize him—if it wasn't absolutely required.

"Then I'll see you later." Patrick smiled at her, an intimate, forgive-me-for-last-night smile that should have surprised her. But she guessed what he was doing. He was staking his claim in front of Sebastian. Now she had only to learn if it was a real claim or one to discourage Sebastian from preying on her.

"Yes, later," she said.

Patrick joined the men at the bore, and she watched as they gestured to him, communicating as best they could over the noise of the machinery.

"Let's go," Clint said.

The three observers were in the Toyota bouncing down the track when they heard shouting. Clint slammed on the brakes, and they all turned simultaneously.

At the drilling site, all the men were whooping and dancing under the iridescent plumes of a glorious waterspout.

"I haven't seen a gusher like that one but twice in my lifetime." On the homestead veranda, Clint thrust his hands in his pockets and stared at another extraordinary sunset. He looked like a man savoring victory.

"The water will last a good while," Patrick said.

"Do you think so?"

"Yes."

"Tell me, how did you know that site would be so successful?"

Patrick considered the question. How had he known? He was still confused by what was so obvious to him and so difficult for others to see. He was coming to terms with his heightened abilities, but only gradually. "I wish I could tell you."

"Then you don't know?"

"Perhaps I've been trained. I sensed that was a good site." That wasn't a lie. He just didn't add that he had seen the water under the earth as clearly as if it had been a mighty river rushing above ground.

"Do you still have no memory of who you are?"

Patrick watched Clint's gaze swerve toward the woman emerging from the garden at the side of the house. Edwina Wallace had a graceful, thoroughly feminine walk. With her arms piled high with oddly shaped branches to make a centerpiece for the table, she was the picture of womanhood. As if he didn't realize—or care—that he was being observed, Clint watched her until she disappeared inside.

"Well?" Clint asked, after Edwina was out of sight. "No memories?"

"Sometimes I see glimpses of my past. Fragments, nothing more. And sometimes I hear ... advice."

"You know, I sent out word all over the Territory that you'd been found and how. Not because it would change my mind about you, but for your sake. I thought perhaps someone might know who you were, particularly because of your abilities with horses."

"And there's been no response?"

"No one knows anything. The police have checked all their records, and no one has reported anyone of your description missing in all of Australia."

"I'll remember eventually."

"You may not." Clint leaned against the railing so he could see Patrick's face. "The doctor said that sometimes, in cases like this, memory never returns."

"A life forgotten." Patrick thought of the slivers of memory that had returned to him. In the jigsaw puzzle of his life, they added up to less than one piece.

"How will you feel if you never remember?"

"How will I feel if I do?" He turned at a noise behind him and saw Mackenzie approaching with a tray of iced drinks. The light from the setting sun turned her eyes to gold and colored her cheeks a warmer hue. He wanted to touch her skin, to renew his acquaintance with its texture.

"Where's our guest?" she asked, offering a drink to both the men.

Clint took his. "Consulting with his team now that they've had a look at the property. They've taken over the office."

"I don't suppose we could lock and torch it with Sebastian inside?"

Clint didn't even flinch. "You mean his aristocratic charm hasn't swept you off your feet?"

"I'd like to sweep him off his feet and dump him in the rubbish heap." She set down the tray and took her own drink without quite looking at Patrick. "The station's buzzing with news about the bore. With that much water, are we going to build drains to carry it a distance?"

"Not if St. Carroll holds onto the station. There won't be money to build them with. And the way he's talking, he won't be running cattle, anyway."

"You don't think he's serious?"

"He's serious to a point," Clint said. "He has to run cattle to keep his leases, but he'll run only the minimal amount. He would have to put too much into the station now to get any sort of real return. And he thinks there are better ways to spend his money."

Patrick couldn't stop looking at Mackenzie. She was wearing yellow tonight, a vibrant, sunny hue that made her hair glow a brighter red. When he looked at her, he experienced sight deep inside himself, in places that had nothing to do with vision. Technically he understood the connection, but nothing could explain the power and beauty of the experience.

"St. Carroll is a man with no concern, no feeling for anyone else," he said, without taking his eyes off her. "He's incapable of feeling. He'll harm anything and anyone who stands in his way. In his short life he's robbed and murdered. He has more at stake here than he's let on. If he doesn't find what he's looking for, he'll be ruined financially. That can make a ruthless man forget any remnants of a moral code."

Clint stared at him. Mackenzie forgot to avoid his eyes and stared, too.

"How do you know these things?" Clint asked. "What proof do you have?"

Mackenzie put her hand on her uncle's arm, but she didn't take her eyes off Patrick. "He's just guessing, aren't you, Paddy? We all sense what kind of man we're dealing with here. Patrick's just carrying it one step further by making guesses about Sebastian's past."

"Accusing a man of murder and stealing is further than a step. How do you know these things?" Clint repeated.

Patrick couldn't answer. Once again he had stepped over the boundary between what was readily apparent to anyone and what was only apparent to him. He still had much to learn, and he didn't even know why.

Mackenzie was torn watching him. She wanted to reassure both men. She wanted to explain Patrick's gifts, but how could she explain what she didn't understand herself? "I think Patrick is just putting our own fears into words," she said. "Sebastian is more than irritating. He's so slick, he hardly seems human. A man like that could do almost anything, couldn't he? Kill . . . steal."

"Is that what you were saying?" Clint asked Patrick.

"When I look at St. Carroll," he said quietly, "I see evil."

"Are you usually right about people? Or do you make mistakes?"

"I don't think I make mistakes."

"You can read the virtues and sins of others, but you can't remember your own history?"

"I think that's called a paradox."

"I think it's called gall."

"That, too." Patrick pulled his gaze from Mackenzie to face Clint. "But don't be so irritated by my arrogance that you discount what I'm saying."

"Meaning?" Clint asked.

"Watch out for St. Carroll. You're a good judge of your fellow man. But you believe there's good in everyone, so you give everyone the benefit of the doubt. There is no good in Sebastian St. Carroll."

"I gave *you* the benefit of the doubt."

"And I thank you for it."

The two men continued to look at each other. Mackenzie could almost feel them measuring each other's will. Then Patrick set down his drink. "I have to check the horses once more before nightfall."

Clint gave a curt nod. Mackenzie was silent until Patrick was out of sight. "Don't judge him too harshly," she said. "He's under a strain. It's difficult not knowing who he—"

"He's right about St. Carroll." Clint stared into the encroaching darkness, stared after Patrick as if he could still see him. "Rumors reach even this far into the continent, but I don't know how they reached Patrick. I'd like to."

"Rumors?"

"St. Carroll was arrested last year in Hong Kong on suspicion of murder. A business associate of his disappeared. Apparently St. Carroll was the last person known to see him alive. They found the man's body in the harbor two weeks later with a bullet in his chest similar to one found in an antique revolver in St. Carroll's possession. The murder bullet vanished from the forensics lab where it was undergoing testing. The case against St. Carroll vanished with it."

"Why haven't you told me this before?"

"Because he wasn't convicted. And because I didn't want you to know what kind of man held Waluwara's future in his hands."

She shivered, although the sun hadn't been down long enough to lower the temperature significantly. "What is Sebastian capable of doing if he doesn't find what he wants here?"

Clint smiled a bitter smile. "You might ask Patrick. I really don't know."

Mackenzie watched Sebastian finish his third after-dinner drink. He liked cognac, in large quantities, and the only sign that he felt it was a slight flush on his cheeks and a more casual posture.

Despite her personal feelings about him, she could appreciate the man's dark good looks, particularly when he was less than polished perfection. She imagined that the path of his adolescence and young adulthood had been strewn with women who hadn't seen beyond his dark eyes and easy smile to the man who was utterly devoid of redeeming qualities.

She looked at the garden, where her uncle was having a conversation with Harry. She was glad Clint had stayed in sight. She didn't want to be alone with Sebastian.

"So tell me what you do for entertainment," Sebastian said. "What does one do without restaurants and the theater?"

"One copes." Mackenzie forced a smile and tried to imagine Sebastian pointing a revolver at a business associate's chest. The image was crystal clear. She found it so riveting that she missed his next comment.

"I said, how do you cope?" he repeated. "Even the television doesn't work here."

With effort she pulled herself back to the conversation. "I read and listen to music. I have friends all over the country, and we stay in touch by mail. I was educated by School of the Air for a time, along with other station children. We're all grown up, but we still correspond. How many school chums can say as much?"

"Such a bleak existence."

"You seem compelled to point that out over and over again."

"Someone should point it out to you. You probably don't know anything different."

"On the contrary," she said, keeping her voice calm, "I know quite a bit. But I fancy this life more than any other I've seen."

"There are things I could show you."

"I'm sure."

"You're a lovely woman. I'm surprised this dreadful climate hasn't ruined your complexion." Before she could react, he touched her cheek. "Still soft and fresh. But what will you look like in ten years, or even five?"

"Like a woman who's lived the life she chose for herself." She stepped away so he couldn't touch her again. "If you care to entertain yourself tonight, Sebastian, I'll be happy to show you our video library. We have no telly reception, but we have some wonderful films and a room full of books."

"Actually, I was thinking about a walk down to the pond."

"Billabong," she corrected.

"Right-o. Waltzing Matilda and all that."

"All…that." She searched the shadows for her uncle, but he was no longer in sight. She suspected he had gone off with Harry to see about something. Harry wouldn't have interrupted unless there had been some crisis or other. "Well, it is a beautiful night for a stroll. I think you'll enjoy yourself."

"You'll come, of course."

He was taunting her; it was as blatant as the unctuous smile on his face. She could refuse to go and brand herself a coward, or she could go and fight off his advances. She wasn't afraid of him, although there was reason to be, but she was afraid of what he could do to Waluwara's future. Was Sebastian a man who would sacrifice his own best interests to revenge a slight? She didn't know, but she didn't want to take that chance.

"I'll come," she said, "but I won't stay long. Patrick will be looking for me."

"That's right, isn't it? He said he would see you tonight. I gather he's your gentleman friend?"

"Patrick's my friend."

"Well, I hope I'll be your friend, too."

She was glad Patrick was the mind reader, not Sebastian. "You might want to fetch something warm to put on. The temperature's dropping."

"I'll be fine."

She couldn't think of any other delaying tactics; she was wearing a light jacket over her dress. Again she scanned the shadows for Clint, but there was no one there. Even the stock dogs, who sometimes hung around the homestead in the evening, had gone elsewhere.

"Well, let's be off." She started down the steps, but not soon enough to stop Sebastian from offering his arm.

"We wouldn't want you to trip."

She managed a smile. "I know every inch of ground. I'm not likely to stumble."

"I might."

As she took his arm she felt the trap closing around her. She experienced an uncomfortable affinity with all the women throughout history who had been forced into situations like this one.

"The stars here are beautiful. I'll give you that," he said.

"How kind."

"You don't like me, do you, Mackenzie?"

She supposed he was the type of man who would find a woman's dislike of him enchanting. She didn't want to give him that pleasure. "I don't know you, Sebastian."

"We can remedy that."

"Let's. Tell me all about your life." She hoped that would keep him busy for the rest of their walk.

"It's rather a boring story, really. Eton. Cambridge. Wealthy upper-class family. Enough money to do anything I wanted, whenever I wanted to do it." He shrugged. "Then, when my parents tired of supporting me, I moved to Hong Kong to make my own fortune."

"And were you successful?" she asked, knowing the answer.

"I've made and lost several."

"I imagine the making was more fun than the losing."

"Oh, I never lost because of anything I did. I'm ashamed to say I was taken advantage of. Part of growing up, I suppose."

The temperature seemed to drop twenty degrees. She forced herself not to withdraw her hand. There had been such an undertone of malevolence behind Sebastian's cultured accent. "Well, perhaps you'll make another," she said.

As they neared the heart-shaped billabong that had been the reason for building the homestead on this section of property, he filled in a few more unimportant details of his life. It was a lovely spot, one of Mackenzie's favorites on the station, a shining stretch of water surrounded by tall, sturdy gum trees and wattle that was just beginning to flaunt its golden blossoms. She heard the staccato call of a large-tailed nightjar in one of the trees as they approached, then a flurry of wings as it flew away.

"Rather a pretty little glen," Sebastian said.

"The variety of land on this station is unusual. We've everything from hills to true desert country. And we're close enough to the Victoria and its tributaries to have the advantage of—" She stopped as she felt Sebastian's arm snake along her shoulder. She tried to move away, but he followed her.

"I thought you might be chilled," he said.

"A bit soon in our acquaintance for that, don't you think?" She kept her tone light.

"Don't tell me you didn't suspect I might want a tad more than a walk in the moonlight?"

"It's a fair cow, isn't it, when a woman can't even trust a good English gentleman to behave himself?" She still kept her voice light; it took as much effort as wrestling a five-hundred-pound heifer to the ground.

"I should think you'd be pleased, Mackenzie. Generations ago my ancestors were at court while yours were on their way to Sydney in chains, but here you and I are, absolutely equal. It's a great day, don't you think?"

"With your gift for blarney, I half believe your ancestors were digging potatoes in County Cork." She moved away, and this time he let her.

"Did your uncle tell you I was considering putting the station up for sale if we don't find ore?" he asked.

It was hard to ignore the message behind such a sudden shift of topics, but Mackenzie pretended to. "He mentioned some such. I'm sure that would be hard for you with all the St. Carroll history tied up in this place."

"Don't be absurd. It won't be hard at all. I despise Waluwara and my family, as well. I'd like nothing better than to set departed St. Carrolls rolling in their graves. You'd like it if I sold, wouldn't you? You and your uncle both."

She walked to a wattle shrub and began to gather branches to take back with her. It was something to do with her hands other than strangle him. "It's not up to me to like or dislike what you do, Sebastian. I'm sure you'll do what you think you have to."

"I can refuse all offers, you know."

She didn't look at him. "Of course. That's your legal right."

"Particularly those from people I don't like."

"Really? I didn't know it was necessary to like the people you planned to take money from."

"And if I keep the station, there might always be the need for a good housecleaning, don't you think? Nothing like a change of leadership to shake everything up and get it moving again."

Her skin crawled. She knew that Sebastian was baiting as well as threatening her. He wanted to see how far he could push her as he pointed out her alternatives. She could yield her body—she supposed those were the stakes they were playing for—or her uncle could lose either his job or his chance to buy Waluwara. The situation was so hopelessly melodramatic she half expected him to threaten to tie her to the nearest railroad track—except that it was hundreds of kilometers away.

She could only think of one possible response.

"A good housecleaning is called for," she said evenly. "I wish you'd do it. Uncle Clint has had offers at bigger, more productive stations. But he's so loyal, he needs a sharp kick to get him moving. That would be just the one."

"Where would you go?"

"With him, wherever that might be. There's a lot of country to explore back of beyond."

"I've observed you for more than a day now. Neither you nor Clint would go without a fight. But you don't have to fight, you know."

"Don't we?" She faced him, the wattle a shield in front of her. "*Who* don't I have to fight, or fight off?"

"I'm going to be here several weeks. I'm a reasonable man."

"How reassuring."

"Must I go on?"

She was shaking. From anger, not fear. "I should think you'd be ashamed to," she said. "This is the twentieth century, not the eighteenth. I am not in chains, and you are not at court. We *are* equal, as any other British or Australian citizen would be happy to explain to you. And as your equal I choose not to become your whore in exchange for some dubious favors you're willing to grant me."

"You have a way with words."

"I also have a way with my fists. And if I scream, I can bring half a dozen men running, men who would bury you six feet under."

He cocked his head, as if assessing how best to get around this sticky stubborn streak of hers. "Wouldn't you find screaming a humiliation? Besides, how much support would you get if you did? Remember, the men on this run depend on me for their livelihood."

"The men on this run depend on me for friendship. That's more important out here."

He moved closer, this time assessing her determination. He smiled, obviously hoping to disarm her. "You're making more of this than I intended. I'm not an animal. I just want a little female attention while I'm here."

She threw up her arms to fend him off, waving the wattle branches in his face. "You just want a little—"

"Trouble?" Patrick stepped out from behind one of the gum trees. "Is it trouble you're wanting, St. Carroll? Because you've managed to find it."

Mackenzie was astonished by the fury in Patrick's voice. In the worst of times he had repressed his emotions, leaving her to guess at them. Now there was no need to guess. "It's all right, Paddy. Sebastian and I were just setting the ground rules."

"Do you know the ground rules, Paddy, old man?" Sebastian asked lazily. "You should, you know. After all, I expect my employees to keep informed."

"Bloody hell, Sebastian!" Mackenzie exploded. "You're a selfish, arrogant bastard who thinks the sun shines out of his own ear! You can take your blooming jobs and shove them in the same blooming spot!"

He laughed, a pleasant, mellow laugh that still gave Mackenzie chills. "I admire spirit in a woman."

"And I admire integrity in a man!" She swept past him. "Don't waste your time defending my honor, Paddy. Sebastian doesn't understand the concept." She didn't look behind her to see if either or both men were following. She started toward the house, and nothing was going to stand in her way.

Patrick stepped in front of Sebastian when he started after Mackenzie. "Don't plan to go anywhere, St. Carroll."

"What sort of man would let her walk back in the dark alone?"

"She's safer with the snakes and the dingoes than she is with you."

Sebastian's attempt at lazy charm disappeared. "Out of my way, horse trainer. You have nothing to say about where I go and what I do. Or whom I do it with. Not if you want to stay on here."

"I know you, St. Carroll. Unfortunately, your type exists all over the universe. You prey on anyone who's weaker and drag down anyone who's stronger. You're a threat in every conceivable way to people like Clint and Mackenzie and the others here. You're a threat to anyone except those exactly like you."

"How about you, horse trainer?" Before Patrick could respond, Sebastian's fist shot out at lightning speed and sank into Patrick's belly. Caught off guard, Patrick doubled over, and Sebastian slammed his forearm against the side of Patrick's head.

Sebastian straightened as Patrick reeled toward one of the wattle shrubs and fell against it. "Where's that trouble you were so certain I'd found? Here's a bit of a bonus, since you won't be picking up your pay this week. Don't make threats you're not man enough to keep!"

Sebastian backed away several feet; then, as if he no longer believed Patrick to be a threat, he turned and started up the path in the direction Mackenzie had taken.

Sebastian had gone three steps before he found himself stretched out on the ground. He rolled, or tried to, but Patrick, who was sitting on his back, anchored Sebastian's arm at a painful angle.

"I never make threats," Patrick said. "It goes against all my instincts." He twisted Sebastian's arm farther when Sebastian tried to pull free. "So here's a bit of a bonus for you. Don't harm anyone on this station while you're here. Take all your festering hatred and your barely leashed violence and turn them on yourself, where they belong. Watch and listen and learn, St. Carroll. Because if you don't, you'll have me to reckon with."

When Sebastian stopped struggling Patrick stood. But he had learned what he needed to know about Sebastian. He watched him carefully, and when Sebastian sprang, he was ready. He stepped to one side, planting one foot against Sebastian's thigh as he fell past him. Patrick snapped his leg forward, and Sebastian went sprawling into the wattles.

"Watch, listen and learn," Patrick repeated.

Sebastian recovered and sprang again, but this time he anticipated Patrick's kick and dodged it successfully while executing one of his own. Patrick countered it as easily as if it had come from a bush fly.

"You watched," Patrick said, dodging as Sebastian spun around for another kick. "But you didn't listen, and you didn't learn. Can you learn, St. Carroll? Or is it already too late?" He brushed off Sebastian's punch, then grabbed his wrist and flung him past his hip into the wattles again.

Sebastian stood, brushing himself off. "You've trained," he said.

"Have I?"

"But not enough!" Sebastian rushed him, spun and snapped a kick in midair. Patrick wasn't there to receive it. Disoriented, Sebastian spun again and found Patrick beside the wattle.

"Not enough?" Patrick asked. "Are you sure?"

Sebastian shrieked his rage, a warrior's ferocious cry, and rushed Patrick again. Once again, Patrick was not where he had been by the time Sebastian reached the place. The third time Patrick was exactly where he was supposed to be, and Patrick was ready for him.

"You watched and listened," he said, holding his hands, palms out, in front of his body. "But you didn't learn."

Sebastian stopped in midair. He couldn't move; he couldn't breathe. Time seemed to stop, and he was powerless to make it start once more.

"Learn," Patrick said. "Or die young." He turned his hands inward and stepped aside. Sebastian fell at his feet in a boneless heap.

Sebastian lay still. Breath filtered into his body. Blood warmed his limbs. Even the ground under his face smelled like life. "I'm not dead," he whispered.

"Consider that a gift."

"Who are you?"

"Someone who knows you, St. Carroll. I know every thought you have, every sick and twisted fantasy. Try any of them, touch anyone here, and I'll feed those fantasies to you one by one until you choke on them."

"Who are you?" Sebastian repeated.

"Someone who never should have touched you." Patrick stepped away from him.

Sebastian took the opportunity to sit up, then stand. He moved slowly away from Patrick. He experimented with shaking his head and flexing his fingers. "Where did you learn to fight like that? What sensei taught you how to hypnotize an opponent that way?"

Patrick shook his head in disgust.

"I want to know!" Sebastian said.

"And whatever you want, you get?"

"Whatever I want, I buy!"

"You don't have enough money to buy anything I possess. No one does."

"I'm sorry I attacked you that way. I didn't understand—"

"That I was more powerful than you? No, of course you didn't. You would never attack someone who had a chance against you. You haven't learned a thing. Get out of my sight."

"Who are you?"

"A horse trainer."

"You're not."

"That's right. I forgot. You fired me."

"No. Of course you're not fired."

"And the others? Mackenzie? Clint? You'll leave them alone now?"

"Yes. I'll leave them alone."

Patrick stared at him, then he shook his head. "There's nothing of me you can have, St. Carroll."

"We'll see." Sebastian sidled away, watching to be sure that Patrick didn't follow him.

"Go back to the house and sleep this off," Patrick said. "I won't follow you."

Sebastian turned and increased the length of his stride. In a moment he was out of sight.

The night was perfectly still; even the boobook owl that had called restlessly from a tree after Patrick's arrival was silent. Patrick stared at the reflection of the moon in the still waters of the billabong until the silver sheen became a face.

The powers you've been given, little one, must never be used to cause another harm. This is a sacred trust you must never disavow. If you are ever tempted to misuse them, even for what you believe to be good, you will be haunted by your failure. That will be your punishment, one without end.

Patrick sank to his knees and covered his ears with his hands. The voice grew quieter, then fell silent, but the face he had seen in the billabong danced across his eyelids.

The face became a door. He reached for the doorknob, aware of what he would find behind it. A thousand voices would scream his past at him, and he might not be able to hear even one. The voices would scream, and he would go mad—or, kinder, perhaps, die quickly. But death or insanity had to be better than not knowing who or what he was.

His hand rested on the knob. Who was he? What was he? The door swung open in his hand, and the voices shrieked all the answers he would ever need to know. The sound, the terrible cacophony of memories, both overwhelmed and deafened him. The agony was worse than anything Sebastian St. Carroll could ever have inflicted. The door slammed shut, and he didn't know, or care, how it had happened. It shut, and he was still alive, still only a shadow of the being he had once been.

He uttered a sound, then another, until the sounds strung together in the outpouring of a musical language. But the face was gone, and the door faded away.

He was left with silence and a moon gone behind a cloud. He had never felt more alone.

Chapter 11

"What happened?" Clint stepped out of the garden as Mackenzie passed. He took her arm.

"Our guest happened!"

In the near darkness Clint squinted, examining her from head to toe. "Did he hurt you?"

"No. He didn't even touch me. Patrick arrived before he could do anything more than make half a dozen threats."

"You'll pack and go off to visit a friend tomorrow. I won't have you here while St. Carroll's on the property."

"No. I'm not going to run from anyone. But I won't take chances and be caught alone with him again. Not after tonight. I wouldn't be surprised if he's everything Patrick said, and worse. He has no conscience."

"A section of fence in the western paddock was trampled. I went with Harry to see what should be done for the night."

"Don't apologize." She smiled wryly. "I should have known better than to take a walk with Sebastian. But I was trying to keep the peace. Now I'm afraid he's about to declare war."

"Let him try. The worst he can do is terminate my employment."

"That's not the worst. He can make life impossible for the people who have no home but this one."

"Just be careful you don't mention that to him. St. Carroll's a man who preys on weakness."

"I've learned that." She lowered her voice. "Here he comes." Mackenzie turned. Her hearing had always been particularly acute. Now she heard Sebastian's footsteps well before her uncle did. She stared in the direction of the sound and watched him materialize just where the veranda light lapped at the garden shadows.

She fully expected Sebastian to pretend he didn't see them. With the boss at her side and a full quotient of station hands within call, Sebastian wasn't at his best. He was much more the kind of man who liked to corner his prey when it was alone and vulnerable.

He surprised her by walking toward them, skirting the shadow's edges. The muscles in her throat tightened; her fists clenched. With confrontation only footsteps away, she knew Sebastian was going to inform her uncle that his services were no longer necessary.

"I've come to apologize," he said, standing several lengths away.

It was too dark to see more than an outline of his face. Mackenzie could read nothing of his expression. "Have you?"

"I don't know what possessed me. I must have had one too many glasses of cognac. Powerful stuff, I'm afraid. I hope you'll forgive me for being such a boor."

She nodded curtly. He glanced at Clint. "I don't know if Mackenzie told you, but I'm afraid I made improper advances."

"I expect you to leave Mackenzie alone while you're here."

"Of course. My sincerest apologies."

He turned away to go inside, but in the second before his back was toward them, Mackenzie caught full sight of his face. He had a bruise across one cheek. The other was scratched, as if by branches.

She started to comment, then caught herself. "Sebastian, where's Patrick?"

"I don't know. He was still at the pond when I started back." He faced them again, and she saw that her quick impression had been correct. "He's an interesting chap. Do you mind if I ask where he comes from? What exactly do you know about him?"

"He's from the States. I'm not exactly sure where," Clint said curtly. "All I need to know is that he's the best horse trainer in the Territory."

"Oh?"

"If all my men had his instincts, we'd triple our output overnight."

"So you would say he has a special instinct with animals? A special touch, perhaps?"

"That would sum it up."

"And he was responsible for finding the site for the bore? The enormously successful bore?"

"Patrick seems to have a bit of luck in whatever he does," Mackenzie said. She tried to resist the next, but her self-control was flagging. "I understand he's quite lucky with his fists, too. When he has to be."

Sebastian attempted a smile; the result could have withered an oasis. "It seems he's a man of many talents."

"Which *he* puts to good use—"

"Have a rest now," Clint said, interrupting smoothly. "We'll have to rise early to get a good start on the surveying."

"Yes." This time, when Sebastian turned, he continued up to the veranda and closed the front door behind him.

"Sebastian and Patrick fought," Mackenzie said, when he was gone.

"Obviously."

"I'd say Sebastian lost."

"Obviously."

"Patrick isn't a violent man."

"Any man's violent if the stakes are high enough. It sets us apart from the angels."

"I've got to find him."

"Do you?"

"How dare he fight for me!"

"High stakes."

She didn't respond. She started through the garden. It didn't even occur to her that Clint hadn't tried to dissuade her.

Patrick didn't know how long he had been at the billabong. It could have been minutes; it could have been hours. The moon had drifted behind the clouds when he heard Mackenzie's footsteps. He knew it was her. Although she wasn't yet within sight, he could see determination on her face, feel her concern and anger. He was still so emotionally chilled that he felt none of the anticipation he always experienced when he knew she was near.

"Patrick," she called.

For a moment he considered not answering.

"Are you out here?"

"Over here." He stood, brushing grass and dirt from the knees of his jeans.

Illuminated by starlight, she appeared on the path near the water's edge. "Are you all right? I just saw Sebastian."

"I'm fine." He took a deep breath to be sure he really was. Sebastian's first punch had been a terrible shock. If he had ever experienced pain like that, the memory was buried inside him again, along with a billion others.

"Are you certain?"

"I'm fine." And he was. No damage had been done. He suspected he wouldn't even have a bruise to show for that agonizing moment—or the ones that had followed.

"What right do you have fighting over me like that?"

"None." He turned away from her.

She was caught off guard. On the walk to the billabong she had prepared herself for an argument, whipped herself into righteous fury. Patrick had no cause to protect her. If her encounter with Sebastian had come down to a physical struggle, she might not have won, but she wouldn't have lost, either. And if she had needed help, it had been her right to ask for it, to scream for it, if necessary. Instead, without her consent, Patrick had taken matters into his own hands.

"Well, that's the bloody truth." She folded her arms. "I don't need help fighting my own battles."

"He's nothing like he appears. He's highly trained in the martial arts. As deadly as that snake you wanted me to kill."

Some of the starch went out of her. She moved closer. "Are you really all right, then?"

He wasn't all right. He didn't know if he would ever be all right again. He saw faces in silver shifting moonlight, heard words in a language unlike any he'd encountered here. He opened doors in his mind and could not endure the answers that were waiting for him. But worse, so much worse, he knew, without understanding how, that he had breached his own moral code. In his anger at Sebastian St. Carroll he had used powers St. Carroll didn't, couldn't, have. He had flaunted those powers to prove his superiority. And by flaunting them, he had opened himself up to St. Carroll's evil maneuvers.

When he didn't answer, Mackenzie moved closer. "Let me look at you."

"He didn't hurt me."

She put her hands on his shoulders and cocked her head to examine his face. "I don't see any bruising." She ran her fingers up his neck to his cheeks. "Do you hurt anywhere?"

He hurt everywhere, in places deep inside him that had no names. He wanted to tell her not to touch him, that he was not worth touching, but her fingers against his skin absorbed his pain, and he wasn't strong enough to deny himself that healing.

Mackenzie knew she should step away, although nothing except her hands moved. Patrick's eyes closed, but he stood perfectly still under her caressing fingertips. His skin was warm, resilient and smooth. Touching him was addictive, a pleasure more than a search for injuries.

She knew she should go. Clearly he hadn't been hurt badly enough to need medical attention. If he had bruises or cuts that she couldn't see, they would probably heal without intervention. But she couldn't force herself to leave him. He was suffering, perhaps not physically, but in other, more powerful ways.

"You hurt him," she said. "I saw his face. He'll be bruised for a week. If he's deadly, then you must be deadlier."

He stiffened, and she felt his pain as surely as if it were stabbing her own heart. "You didn't know that about yourself, did you?" she said. "And it frightens you."

"Not frightens."

"No? What then?" She rested her palms against his cheeks.

He opened his eyes. "You'd better go."

"Are you horrified that you can be violent, too?"

He covered her hands with his, but he didn't have the strength to push them away. "All of us have that capacity."

"But you thought you were better than the rest of us, didn't you? You thought you were in perfect control of your instincts."

"My instincts control me."

She looked deep into his eyes and saw that he wasn't talking about violence alone. Passion flared there, and need. He needed her in a way he had never needed anyone. He needed her passion to flame with his, to extinguish the pain, the terrors, the anguish. And he despised himself for it.

"If your instincts controlled you completely," she said softly, "we would be on the ground right now, our clothes torn off, making love."

He made a sound low in his throat that could have been a denial or an affirmation. It was more vital than either, a plea for her to walk away, or perhaps a plea for her to stay.

She rose on tiptoe. He had fought for her, and now he denied himself what he wanted most. She wanted neither protection nor denial, yet both were a measure of the man. She swayed closer, and for that moment they were only heartbeats apart. Then he pulled her closer, groaning a futile protest, and touched her lips with his.

She was sucked into a whirlpool of sensation. She could feel his desperation, his ambivalence, his desire, as her own desire swirled hotly through her. Her thoughts were a wild jumble, flashes of places she had never seen, kaleidoscopes of feelings and instincts and memories just out of reach. She could feel herself and everything she knew herself to be spinning uncontrollably. She clutched him, terrified and aroused simultaneously. She wanted him gone, and she wanted him inside her so their merger was complete. But if she truly wanted the first, she couldn't make herself ask for it.

He clasped her harder. His tongue sought hers; his hips cradled hers; his hands roamed restlessly. He kissed her and absorbed a lifetime of feelings: sorrow and joy and a strong yearning for more than life could provide her. He murmured his understanding against her lips. He knew what it was like to want more. At that moment he wanted more than he had ever thought possible.

"Patrick, what's happening?" She gripped his shirt as if he could save her from drowning in the tumultuous sea of their emotions.

He didn't know. He had no memory of this, not even the vaguest recollection that this wedding of body and spirit by passion was a possibility. If he had ever kissed another woman, that moment was gone. But he knew, instinctively, that if he had ever shared this glory with one, he would remember it still, even if he never remembered anything else.

"Run away, Mackenzie." He tried to start her on her journey, but his hands held her closer; they could not push.

"Where would I go that you couldn't follow?"

"If you go, I won't follow."

His eyes were dark with desire. She saw a million questions veiled behind need and yearning. She shook her head slowly. "I don't want to go."

"Neither of us understands this."

"It's as old as forever." She dug her fingers into his hair and let it spill over her fingertips.

"And we aren't." He had given her a chance, although not much of one. His hands had never left her body; the power of his will had never faltered. He wanted her, and he had only a fragment of self-control.

"I'm not sure about you." She didn't smile. She wasn't sure who or what he was. He could be as old as forever or as young as the dawn of the day she had found him. She only knew he was good, a man who struggled with all the forces inside himself. A man struggling now.

He bent his head to hers, and the struggle was over. He wanted her; she wanted him. Fear took wings, and with it, self-denial. She tasted like freedom, like all the good things that waited for both of them. He wove his hands through her hair and tasted her cheeks, her lips, the wildly fluttering pulse at the base of her throat. He heard her responsive moan and saw it in colors no artist had ever painted.

The air was cool, but the earth was still warm. They sank to the cushion of grass beside the water. He lay with one leg over hers to feel the slender lines of her body against his own. He pillowed her head on his arm and drew her closer.

"I've wanted you forever," he said, kissing her cheeks, her forehead. "I've wanted you for eternity, but I didn't know it!"

She had wanted him, too. All the times she had put barriers between herself and others, she had been waiting for Patrick. She hadn't dreamed foolish, maidenly dreams of a knight in shining armor. She had repressed all her feelings and told herself that loving a man would chain her spirit. Now she knew that she had lied. She had never felt freer, never truly known that the universe stretching before her was hers to conquer.

She kissed him and felt both his yearning and hesitation. She touched her lips to his chin, the corner of his mouth, the roughened texture of one cheek. "If you want me now, show me," she said. "For a different reason, I don't have any memory of this, either."

"Two beginners, then."

"One beginner and one . . . rusty pro?"

He kissed her hair. When he kissed her, wherever he kissed her, he felt no release, only a stronger desire. "An assumption."

"Worth a bet, I think."

"We'll see."

"Will we? How will I know if I've won?"

He brushed her lips with his, once, twice, three times. Her expression—a touch of shyness, a touch of wonder—changed to something more elemental. At the fourth time she lay back, taking him with her. She clasped him to her as he kissed her again. She could feel the warmth and weight of his body pressed against hers. Every inch of him caressed her.

She felt his hand skim her neck and pause at her shoulder. His fingertips began a slow, sensuous massage, at first through her jacket, then under it to the bare skin at the neckline of her dress. His touch was electric. It pulsed through her like a current, sending small shock waves along her spine.

She moaned against his lips, not sure what she was asking for. She only knew she wanted, needed, more.

More was his hand between them, skillfully unfastening the buttons at the front of her dress. More was his hand against her bra, then against the bare skin of her breast. More was his fingers, his long magical fingers, touching her in places she had denied him before.

She felt no shame and no caution. She moaned again as he slipped her dress down her arms. His lips traced the delicate line of her collarbone as his hands explored her. In one fleeting moment she thought of her mother and understood for the first time how Mary Kate had given herself to a stranger, then mourned his absence for the rest of her brief life.

"Mackenzie."

She heard Patrick whisper her name. The sound sent a fierce wave of pleasure through her. It was *her* name he said at this moment. *Her* name, not the name of another from deep inside his memory.

"Only you," he said, as if he had read her thoughts.

"Only you," she said. And she knew, somehow, that it would always be only him. Only Patrick, no matter what happened in the future or where he went when his memory returned.

Her hands were trembling, but she found the buttons on his shirt and made short work of them. With his help her dress fell to her waist, and she felt the shocking impact of his skin against hers. She wound her fingers in his hair and pulled his mouth hungrily to hers.

He fed her hunger and his own. Her soft breasts flattened against his chest as if her body had been made to lie against his. Touching her was like absorbing in one moment all the wondrous things he knew of the world. Like early morning rays of sunshine against bare arms, sparkling diamond drops of water, the chirruping song of a magpie, the velvet coat of a newborn colt.

He felt himself falling through space with her, through dark, star-dazzled skies into undiscovered realms. He held her tighter in prayerful gratitude and shut his eyes.

Colors filtered from three bright spots in a hazy mauve sky. Forms, beings, of such iridescent beauty that they pierced the haze like the suns above them, stood in a wide, silent circle. Two beings emerged and started slowly toward each other.

Mackenzie felt a change in Patrick. He started and stiffened, as if she had hurt him. She murmured against his lips. She used her fingertips to massage away his sudden tension. She didn't want him to have any doubts about what was happening between them. She didn't want him to worry about her. "This is right," she murmured. "It's right!"

He wrapped his arms around her and held her closer. The resulting kiss went on and on, a passionate question, then a promise. She could feel the heat of his arousal through their clothes. Boldly, her hands traveled there, slipping between their bodies to explore this new promise.

He didn't close his eyes. But this time the vision came without it.

The forms glided closer and closer to one another. Yards apart, they stopped. A third form, one of older, more ad-

*vanced knowledge, broke from the circle and started to-
ward them. Those gathered around began a rippling,
melodious chant. The master—he had always been called
master—glided, floated, moved across the ground as
smoothly as if he were an ark sailing through the water.
When he reached the two figures he began to speak.*

Patrick gave a small cry and broke from Mackenzie, but
he could not leave her. He fell to his back on the ground beside her. Confused, she sat up. Her hand stroked his cheek.
She could feel his doubts, his questions. She thought she
understood them.

"You won't hurt me," she whispered. "You couldn't."

She saw his gaze flick to her breasts, pearly white in the
moon's reflection. He tried to turn away; she knew he tried,
but he couldn't. She smiled a little. Her hands trembled as
she pushed her dress lower; then, as he watched, she knelt
and let the dress fall lower still.

"Mackenzie." His voice was agonized.

"You won't hurt me," she repeated. "I know you won't."

He couldn't answer. She settled herself against him, naked now except for a scrap of lace that stretched from hip
to hip.

Memories and feelings whirled in his head. The woman
beside him was everything a man could ever hope for. Her
body was the lush wellspring of femininity. His body called
out to her, agonized, tormented beyond his endurance. He
wanted her, wanted to sink inside her and unite them in a
way that had nothing to do with centuries of civilized
thought and everything to do with primal urges that connected them to the earth itself.

He groaned as she slipped his shirt over his shoulders. He
sensed the sweetness of her touch, the untutored yearnings
that compelled her to take the lead. He sensed the whole-
ness of her giving, the faith that shut away her own questions.

The sweetness, the fumbling, trembling glide of her hands
across his chest, the faith that had brought her to him, dissolved the power of his memories. He was overwhelmed
with emotion, swollen with it until he thought his body

could not contain it. He felt his blood running hot inside him, and the part of him that yearned for solace, for burial and renewal inside her, was heating along with it.

He felt the snap on his jeans give way and the cool flow of her hands over that place. He released a groan, because he thought he would die if he didn't release this unbearable tension.

"Make love to me, Paddy," she whispered.

He heard the command, the plea, the hesitance. He knew she needed his reassurance. She was giving herself, and he was giving little in return. He couldn't explain what he didn't understand, but neither could he bear for her to be hurt.

Nor could he bear the exquisite, unrelieved agony of her hands stroking him.

He groaned and knew that this time it would do no good. She arched against him, and he turned her to the grass once more. Impatiently he kicked away his jeans and briefs. He could feel her melting against him. Their bodies were merging; their spirits were merging before he could even part her legs to make them one. He felt a hosanna resounding through him. Nothing in his life had ever been this right. Nothing had ever been this foreordained.

He slipped his arms beneath her and stared into her eyes.

The master held out his hands. Each of the two figures accepted one. As the three beings touched, there was a rainbow of exotic, indescribable color that soared through the air. Then the master linked the hands of the two beings and turned away from them. Each person in the circle turned away, too, and the two beings were left alone, in the center. There was another explosion of light, of rainbow colors. The chanting grew louder....

"No!" Patrick sat up and rested his head in his hands. "God, no!"

For a moment Mackenzie didn't know what had happened. She was so immersed in her feelings that she couldn't believe he had separated himself from her.

"I can't! My God, Mackenzie, I can't."

She sat up. She had never been more aware of her nakedness. She was naked in every way, and in the darkness, she could find nothing to cover herself. "What is it?" she asked.

He heard her fears and the beginnings of shame. He couldn't tell her what he'd heard, what he'd seen. He was a madman. He saw beings who weren't there, heard voices in his head.

"I just can't!"

"Was it something... Is it..." She couldn't go on. The voice she heard was scarcely her own. There was no confidence in it, nothing but a puling, whining plea. Tears sprang to her eyes. "I'm sorry if it's not what you expected," she said woodenly.

"That's not it!"

"Then what is it?" She began to feel around on the ground. Her hands were unsteady, and her eyes were filling with tears. She cursed her own weakness, would, she supposed, curse it forever now.

He couldn't answer. A worse thought than his own insanity gripped him. He was not insane. And it was so much worse not to be insane. Because if he wasn't insane, then there was another, infinitely more frightening explanation.

He wasn't human.

He drew a deep, agonized breath. He moved away from her, convinced he would somehow hurt her by his presence alone. He was still on fire from their lovemaking, and perhaps that was proof of his humanity. But if it was evidence, it was the only evidence.

He saw colors that didn't exist, saw beings who weren't there. Saw ceremonies... What kind of ceremony had it been?

He knew the answer as quickly as he'd asked the question. It had been a mating ceremony, brought to his consciousness because he had almost mated with Mackenzie. It had been a mating ceremony. His? *His?* Who was he? *What* was he? And was he somehow, on another world, or in another dimension of time, mated with another being?

Could he hurt the woman he loved here, in this place, in this time? The woman who, in every way, was the other half of his heart?

"You've remembered something, haven't you?" she asked. She had successfully pushed away the trembling, the tears. Now anger filled her. "Answer me, Patrick, damn it. Do you know who you are?"

"No."

"I see." She found her dress and pulled it over her head. She wanted nothing more than to cover herself. All of herself.

"I have no right to . . . make love to you. I could hurt you!"

"Yes. You're perishing good at that."

"Mackenzie."

Something inside her knotted and unknotted at the pain in his voice, but she steeled herself against it.

"I don't want a man who doesn't trust me," she said. "I'm glad you put a stop to this."

"Trust you?"

"That's what this is about, stranger. You don't think I'm woman enough to take whatever it is you're afraid you'll dish out. You fought Sebastian for me, now you've fought yourself. You don't want a partner, you want somebody to take care of."

He tried to read her feelings, to understand the struggles inside her, but she was successfully blocking them. He reached out to touch her, to make a link with her that she couldn't sever, but she slapped away his hand.

"Stay out of my mind. Stay out of my life," she said. She stood, found her shoes and slipped them on. "You're not better than Sebastian, Patrick. At least he's honest about what he wants when he goes after it."

There was the tiniest break in her voice, the tiniest break in her defenses. For a moment Patrick was overwhelmed by her sorrow, her anger, her sense of betrayal.

He reeled under the blow, shutting his eyes against her pain. When he opened them, he was alone.

Chapter 12

Sebastian had such finely honed instincts that it took him less than half a day to find the right man to tell him about Patrick. Jack, the bookkeeper, was a bearded, spindly misanthrope who had come to Waluwara because there were fewer humans per square mile than there were cattle—and there were blessedly few of those, too. He kept to himself so completely that even in a place where almost everyone craved solitude, Jack was considered a loner.

Because of his natural inclination for the solitary life, and because he worked exclusively with figures, Jack tolerated his fellow employees but had no personal loyalties. And even though he preferred isolation, he was still, by virtue of his position, privy to a quantity of information about the others who lived on the station.

No, he told Sebastian—without once looking up from his work—he didn't know any more about Patrick than anyone else did. Seemed to him that Patrick was just another bloke who'd made a muck of his life. No, he didn't have a clue where Patrick had come from, other than the heart of a dust storm. But no one knew that, did they? After all, a man who couldn't remember his own name wasn't likely to remember anything as complex as where he'd been born. Yeah, that was true, fair dinkum. The poor bloke didn't even have a last name. For accounting's sake, they were calling him Smith, to keep things tidy.

"Smith." Sebastian stood on the steps of the station office and peered out over the small settlement that was the last gasp of the St. Carroll financial empire. Once there had been property holdings throughout the world, coffee plantations in Kenya and tea in Sri Lanka, miles of fertile rice lands in India and Thailand, wheat fields in Iowa rippling as far as the eye could see. His family had been farmers at heart, he supposed, serfs raised up by luck and cunning into positions of power. They had never dared venture beyond what they knew best, land and its natural bounty. They had never had a different vision.

He had been the one with a different vision.

Now there was only Waluwara to show for the St. Carrolls' careful harvesting of the earth they had never purged from their blood. Waluwara, whose parched, barren soil sailed miles each day in spirals of dust. Waluwara, which he could no longer hope to maintain, even if that had been his wish.

There were footsteps behind him. He didn't look to see who had joined him. He smelled tobacco and spearmint and knew that Brent Caswell, the spokesman for the consultants from Perth, was beside him.

"You're going to have to decide, St. Carroll. We've given you our best estimates on where we might find ore. Your time and resources are limited. And the Wet is coming."

Sebastian didn't turn his head. He inclined it, aristocrat to lackey. "I believe I hired you, Caswell. Since when do you give the ultimatums?"

"Since the deposit for our services is about to run out."

"You'll get your money."

"We will, or we won't stay on. We agreed to come for two weeks. Our equipment arrives tomorrow. When it does, you'll need to tell us where you want us to move it. North, south, east, west, it makes no difference to us. But if we don't start soon, what money you've already spent will be wasted."

This time Sebastian turned. Caswell was a short man, big-boned and muscular, with a rib cage wide enough to house an emu. He had come highly recommended, but Sebastian had disliked him on sight. Caswell was a fair man, basically an honest one. And he had taken Sebastian's measure immediately.

"I'll tell you tonight," Sebastian said.

Caswell narrowed his eyes. "We'll have the rest of our money before we touch a drill bit to the ground."

"That wasn't our arrangement."

"That's our arrangement now. No money, our equipment goes back to Perth, and we go with it."

Sebastian calculated what cash he had left. It would cover the agreed-upon two weeks, but when it was gone, there would be just enough to get him back to Hong Kong. Whether he would go with his tail between his legs or sipping Dom Pérignon depended on this man and his crew. He smiled his toothiest smile. "So be it. You'll have the remainder of your funds tonight."

Caswell didn't smile back. "We won't stay longer than we agreed upon."

"Not even if you're on the trail of a rich deposit?"

"I don't like you, St. Carroll. I'll do the job I said I would, but I won't work even an extra minute."

"You have so much business you can turn down offers of employment?"

"I'm a free man. I can turn down anything . . . or anyone . . . who doesn't suit my fancy." This time Caswell smiled, just before he disappeared into the office.

"Smith." Sebastian stared at the horizon, shimmering like a lake in the noonday heat. Smith, a man who could find clear, flowing water under the ground. A man who could hypnotize an opponent with the twist of his hands. A man with a special affinity for animals, such an unusual affinity that even in this wasteland filled with horsemen, he stood alone.

"Patrick Smith, alias St. Patrick my deliverer." Sebastian smiled again, but this time the smile was for his benefit alone.

The colt was a roan, with a glowing red coat that reminded Patrick of Mackenzie's hair. He watched the colt's mother nudge it to its wobbly little legs. Then he watched it find its own version of life support and begin to nurse greedily.

"I reckon it's always a miracle."

Patrick looked up to see the boss standing in the barn doorway. He had been so totally absorbed in the drama of birth that he hadn't heard Clint arrive.

"Where's Dr. Al?" Clint strolled to Patrick's side and peered over the stall door.

"Busy on the other side of the run, I think. He went off with Harry this morning. Nobody guessed the mare's time had come."

"No problems?"

There had been problems, major ones. Patrick had taken care of them himself. But he didn't elaborate now. How could he explain that he could heal animals as well as people? He didn't understand his own gifts. He couldn't expect understanding from others.

"A few. But everything's fine now."

"His bloodlines are faultless. Raise him right and he'll win for us at a race meeting or two. If we're here to race him."

Patrick sifted through all the other man's doubts and fears, along with his powerful yearnings. "What are the chances St. Carroll will find manganese?"

"I don't know."

Patrick searched his mind for an answer to his own question, but Waluwara's future was veiled to him.

"If he finds a large deposit," Clint said, "it will be the end of this place."

"And if he doesn't?"

"It will be the beginning of me."

Patrick imagined both possibilities. "Yes, it would be. If you stayed, your children and their children would grow courageous and strong here, just like Mackenzie has."

"I have no children."

"Mrs. Wallace is still young enough to give you several."

Clint frowned, raking Patrick with an expression other men had come to fear. "You're taking a fair bit on yourself there, aren't you?"

"Am I?" Patrick shrugged. "She loves you. You love her. You've denied yourself that love since her husband died because you're a hard man who's afraid of anything gentle or soft."

"You don't know anything about it."

"Her people are from the village, aren't they?"

Clint hesitated, as if he had no intention of answering. Then he said gruffly, "Her mother."

"And her father was white?"

"What of it?"

"She has the gifts of both. The strengths of both. But she believes you don't want her because her blood is mixed."

Pain settled over Clint's features. "How do you know all this?"

"My eyes are open."

Clint gripped the stall door. "Too bloody open, mate."

Memories of the past evening had haunted Patrick all day. "Believe me, I wish they weren't."

"Turn that extraordinary vision on yourself, Patrick, and what do you see?"

What could he say? That he saw a man who was different from everyone around him? That he saw a man who seemed human enough but who had abilities far outstripping those of his fellow men? That his memories were of beings formed from light, of disembodied voices offering advice he couldn't seem to follow? And that now his memories included a woman so beautiful, so stirring, that he would never be able to forget the look on her face when he had refused the precious gift she had offered him?

"I think there are things inside me I'm afraid to see," he answered.

"I think there are things inside you that would frighten even the most courageous man."

Patrick looked up. Clint's gaze had softened. There was understanding there, an understanding Patrick had never really hoped to find in anyone.

"Things that will take you away from Mackenzie," Clint added.

"I don't want to hurt her."

"As you've pointed out to me, we don't always know what will hurt those we love. Not until it's accomplished."

Patrick considered that piece of wisdom after Clint had gone. The little roan colt still suckled noisily at its mother's teats. He saw Mackenzie in the colt's shining red coat, in its exuberant, jerky grace, in its enthusiastic joy in a life it hardly knew.

He was afraid that from now until the end of his existence, he was doomed to see Mackenzie Conroy in everything.

Sebastian watched the man on the horse. He had witnessed equestrian events from Ascot to Churchill Downs, but he couldn't remember ever seeing anyone more in tune with his mount. There were moments, as he watched Patrick, when he wasn't sure where the man ended and the horse began. Together they were fluid motion, seamless grace. All without a saddle or reins.

He swung himself over the side of the riding ring and perched on the top rail. When Patrick completed putting the horse through its paces, he guided her toward Sebastian.

"What are you doing here?" he asked with no preamble.

"Watching you. Watching my horse. That is my horse, isn't it?"

"No. This horse is the personal property of Reg, one of the stockmen."

"Why are you training her, then?"

"Don't worry. I'm not wasting your time or money. I've finished my own jobs for the afternoon."

"Don't jump to conclusions. I just like to keep abreast of what's going on. That's a beautiful animal. I'm sorry she's not mine."

Patrick heard the false cheer. His expression didn't change. He waited for Sebastian to say what he had really come to say.

"Do you have a moment? I could come back later."

Patrick slid off the horse's back and gave her a slap on the rump. She moved off to see if there was anything to graze on at the opposite side of the ring.

"Let's walk," Sebastian suggested. "When I stand still, the damned flies settle all over me." He led the way, heading toward an open field.

Patrick knew that Sebastian hadn't come to apologize or to fire him. But he wasn't sure what his motive might be. Sebastian St. Carroll was a man of many talents. Now that he had an inkling of some of Patrick's gifts, Sebastian was using his own to shelter his thoughts.

"I found out a bit about you today."

Patrick had no intention of wasting time. "There's only a bit to find out."

"Is it true you don't know who you are?"

"I'm Patrick Smith, Waluwara horse trainer."

"And before that?"

"As far as I know, there was no before that."

"No memories at all?"

"What exactly do you want, St. Carroll? I told you last night that you could never possess anything that belonged to me."

"So you said."

They continued to walk. The sun was low in the sky, and there was a gray haze surrounding it, almost as if rain clouds were struggling to form.

"I heard one of the stockmen say that the Wet will come early this year." Sebastian found shade in a clump of eucalyptus at the field's edge and leaned against one of the trees for a better look at his companion. "Do you think so?"

"I don't know."

"It won't be possible to look for ore if it does, you know. The tracks will bog, equipment could be lost. Possibly even lives."

"Then you really should get busy."

"My thoughts exactly." Sebastian stripped off a piece of iron-gray bark. The wood beneath was smooth and silvery. He wondered if the tree had been waiting expectantly for this opportunity to transform itself into a thing of beauty. Waiting like the land, the vile, scrub-ridden miles of Waluwara, which harbored bountiful treasure.

"But I have a problem," he continued.

"Only one?"

Sebastian threaded the bark between his fingers. "I had hoped that the team I brought with me could tell me exactly where to look. It is that easy sometimes, I'm told."

"And you like things to be easy."

"Don't we all? But, of course, things rarely are. And this time they're not. There are many potential sites. The team has recommended six. My job is to select the one I want to gamble on."

"A task you should be well suited for."

"What does that mean?"

"You're a gambling man by nature."

"One whose luck hasn't been good of late, I'm afraid."

"And that's why you murdered Walter Chinn at his home in Kowloon last year. Because your luck had run out, and he was going to make sure you were never lucky again."

Sebastian turned pale. "Who are you?"

"I told you last night, I know every thought you have, every sick and twisted fantasy that's ever crossed your mind, St. Carroll."

"Then you know why I'm here."

He did know. Now. Sebastian had become good at protecting himself, but not good enough. There had been a moment's lapse in that protection, when Patrick had accused him of murder. It had been plenty of time for Patrick to see into his mind.

"You're here to find out if I'll help you choose a site," Patrick said.

"I believe in your abilities."

"Do you think I'm flattered? That I care what you believe in? I told you last night that nothing about me was for sale."

"Obviously, then, you're sure you have something I'd want."

"It doesn't matter if I do or don't."

"But you see, Patrick, it matters to me. If you really can read my mind, you know I'm about to lose everything I have. I will lose everything if I don't find manganese. I believe you can help me find it. *You* believe the same."

Sebastian pushed himself away from the tree. The bark in his hands fell to the ground unnoticed. "Can you see minerals under the earth? Can you see deposits just waiting to be mined the way you see water? I think you can. I think you have extraordinary powers. I've seen them before. Perhaps none exactly like yours, but powers that convince me the world isn't exactly the place most poor fools believe it to be."

"What kind of powers?"

"Men whose souls can travel from place to place while their bodies never move. Men who can find disease and injury simply by running their hands over a chest, an arm. Men so powerful they have only to look an opponent in the eye to send him screaming into the night. I've seen these things in Hong Kong. The Orientals have knowledge that Westerners will never understand."

"And you've studied some of their techniques."

"There is only so much they will teach a foreigner."

Patrick heard the things that Sebastian left unsaid. There was only so much that even the most evil sensei would teach a man like Sebastian. There were moral precepts that even corrupt men felt compelled to follow.

"So you believe in more than the eye can see," Patrick said. "Yet you're not frightened by the possibility that powers like the ones you've described could be used against you?"

"No. I have my own powers. In this case, they reside in my hold on the pastoral leases here. There's nothing you can do to change that. I hold the cards, and I'll lay them out for you, if you're interested.''

"You don't have to." Patrick knew that Sebastian was purposely allowing his thoughts to be read now. He saw the other man's plan as surely as if he had spoken. If Patrick helped Sebastian find manganese, Sebastian would not oust Clint from his position at Waluwara. The village and its people would remain untouched. Clint could continue to manage the station, perhaps even with a more bountiful budget, if the find was good enough.

Although this went against Sebastian's greediest instincts, it did have some benefits for him. If the property was maintained, he would be in no danger of the Territory stepping in to strip him of his leases. He could continue to mine the land until every trace of valuable minerals had disappeared.

"But if you don't find ore for me," Sebastian said, "I'll sell the land, and it won't be to Clint Conroy. I'll sell it to the owner of Silver Tree, Matthew Fraser. We've already discussed it."

"Even if the price is lower?"

"Of course not, but it won't be. I've checked into Conroy's finances. He'll offer low. He'll have to. He doesn't know that there's someone with considerably more assets who might want the property, too."

"Someone who would surely keep Clint on as manager."

"No. Fraser would want his son to manage the property. Seems the lad is a tad bit spoiled. His father wants him toughened up, and quickly. He thinks Waluwara is just the place to be certain that happens. And he has no use for your precious village, by the way. Of course, he can't throw the Aborigines off the land, but he can make conditions less than pleasant for them."

"I can see why you sought him out. Birds of a feather."

"Yes. I visited with Fraser in Darwin, before coming here. He and I hit it off immediately."

"So, you think you have me in a trap."

"You're loyal to the people here because they saved your life. It pours out of you like sweat in the afternoon sun. But

I can bait the trap even more effectively, Patrick. I can make it truly worth your while to help me.''

"Can you?"

"I will give you thirty percent of the profit if you succeed in locating ore for me. And after that, the sky's the limit."

"I sincerely doubt it."

Sebastian frowned. "Pardon me?"

Patrick shook his head. "What's the rest of the offer, St. Carroll?"

"Partners. We'll use the profits from this strike to locate other mines on other properties. Opals, gold, diamonds." He shrugged, as if he couldn't bear to continue such a pleasurable train of thought. "With your...special talents, and my experience and position, we'll be able to make billions. And if I'm making billions, there would be nothing to stop me from making this station a model for the Territory. No expense would be too great. Everyone here would benefit."

There would be nothing to keep him from making the station a model except his powerful greed. Patrick touched Sebastian's arm. Immediately his stomach knotted in revulsion. "You forget, St. Carroll. I know you well. What would keep me from ending up like Walter Chinn?"

"Would I harm the man who was responsible for my own good fortune?"

Patrick dropped his hand. "I'll consider it."

"Consider it quickly. My window of opportunity is limited."

"If I helped you, I'd make one demand."

"Consider it done."

"You'll leave Mackenzie alone while you're here."

"That's a decision I'd already made."

Patrick knew Sebastian was lying. Despite his smooth manners and false cheer, he was seething internally. He held Patrick and Mackenzie responsible for his humiliation of the night before, and at the first opportunity he would punish them both. The feelings were buried so deeply under his present problems that Sebastian had yet to form them in his mind.

But Patrick knew.

"I don't suppose you'd give me a demonstration of your abilities, would you?" Sebastian asked. "After all, I have a lot pinned on your decision."

"A demonstration?"

"Something to show me that you can find more than water under the ground."

Patrick stared at him.

"I didn't mean to offend you," Sebastian said, backing toward the tree.

Patrick's gaze flicked past him, settling on a faint depression just beyond the shade of the largest gum. "Dig there," he said.

Sebastian followed his gaze. He backed toward the spot, as if afraid that Patrick might attack him. He stopped and pointed with his toe. "Here?"

Patrick pointed several feet to his left.

"Here?"

Patrick nodded.

Sebastian squatted, still facing Patrick. Slowly he began to scoop away the dirt. "How deep? Should I get a shovel?"

"Just dig."

Sebastian began to sweat. Patrick absorbed the other man's distaste for getting dirty, his skepticism, even his fear that Patrick was making a fool of him. Then Sebastian's fingertips struck something hard. He began to scoop faster. "There's something here."

"I know."

Sebastian struggled to uncover the object. It wasn't a rock, at least he didn't think so. It was smooth and possibly hollow, the color of the dirt it had been buried under. He dug around it and discovered it was larger than he'd thought. Finally, after a battle that left him soaked with his own sweat and dirtier than he had ever been in his life, he dislodged the object. Only then did he realize what he had uncovered. He dropped it back into the now substantial hole, as if it were radioactive.

"A cow skull," Patrick acknowledged. "The poor beast died of thirst on this spot during a drought almost thirty years ago."

Sebastian got to his feet, wiping his hands on his pants. He wiped them for a long time without looking up. When he did, his eyes were carefully blank. "You'll let me know your decision by suppertime? We can fly over the sites tomorrow morning."

"I'll let you know." Patrick followed Sebastian with his eyes as the other man turned and started toward the homestead. Patrick hoped that when Matthew Fraser learned that Waluwara could not be his, he would find another station that would make a man of his son. There were too many Sebastian St. Carrolls already. The world did not need another.

Chapter 13

The early morning sunshine was already warm on Mackenzie's bare head, but she hardly noticed. The parched air was still and so quiet she could almost hear the trees grow. The stockmen had risen and departed while it was still dark, taking their dogs and horses. The station hands were busy inside or in places far from the homestead. As she strode toward the men's quarters, Mackenzie felt the eerie silence down to her bones. It only made her walk faster.

The quarters were simple, almost primitive in architecture: four whitewashed walls, a rusting metal roof and a veranda that served as a place to smoke or watch the world pass by. The married men lived elsewhere. The men who shared these walls divided up the space according to their own whims. Only rarely had she been inside.

She was going inside today.

On the veranda she pounded her fist against the door. The door shook; the quarters shook. She shook with anger.

There were footsteps inside. She knew whose they were before a figure appeared in the doorway.

"I want to speak to you," she said with no preliminaries. "Right now."

"Would you like to come in?"

She changed her mind; she did not want to confront Patrick on his own turf. "No."

Patrick opened the door. He devoured her with his eyes—he hadn't seen her since their encounter by the billabong. She wasn't dressed for work yet. She was wearing a filmy blouse of patterned turquoise and shorts that showed every inch of her long legs. Obviously she had thrown on the first clothes she'd found.

"Are you all right?" he asked. He put his hand on her shoulder, but she squirmed away.

"Keep your hands to yourself."

"You're angry."

"Bloody hell, the man's a mind reader!" Disdain shone from her eyes; her mouth was a grim line.

He was confused. Her feelings were a jumble he should have been able to sort. But his own feelings made that impossible. He was so filled with yearning, with an ache inside him and a need to hold her, that nothing else could seep through.

"I didn't mean to hurt you," he said.

"Do you think I'm angry about the other night?" She turned her back to him and stared at nothing. "I don't care about that," she lied. "I don't need your affection. I reckon I learned a thing or two about men at the billabong that I won't soon forget."

"You're furious."

She whirled. "It's what I've learned since that night that makes me furious, stranger."

"Stranger, is it?"

"You're helping St. Carroll find ore! I heard it from Edwina. She heard the two of you talking last night."

"I knew she was nearby."

"Then apparently you don't care who knows, because she, at least, has some loyalty. She told me what she'd heard, then she went to tell my uncle."

"I hope it gave them something to talk about."

"What's that supposed to mean?"

He didn't elaborate. "I am helping Sebastian."

"Why? With all your sensitivity to what other people are feeling, haven't you figured out that we don't want Sebastian to be successful?"

"I know."

"You know, yet you're planning to help him anyway? Why? Is he offering you money?"

"Yes. A lot."

Her eyes widened. He could see he had caught her off balance. Despite her anger, she hadn't really expected to discover he was taking a bribe.

"And that's the reason?" she asked.

"What do you think?"

"I think you're scum!"

He put his hands on her arms. When she tried to pull away, he tightened his grip. "No, you don't."

"Don't I? And why not? Is there a better word for a man who sells out his mates?"

"No one's been sold out."

She kicked at his leg, but he held her away easily. "What do you call it, then?"

"I call it working for the man who pays my salary."

"You wouldn't have a salary if it weren't for my uncle."

"And your uncle wouldn't have a salary if it weren't for Sebastian St. Carroll. This is his station, and I'm his employee. How can I refuse to do what he asks?"

"How can you refuse not to!" Mackenzie was successful in wriggling out of his grip. She put her hands on her hips. "Nothing good will come out of Sebastian finding manganese. Not for us, anyway. You'll be richer, though, won't you?"

"Is that what you think?"

She struggled to get herself under control. She was conscious enough of her own emotions to realize that part of her fury came from the fact that in twenty-four hours he had twice rejected her. She had given herself to him, and he had said no, thank you. Now he was saying the same to her loyalty and trust.

"Is that what you think?" he asked again. He moved closer.

"What else can I think?" she asked. "Are you doing it to lead him in the wrong direction? Are you promising to find ore just so you can keep him away from the most promising spots?"

He moved closer still. "You're asking if I'm planning to cheat and lie?"

She had thought she knew Patrick well enough never to suspect him of either. But now, with her belief in herself in shreds, she wasn't sure if she knew anything about him at all. "That's what I'm asking."

"I'll find Sebastian his manganese."

"Don't."

He heard the plea stirred in with the anger. He couldn't reply. There was something sharp inside him, cutting away pieces of his heart.

"Don't, Patrick. I'm begging you."

"I have to do what I think is right."

"Right for whom?" When he didn't answer, the sadness, the plea in her eyes hardened. "I guess I can answer that myself."

"Think hard before you do."

"I don't have to think hard. I can see the answer. Maybe you have some distorted sense of loyalty to Sebastian because he employs you, but that could have been dealt with easily enough by just quitting your job. Since you didn't, I can only assume the offer he made you was too good to pass up, even for the sake of every living soul on this station."

"Mackenzie..." Against his own best judgment, he stepped closer.

"Don't!"

He reached out to her, but she turned away. "I thought I knew you," she said, choking on the words. "I thought I could feel what you feel. I'd never had that experience with anyone."

"Mackenzie." His hands hovered above her. He didn't know if he could bear to plumb the depths of her sorrow.

"But I was wrong. I don't know you any more than you know yourself. You're not the man I believed in. You're not the man I tried to give myself to. That man doesn't exist."

"You're right about that." As gently as he could, he rested his hands on her shoulders.

She stiffened. "Now I think I understand how my mother felt when my father left her to fend for herself. He wasn't the man he appeared to be, either. Mary Kate and I have that in common."

"You don't know that he left her."

She jerked away from his touch.

"Maybe your mother just didn't have the courage to stand beside him, to go with him," Patrick went on. "Maybe she left him."

"Then we have that in common, too. Because I'm leaving now, and I'm not looking back. Best of luck to you, stranger. Find your manganese. Take your blood money and run with it. Maybe it will buy you memories. You'll never make any of your own worth savoring."

The sun was already warmer as Mackenzie hurried toward the homestead. It dried her tears before they could streak her cheeks.

The plane was a single-engine Cessna just large enough to seat six. Patrick felt it climbing toward the sky as the earth fell away beneath him. He shut his eyes against the sheer exhilaration flooding through him. This was nothing like the choppy helicopter ride he had taken with Mackenzie when he had still been disoriented and anxious.

This, he knew. This, he had experienced. Many times. So many times that it was as if he had once lived in the air, dwelled there and felt this glorious sensation as often as he felt breath expanding his lungs.

"Are you a white-knuckle flier?" Sebastian asked from the seat beside him.

Patrick reluctantly opened his eyes. "No."

"Have you flown in a small plane before? Oh, I'm sorry, of course, you wouldn't know that, would you?"

Patrick didn't answer. He had agreed to help Sebastian find ore, but he hadn't agreed to subject himself to the other man's inquisition.

"We'll be flying over the first potential site in a few minutes," Sebastian said. "I've told the pilot to fly as low as he can without putting us in danger. Will that be sufficient for your needs?"

"We'll have to see."

"I had a little chat with Mackenzie this morning." He smiled a little as Patrick's expression changed. "Nothing for you to be concerned about. Her uncle was there. I'm living up to my promise."

Patrick turned away to gaze out the window.

Sebastian continued as if he hadn't noticed. "It seems she knew you were coming with us this morning. She's furious, of course. Not that she said as much. She's reining in her emotions, but she's easy to read. I suppose I have a few of your talents myself."

Patrick watched the landscape glide beneath them. Here there were clumps of scrub, there a cow or two. He could see a fence stretching into forever, the distant sapphire gleam of a tributary of the Victoria, a shed much like the one in which he and Mackenzie had waited out the dust storm.

His eyes closed again. Immediately he could see stars and dark velvet skies, a vessel winging through space in exploration, a crew of beings as radiant as the ones he had seen when he had been wrapped in Mackenzie's arms.

"I suppose she feels that you've turned against her," Sebastian continued. "She does so want her uncle to buy Waluwara. I shouldn't want to be the one to explain your motives for helping me."

Patrick opened his eyes. Perspiration dampened his skin. His breath came and went in small gasps. He forced himself to calm. Sebastian was right about one thing; he was good at sensing feelings. Patrick did not want his own sensed now.

Below him, the land flowed into tomorrow. He saw a track, nothing more than a faint scar on the earth's surface. A lone kangaroo bounded across it, and far to the west a flock of emus, startled by the plane's engine, ran through the brush as if making for a distant rendezvous.

Sebastian seemed unaware of his struggle. "Clint, of course, had nothing to say. I don't trust him, you know. He's not a man who can be bought. I've never understood why he stayed on here when other, better opportunities presented themselves. I wonder if he knows that if it weren't for him and his excellent management, I would have lost this property years ago."

Patrick stared at the earth sliding from his view. And then he was staring at green trees and fields, verdant, emerald green surrounded by water so blue it seemed like a piece of the sky. He was not in the plane, but in a more complex vessel, and although his eyes were still open, and the Australian countryside unfolded beneath him, it was another vision he saw.

"Lindsey," he whispered.

"Pardon me?"

Patrick shut his eyes, and the vision grew as sharp as reality. An island in a lake. A woman as different from Mackenzie as moonlight to sunshine.

She danced along his consciousness now. He reached for her, but only light arced through the air. Then the light was flesh. He was flesh. But not quite.

"Stefan," he whispered.

"Patrick," Sebastian said, "what's wrong? If you're not going to be any good to me, for God's sake, say so now. I'll tell the pilot to turn back."

Patrick sifted through a hundred separate languages and a million different realities to find the answer. "No."

There was a door in his mind, a door he had held shut with every ounce of strength. Now it swung slowly open. It was a heavy door guarding all the secrets of his existence, a door with a thousand screaming voices behind it. But now the voices no longer screamed in unison. He heard one voice, the voice of a man. Stefan's voice.

This race of yours. Are they all like you?

His own. *Are you ready to find out?*

Lindsey's sobs. An unspoken protest.

Then his own voice again. *Close your eyes. Clear your mind.*

He opened his eyes, but his vision swam.

He heard Sebastian's voice as if from a great distance. "I say, Patrick, are you sure you're not ill? You're as white as a sheet!"

The door swung wider. Patrick looked down at his legs, touched his thigh, then his arm, with his fingertips. He was flesh, as was the man beside him.

But he hadn't always been so.

He heard another voice, the one that all along had been too powerful to be barricaded from him.

The truth is there in every moment we live, every place we visit, every vision we see. But it's only there if we're ready to take it as our own. If we aren't ready, little one, the moment is like any other, the place just a place, and the vision passes before our eyes unnoticed. Only when we are ready to pluck the truth and hold it to our hearts, does it become anything more than a dream.

Now he voiced his understanding and thanks to the master who had once spoken those words in the language of his people, a language that came as fluidly to his lips as water flowing to the sea.

The door closed softly, but he knew that now he could open it any time. He felt blood pumping through his body, and his vision cleared. He turned his head and saw the man beside him nod in satisfaction as his color returned. He heard the soft roar of the plane's engine and the terse conversation of the consultants seated in front of him. The air inside the cabin was growing warmer. Obviously they were approaching the spot Sebastian had mentioned, dipping lower so that he could have a closer look.

"What was that language you were just speaking?" Sebastian asked. "It's certainly not like anything I've ever heard."

Patrick turned to the window. The answer was clear to him. So much was clear.

"The language of truth," he said.

Mackenzie paused in the doorway before stepping out to the veranda. She heard voices, the voices of two people who were hidden in the lavender shadows of twilight. Voices near the place where vines as old as she was twined along an iron grille to shade the veranda from noontime sun.

"Edwina, how could you think I cared that your mother was from the village? Aren't I part of the village, too? Wasn't I made a member of the tribe along with Harry when I was a young man?"

Mackenzie recognized her uncle's voice, just as she recognized the musical tones of the woman with him. "If you're truly one with my people, Clint," Edwina said, "then you must know how difficult it is to walk in both worlds."

"I've never come to you because I didn't believe you could want me."

Mackenzie heard a gasp. "Not want you?" Edwina asked.

"I'm not an easy man."

"I've never asked for anything to be easy."

There was a sudden hush. Mackenzie backed away, letting the door fall silently shut.

Her world spun on its axis. She had lived almost all her years in this house. She had never guessed that in the eight years since the death of Edwina Wallace's husband, Edwina and her uncle Clint had fallen in love.

Her heart seemed to constrict. She could hardly breathe. She was filled with joy for the two of them and such sorrow for herself and her own shattered hopes that she could hardly contain it.

Had she sounded like Edwina at the billabong with Patrick? Expectant? Exultant? So sure of her own feminine powers that she had known she could conquer any and all barriers that stood between them? For that moment, had she ignored all the problems that were to come, scorned them because she believed so fiercely in what was right, what was inevitable, that problems seemed a mere blink of the eye?

She heard a scuffling on the porch, four feet trying to learn to walk as two. She drew a deep breath and backed into the hallway so that when the front door opened, it looked like she was just coming out of the parlor.

"I was just going out to get some fresh air," she said.

"You were just trying not to disturb us," her uncle said dryly.

She smiled, pushing down her own pain so as not to intrude on their joy. "I'm sorry. I wasn't trying to spy."

"Edwina's agreed to become my wife," Clint said.

Mackenzie smiled at the other woman, the woman who had given her the only taste of mothering that she could really remember. "Thank you," Mackenzie told her. "It will be a right bear of a job, but there's nobody any better to take it on."

She stood on the veranda after the hugs were over and Clint and Edwina had left to go to the village to tell Harry and Edwina's family. The twilight shadows deepened into night. For hours she stood quietly and watched the stars emerge, one by one, until the sky was a resplendent canopy. Just before midnight one star blazed across the sky, then burned away, followed minutes later by another.

The third falling star seemed to trail fire in its wake, lighting the sky with visions of glory. She could no longer face the mythic beauty of the night, the stars with their message of hope and endurance, the meteors with their brilliantly memorable finales.

She turned and went inside to spend the rest of a sleepless night alone.

Sunfisher pawed at the ground, restless and uncharacteristically skittish. Patrick patted his neck. The horse was afraid, as well he should be, but he trusted Patrick, and he knew that Patrick would protect him from harm.

Since finding his way to this spot, Patrick had counted two falling stars. He knew he could sit this way forever, communing with the sky above him. He also knew that communion was not why he had been called to this place.

Music filled his mind, notes from instruments unlike any he had heard on earth, tones and clusters of tones that evoked immediate pleasurable responses inside him. Music filled his ears, and Sunfisher's ears shot forward in response. The horse danced under Patrick, but not in fear, more as if he danced to the music his rider heard.

Patrick looked above him. Another star appeared in the sky, blazing toward them so suddenly that he didn't have time to react. Sunfisher grew still, but his body tensed as if he wanted to run.

Patrick soothed him with words the horse seemed to understand. The star drew nearer, the music louder, and the sky was suddenly filled with eerie, pastel light.

The star came gently to earth two hundred yards away.

Patrick slid off Sunfisher's back. He patted the horse's sides and spoke to him. Sunfisher moved off, but only a short distance.

Patrick started toward the spacecraft. One hundred yards from it, he began to run.

An opening appeared in the side. He threw up his arms and let himself be drawn through it. Inside, he was surrounded by the language he knew best, surrounded by beings of light. He was cocooned by them, wrapped in their joy at his coming, wrapped in their musical apologies. Wrapped in their love.

The beings parted, circling him, but not too closely. One stood alone. Patrick bowed his head. His very human eyes filled with tears.

"Master," he said.

"You've forgotten. I'm called Captain here," the being said.

"Captain, then."

The being stepped forward. His form was nearly human, but his body glowed with an unearthly brilliance. "You are well?"

"Yes, I am."

"Do you know how you came here tonight?"

"Yes. You sent for me, called for me. I heard you."

"We've searched for you. This place was not where we expected to find you."

"How long have you known where I was?"

"A little while. How long have you known *who* you were?"

"A very little while."

"Do you know exactly what happened to you?"

"Not everything."

The captain brought his arms together in a circle. "Are you ready to know?"

"Yes."

"We were on a mission of exploration and diplomacy. We come here from time to time, to see if the people of this world are ready for our knowledge. They aren't."

"I've seen that for myself."

"We had problems with the ship, so we landed on the other side of the planet, on a small island, Kelley's Island."

Patrick remembered. "In Lake Erie."

"A woman saw us land, and we brought her on board. But she was harmed by the experience, and so we sent you to watch over her."

"Lindsey," he said. "And I called myself...Alden."

"Alden Fitzpatrick," the captain said.

Patrick smiled at the irony. "Well, a part of that stayed with me, at least."

"Lindsey was dying, despite everything you did to save her. You're a healer. Do you know that?"

"Yes."

"To save her, you merged momentarily with her husband, Stefan. It had never been tried in quite that way with a human. You shared your knowledge with Stefan so that he, with his greater understanding of human physiology, could try to find a cure for her."

The vision of that moment was suddenly clear to Patrick. He remembered the terrible responsibility, the fear that he would do more harm than good, the agony of bonding with another who was different than himself. Then...

"I have no memories of what happened next," he said.

"Stefan survived. Lindsey is recovering now."

Patrick bowed his head. Joy filled him. "Then it was worth whatever came afterward for me."

"Afterward you tried to reach us, but in the merging, you had changed. You became like Stefan, just as he became like you." The captain stepped forward and touched Patrick. Patrick gasped. The sensation was one of heat pulsating through him. "You are human now," the captain said. "No longer only in human form. Human."

"For how long?"

The captain didn't answer. "Do you understand why you were drawn to this place, this small dot on the planet?"

Patrick looked deep inside himself, but no answer emerged. "I was trying to reach you. I remember falling through space. I remember a great, searing heat that destroyed my clothes and burned my skin. That's all I remember. Were you here? Were you calling me?"

"I've never before been to this part of this continent."

"Then I don't know."

"You may never know." The captain turned away. "What have you told the people you've met? What do they believe about you?"

"That I have no memory. That I'm a man with certain talents, which I can use to make their lives better if I choose to."

"Have you healed anyone?"

Patrick gazed from face to beloved face. "Yes."

"Have you used your powers to make changes that will affect the course of life on this planet?"

"I don't know."

The captain turned. "Because if you have, you must make amends before you come with us."

"Can I come with you in this form?"

"Will you make amends? Can you?"

"Amends?" He thought of the things he had yet to do.

"You have no right to change life here to suit your own vision."

Patrick closed his eyes. "I have things I must do before I leave."

"Must you?"

"Please!"

"You were always the child who was certain he knew what was best for everyone."

"So I've heard you tell me in the past weeks. Over and over in my head." He opened his eyes. "Please, trust me to know what is best this time."

"You were always the child who made that plea."

"I can't leave yet."

"I feel a great stirring inside you at the thought."

"My business here is unfinished."

The captain turned. The two, different in form but still much alike, gazed at each other.

"I understand what that means, and how it will eat at you forever if you disappear from this place now. But I can't let you go back unless you promise you will return to the ship when you've finished."

Patrick thought of Mackenzie. He would return to the ship and leave her light-years behind. And when he did, he would never be allowed to return to her. She would be dead to him, an eternity away from his side. He would never again feel her soft skin against his, never again see the bright blaze of her hair, never sink into her feminine depths to lose himself in her arms.

"That's the only way it can be," the captain said. "Go and promise to return to us quickly, or come with us now."

"I promise I'll return. Just as soon as I've completed my stay here."

The captain put his hands on Patrick's shoulders. Patrick felt the heat radiate through him.

"Then go, little one," the captain said. "And hear my voice in your thoughts no more. What you do now, you must do from the very depth of your own soul."

"I haven't been 'little one' for a long, long time, Master."

The captain nodded. "Nor have I been your master. Son of my dearest boyhood friend, child of my heart, you are your own master now."

Chapter 14

The Wet came early, not with wildly howling fronts that marched on the homestead like conquering armies, but with a gentle soaking rain that coaxed wildflowers from their underground hiding places and turned the grass green overnight. The dry river and creek beds, nothing more than depressions in the earth, did not fill; the Victoria, miles from the homestead, did not overflow her banks. The station tracks did not wash out completely, and the stockmen were not forced to rescue or shoot cattle bogged down in mud or marooned on islands. But the rain was a reminder that those things were to come. And soon.

From a short distance Patrick watched Sebastian pace back and forth on the far east end of the station as stockmen, station hands and consultants alike struggled to move another piece of equipment into place so that the drilling for manganese could begin. There had been a three-day delay in the arrival of the equipment, then a similar delay in getting the equipment to the spot that Patrick had selected. The rain hadn't made the track impassable, only nearly so. If the track had been properly graded after the last Wet, as it should have been, the rain would only have slowed them down a little. As it was, Sebastian was experiencing first-hand the consequences of allowing the station's equipment to deteriorate. There would not be time or money to try another site if this one was a failure.

"You're sure this is the best place?" Sebastian slowed his pacing long enough to toss the question at Patrick.

Patrick heard shouts and knew the time to drill was at hand. "You'll find manganese here. Lots of it."

"Caswell says it's never that certain."

"You're welcome to trust Caswell, if you prefer."

"You know I'll be ruined if this doesn't produce, don't you? The damnable rain has cut our time short."

"I know you think you'll be ruined."

"What does that mean?" When Patrick didn't answer, Sebastian began to pace again. "If I find you've cheated me..."

"You'll what?"

"You'll live to regret it."

"A somewhat better fate than Walter Chinn's."

"He threatened me!" Sebastian stopped and faced Patrick again. "He was going to take away everything I'd worked to build."

"And so you killed him?"

Sebastian looked away. "I didn't mean to."

"No?"

Sebastian stared into the distance, as if he was reliving that night. "I was there to make peace. Walter had always admired my gun collection, particularly a nineteenth-century six-shooter, a Colt Whitneyville-Walker, to be precise. Walter was a great fan of the American West. I presented it to him, hoping a gesture of goodwill would keep him silent until I could straighten out some business matters. He accepted the Colt, thanked me, practiced loading it, then told me he was going to expose me anyway. When I discovered he'd been playing me for a fool, I lost my temper and we began to fight. I lunged at him and grabbed the gun to hit him with the butt. It discharged in my hand."

Patrick's expression didn't change. "Why are you telling me now? Isn't it to your advantage to make me think the worst of you?"

"You knew the truth already, didn't you?"

"I know that when Chinn died by your hand, you felt only fear that you'd be discovered."

"Then you're not infallible."

"No?"

"I never meant to kill him."

For the first time Patrick felt the other man's regret, a thin ray of light piercing the roiling darkness inside Sebastian. "I've misjudged you," he said, "though not by much."

"You don't know what it's like to be me."

"For that, I'm thankful." Patrick dismissed Sebastian with a curt nod and started toward the drilling site.

"There had better be manganese here," Sebastian shouted after him.

Patrick strode on. Now he had seen the totality of the other man's soul. Next to that thin ray of regret had been a full measure of cowardice. Sebastian had not meant to kill Walter Chinn, largely because Sebastian had been terrified of discovery. He was a man ruled by greed, but that greed was balanced by a dread that his freedom might someday be taken from him. It was that dread that kept him from being truly dangerous.

For the first time Patrick was sure that no one at Waluwara had anything to fear from Sebastian St. Carroll.

"Is your uncle here?" Sebastian stood in the doorway of the homestead parlor as if he were really seeing it for the first time.

Mackenzie thrust her hands in the pockets of her moleskins and stepped aside. "We expected you day before yesterday."

Sebastian pushed past her. "We got bogged down coming back. Of course, you must have assumed we would."

"I didn't assume anything of the sort. Even my dislike for you doesn't give me control of the heavens. You took your own chances when you decided to go for a treasure hunt this time of year."

"I'm here to see your uncle."

"He's in his study. I'll get him. Would you like to wait here?"

"I'll wait. I won't like it. There's nothing to like on this whole bloody continent."

Mackenzie felt a thrill run through her at his words. "Nothing? What about a manganese deposit on the eastern end of the run?"

Sebastian didn't answer. She searched his face and found her own answers. "I'll get the boss."

"Do that."

She found her uncle gazing out the study window at the men, muddy and obviously exhausted, coming back from Sebastian's treasure hunt. He didn't turn when she came in.

"I suppose he wants to see me."

"I'm not sure the news is what we were expecting."

This time he turned. "No?"

"I'd like a favor."

"What?"

"May I come with you to hear what he has to say?"

Clint studied her before he rose. "If he'll allow it."

"Thanks."

In the parlor, Sebastian was fingering half of a carved emu eggshell, a particularly fine example of bush craftsmanship presented to Clint before Dilly Dan took his leave.

"I'm sure you're tired," Clint said, wasting no time on greetings. "Would you prefer we talk after you've had a bit of a rest?"

"Do you still want the station?"

Clint paused. "At the right price," he said at last. He sounded neither eager nor reluctant. Mackenzie struggled to control her own feelings.

"I've offered it to Matthew Fraser, too."

"Surely his resources are greater than mine."

"But his desire to own Waluwara isn't as great." Sebastian gripped the eggshell with his considerable strength.

Mackenzie watched in fascination, but the shell didn't crumble under his fingers.

"Isn't it?"

"No." Sebastian dropped the eggshell to the table. It remained intact. "He has other possibilities, it seems. And you have only this."

"Then you didn't find manganese?"

"On the contrary. We found a large deposit."

"Then what's your reason for wanting to rid yourself of the property?"

"The manganese is virtually worthless." Sebastian faced them. His smile was completely devoid of warmth. "It's of such a poor grade that it would cost more to mine and ship than it's worth at this time. My consultants say there's no profit in it. Not a cent."

"I see."

"Do you?" Sebastian laughed humorlessly. "You're witnessing the dismantling of an empire, Conroy. Do you see that, too? And does it please you? Have you and your people rooted yourself to this land solely to wait for the day when you could drive me off it?"

"If I had lived my entire life hoping to get the best of you, St. Carroll, that would make you a very important man indeed."

"You must realize I can put the land on the open market and wait for a better offer."

"You can. But, of course, if you do, you may lose everything you still have while potential buyers scour the run to see if you left anything of worth for them. And what will they find? Ungraded tracks and rusting equipment, fences held together by hope, wild cattle that outsmart even the best stockmen."

Sebastian didn't try to deny it. "That's what they would find."

Mackenzie stood there as the two men negotiated, but all she could hear was Sebastian's voice announcing that the manganese had been of such poor grade that it was unprofitable to mine and ship. No profit in it. No profit.

Her gaze flicked to the window. The consultants were climbing the steps to the veranda. Patrick wasn't with them.

"Then Patrick failed," she said out loud.

The two men stopped their discussion.

"Mac..." Clint said.

She turned, realizing that she had spoken her thoughts. "I'm sorry," she said. "I'll leave you to your discussion."

"Did Patrick fail?" Sebastian asked, before she could go. "An interesting question. He found manganese, just the way he promised. I demanded the largest deposit on the property, and he found me a large deposit, even if it's quite worthless. I suppose we can ask if he knew I wouldn't be able to mine it, but even the question credits him with incredible power. So whether he failed or not depends on one's viewpoint. For my part, I won't be asking for his help again."

"Then you think he led you on?"

"I think he gave me exactly what I asked him for. And by doing so, he ruined me."

She couldn't accept the fact that somehow Patrick had known the manganese had no value. But she couldn't rule it out, either.

"Do you know where he's gone?" she asked.

"I've no idea. And I don't care. I only want him to stay away from me until I leave, which will be immediately, if the weather holds long enough."

"Shall I tell your pilot to ready the plane and stand by?"

"Do that." He dismissed her and turned back to Clint.

She thought of a dozen parting comments, but suddenly none of them seemed important. Sebastian St. Carroll was simply a poor example of a man.

But possibly Patrick was something more.

She found Edwina and asked her to relay Sebastian's message to the pilot and the consultants. The sound of Sebastian's plane taking off was going to be the sweetest music anyone on the station had ever heard.

Outside, the hot afternoon breeze held the promise of a storm, perhaps as early as that evening. She thought of another storm, when dust had swirled instead of rain and the air had been as dry as sun-bleached bones. Fear gripped her, irrational, primitive fear. Patrick had come to her on a storm, and he would leave on one, too. She didn't know why or how, but the feeling was as solid as the ground under her feet.

Perhaps he would convince Sebastian to take him to Darwin, or use part of the money Sebastian had paid him to find his own way there. Perhaps he had remembered who he was, and he would be returning to his previous life. Perhaps he would just walk into the desert again and disappear as he had appeared. But however he took his leave, he would be going. She knew this in every fiber of her being.

"Bloody hell." She pushed a lock of hair behind her ear and stared out over the station. Patrick would be leaving, but wasn't it for the best? Once he was gone she could return to the life she had always known. She didn't need him or the endlessly complicated twists and turns he had brought with him. She didn't need to offer herself again to a man who didn't want her, and she didn't need the upheaval of emotion that came every time she thought about him.

He had refused her love, taken money to help Sebastian find manganese . . . healed a seriously injured child, discovered much-needed water, saved her uncle's life. She looked toward the riding ring and in her mind saw him with Sunfisher, although the ring was empty. She saw him with Brother on his shoulders, with the mulga snake, with the new roan colt that followed him like a pet dog whenever he was near. There was no darkness in this man. No greed, no temptation to hurt any living thing. That temptation had been hers.

She shut her eyes and saw Patrick's face the night he had refused to make love to her. He had been tormented, and in her humiliation she had been unable to accept that torment for what it was. He had not wanted to hurt her, but he had believed that by making love to her, he would hurt her more than by refusing.

And the manganese. Somehow—she still couldn't comprehend the scope of his powers—he had done exactly what Sebastian had asked of him, and by doing so, he had as much as presented Waluwara to her uncle. She couldn't believe his powers were so great that he had known all along how the search would end, but neither could she now believe that he had acted from greed. What signs had she ever witnessed that he was anything but a man driven by the highest morals?

A shout in the distance forced her to open her eyes. Harry and Reg were riding toward the homestead. She took the steps two at a time and started in their direction.

"Harry!" she called when she was near enough. "Have you seen Patrick?"

"Not since he got back an hour or more ago. He was on his way to the men's quarters."

She waved her thanks and started in that direction. At the quarters the narrow veranda had an occupant, but it was Jack the bookkeeper, not the man she sought. "Have you seen Patrick?" she asked from the ground below.

"Uh-huh."

She pushed down her annoyance. "Mind telling me where and when?"

"Here. Took off about half an hour ago," Jack said, scratching his bearded chin.

She started a goodbye, then thought better of it. "Is anyone inside?"

He shook his head.

"Would you mind if I looked around for a moment?"

Jack shrugged. He lived by himself in a two-room house beyond the homestead. Mackenzie knew she could have asked his permission to burn the quarters down and she would have received the same wordless reply.

Inside she scanned the large sleeping area for Patrick's cot. She found it against the far wall. It was unmistakably Patrick's, impeccably made and Spartan. The few items of clothing he had purchased from the station store were neatly folded on a carefully made bed, along with half a dozen books he had borrowed from the homestead library. She fingered the knobs of the small dresser beside it, then pulled one of the drawers open. It was empty except for a few toiletries, and so were the others.

She tried to picture all Patrick's worldly goods. With the exception of the clothes he was wearing, he had taken nothing with him. But obviously, quite obviously, he was leaving these few items for anyone who could use them. She rejected all the other explanations. She didn't believe he had just finished his laundry and forgotten to put it away. She didn't believe he was preparing to move to a different part of the quarters, a different building on the homestead. Patrick had gone away, and he didn't expect to return.

"Which direction did Patrick go?" she asked when she was on the veranda again.

Jack shrugged.

"Don't act the angora with me, you old billy goat. You can point as easily as you can shrug."

He looked aggrieved. Then he tilted his head to the left.

"I hope your neck locks in that position." She leaped to the ground and started toward the paddock where the horses were kept. Before she was out of shouting range she whirled. "Was he on horseback?"

His voice just barely carried the necessary distance. "He was."

"One word more than necessary," she muttered. "A blooming world's record."

She caught and saddled Bounder, then left him at the gate while she went for her swag and a water bag. She didn't know how long she might be gone. Perhaps only an hour, perhaps longer, if she was caught in the storm. She was fastening her provisions to the saddle when she saw the parade from the homestead begin. The consultants were first, heading toward the airstrip by foot. Then as Harry brought the Holden to the front, Sebastian emerged and had a few final words with her uncle on the veranda before he climbed into the car.

She watched the car disappear around the back of the homestead and take Sebastian St. Carroll out of sight. In the distance she could hear the hum of an airplane engine. She was in the saddle when the hum grew louder. She shaded her eyes and watched the plane appear and climb toward the clouds.

Sebastian St. Carroll was out of their lives.

She steered Bounder toward the house, where her uncle waited on the veranda. "Is he going to sell it to you?" she asked.

Edwina came out to join him. Clint put his arm around her shoulders. "He's having the papers drawn up in Darwin."

She saw his happiness; she saw his worry. Despite the station's run-down condition, it would still cost every penny her uncle had saved and borrowed to buy it. And then some. It would be a long time before there would be any money to make the necessary improvements. And only then if luck was with him and everyone worked twice as hard as they had before.

But sometimes miracles happened.

She thought of Patrick. "I'll be leaving for a bit," she said.

"Where are you going?"

"Seeking treasure." She gazed at the two on the veranda, obviously so content in each other. In the past weeks everything had changed. Waluwara would never be the same place again.

And that was good.

She smiled. "You've found yours. I still have to look for mine."

"I hope your luck's in," Edwina said.

"I think I'll have to make my own." She turned Bounder toward the west and started away from the house.

Parallel to the edge of the garden she turned and looked at them once more. Neither her uncle nor Edwina had moved. They were framed by vines just beginning to turn green, while above them silver-edged clouds gathered for another shower. The homestead suddenly looked particularly dear. Had she ever really appreciated all she had been given here, or all that she had learned?

"I love you both," she shouted.

Her uncle lifted his hand in farewell. Tears sprang to her eyes, although she didn't really understand why. Then she nudged Bounder's sides, and he leaped forward.

In a few minutes the homestead was no longer in sight.

Chapter 15

His business here was finished. Patrick watched the sun sink behind the thick horizon clouds in a haze of iridescent light. Earlier in the afternoon he had watched Sebastian's plane vanish behind clouds, too. Only rarely in his lifetime had he paid attention to endings. Beings of his race lived for millenia, and his own life had always stretched without end before him.

Now endings seemed a thing to contemplate at length.

Beneath him, Sunfisher whinnied softly. With the sun's disappearance had come the first soft drops of rain. The rainfall wasn't unpleasant. It splashed against his skin and dampened his shirt, but he knew that as night fell, it would grow colder. He slipped off the horse and reached for the cape-shouldered stockmen's raincoat he had rolled and brought with him. He had saddled Sunfisher for the ride because the horse would be going home alone. When Sunfisher arrived at the station without a rider, someone would unsaddle him. And that person would find Patrick's letter to Mackenzie and Clint.

Another ending would be completed.

After he pulled on the coat, he didn't mount immediately. He listened, sending out tendrils of his mind to the far reaches of the run. He listened, but the two beings he longed most to hear weren't within his reach. He had not been able to feel Mackenzie's presence or visualize her form since he had ridden out of sight of the homestead. And his captain, somewhere out in space, was beyond his grasp, too.

Where was Mackenzie, and why couldn't his mind touch hers? Panic welled inside him, a feeling as foreign as his body had been to him at the beginning. He had left the homestead without a word, but he had believed he was taking at least a part of Mackenzie with him. Now he knew that wasn't true. She was as dead to him as she would have been to anyone with only a human's capabilities. How did humans tolerate this separation from the ones they loved? How was he going to tolerate it?

The captain was another matter. The captain would come when the time was right, and when that time arrived, he would signal where he was to land. The meeting would be out here somewhere on Waluwara's vast acreage. Patrick knew that he was near enough to the ship's eventual destination to make that journey a short one. Now he had only to wait. Wait and wonder what the future held for him.

As the rain began to fall harder, Sunfisher whinnied again. Patrick had expected to contact his ship before this. Now he gave some thought to where to wait. Had the weather been dry, he would have found a stretch of grass to lie on. His all-too-human form needed sleep. He'd had little since his confrontation with Mackenzie. Her words, her loss of faith in him, had rung through his head in the hours when others slept, just as once the captain's voice had rung through his memories.

The rain made sleeping outside impossible, and he was miles from the homestead. But off to the south there was a shelter of some sort. He concentrated, using his powers to scan it, and found it was uninhabited now. It was larger than the hut that Mackenzie had taken him to after she'd found him. Larger and in better condition, but still only a hut. The stockmen sometimes used it when they were out on this end of the run, and not too many years before, one of the men had taken his new bride there to live for a year until she had persuaded him to seek greener pastures.

"There's a place for you there, too," Patrick told Sunfisher, stroking his neck in encouragement. Then he mounted and turned the horse's head.

There might be a place at the hut for both of them. But as he rode toward it, Patrick wondered if there would ever really be a place for him anywhere again.

Rain bounced off the oiled cloth of Mackenzie's stockmen's coat and the wide brim of her hat. There were still thin shards of sunlight shooting into the clouds from a sun that had nearly set, but soon it would be too dark to continue her search.

She had trailed Patrick to this spot by following Sunfisher's distinctive hoofprints. One, the right foreleg, had a small dent at the bend of the shoe. Now the rain was washing away the best evidence she had, and by morning Patrick could be far from the homestead and impossible to trace.

"I wish I could ask you for help," she murmured, patting Bounder's neck. "Patrick would know what to say."

Bounder whinnied, almost as if in sympathy.

She dismounted and searched the ground. The rain splashed against her neck as she bent to investigate. There were men in the village who were such astute trackers that one leaf, one nearly invisible smudge in the sand, could preach volumes to them about what had happened in that place. When she had been young, she had showed a talent for tracking herself. A village elder, Harry's father, had taught her some of his secrets—a remarkable gift to give a white girl child. Now she used that gift to find the last fading hoofprints.

Through the haze of rain she could see the sky was deepening into dusk. She scanned the horizon with binoculars for a figure on horseback, as she had since she had left the homestead. But Patrick had gotten just enough of a start to elude her.

Would he travel in the dark or the rain? If she knew where he was going, or why, the question might have been easier to answer. As it was, she knew so little that she could only guess.

He wasn't familiar with the vast expanses of the station, and surely by now he had heard all the horror stories about men dying for lack of water during the Dry or drowning in madly rushing rivers during the Wet. An intelligent man would be cautious.

No, he wouldn't keep traveling. He would stop for the night. Suddenly Mackenzie was so certain of his choice that she forced herself to pause and consider it again. The same certainty filled her. He would stop, but not in the open. He probably wouldn't be prepared to camp in the rain. He would seek shelter.

She searched her mind for potential havens. The station was dotted with huts, and there were several ramshackle cottages that had once housed men, and sometimes families, to watch over vast expanses of the property. She reviewed all the possibilities and settled on a hut about a kilometer to the west. It was a bit south of where she stood now, not on a continuous line with the trail she had been following. But it made more sense than any other destination. In a quarter of an hour, with some hard riding, she would be able to see it.

She gave Bounder his head and let him cover the distance at his own rough trot. Almost as if he sensed company ahead, he broke into a smooth canter as they neared the place where she knew she would have her first view. At the top of a low hill she looked into the distance and saw smoke curling toward the darkening sky.

She had found Patrick. What else she had found remained to be seen.

The rain fell harder as she rested for a moment. Then, at a touch of her heels, Bounder descended the hill.

One moment Patrick's mind and heart were empty of everything that mattered, the next he was filled with Mackenzie's image. He dropped another piece of wood on the fire he had started, then stood to wait for her on the porch.

Lightning split the sky, but he didn't need its fierce glow to see Mackenzie's approach. He saw it in his mind, felt her hope, her trepidation, her half-formed desire to turn back. She had come because she'd had no choice. But now choices were occurring to her. Now, when she had almost found exactly what she'd sought.

When Bounder reached the porch, Patrick stepped into the rain. She sat tall and unflinching in the saddle, despite the water sluicing from her hat to run in streams down her coat.

"I didn't know you were coming. Not until you were almost here," he said.

She held the reins tightly, as if she was afraid that Bounder—or she—might bolt. "I thought you knew everything about me."

"Come inside."

She sat still, contemplating the invitation. Then she swung her leg over the saddle and dismounted.

"I'll put Bounder in the back with Sunfisher," he said. "Go on inside."

"I'll see to my own horse."

"I'll see to him." He took the reins from her hand before she could protest and led Bounder behind the hut.

Mackenzie stood in the rain for a moment before she stepped up to the porch. One moment water was running across every surface of her clothes and body, the next the same rain was striking the iron roof above her head and sliding in streams down the corrugated rows to deepen a ditch circling the hut.

The memory of the smoke that had guided her here forced her inside. She was shivering now. The air had cooled quickly, and despite her coat she was wet. Before she removed it and went to stand by the fireplace, she looked around the two rooms and remembered that a painfully shy young woman had once lived here with her husband. There were still feminine touches blooming against the corrugated walls, dried wildflowers in an amber bottle, a 1988 calendar sporting a dust-streaked photograph of a rainbow. There was a straw carpet on the glassy-smooth dirt floor, and recent visitors had swept the place clean—perhaps in deference to the woman's memory.

"There's a shelter for the horses behind us. Bounder and Sunfisher just fit." Patrick came in as he spoke and put his coat on top of hers.

Mackenzie held her hands out to the fire and found they weren't quite steady. "Nice place you have here."

"How did you know where I'd be?"

"I didn't. I made a calculated guess." But even as she said the words, she knew that something more than guesswork had drawn her to him.

"Why did you come?" he asked.

"Why did you leave?"

He moved closer. "It was time for me to go."

"Time now that you've done all you could for everyone concerned?"

"Have I done all I could?"

Mackenzie rubbed her hands together. She didn't look at him. "How much did Sebastian pay you, Patrick?"

"You find that an important question?"

"Yes."

"Has he gone, then?"

"He's gone. He sold the station to my uncle."

"That's as it should be."

"You're not surprised?" Mackenzie asked. "Was that the way you had planned for it to happen?"

"I'm not God. No more than any other man. I can't cause anything to happen."

She faced him. The flames were warm against her back, but she scarcely felt them. "Then you deny that you purposely found a grade of manganese that Sebastian wouldn't see fit to mine? You had no idea that it was of such poor grade when you identified the deposit?"

He didn't answer.

"What did he pay you?" she repeated. "Tell me what he paid you."

"What do you think he paid me?"

"Stop answering my questions with questions!"

He smiled, and the sadness in it made her throat close. "I'm afraid I take after a friend of mine. A man named Stefan Daniels."

"I accused you of accepting a bribe, Patrick. I have to know if I'm wrong."

"You know you're wrong. You've known it all along."

She lowered her gaze. She *had* known it. She had never truly believed that Patrick was capable of such greed. But neither had she been courageous enough to believe the best of him. It had been easier to suffer the rejection of a scoundrel than a saint.

"Yes," she said softly. "I've known. Bloody hell, I've known all along, haven't I?"

"He offered me a share of what we found."

"And you could have found anything for him, anything you wanted."

"I found exactly what he asked me to."

She looked up and tried to smile, but she couldn't. "Why didn't you tell me? Why didn't you spend a few minutes with me to help me see the truth?"

"Because if you had seen it, Sebastian would have, too. Your anger was a smokescreen to hide the truth behind. If you hadn't been concerned that I was helping Sebastian, he would have been suspicious. He was so accomplished at lying, he recognized any kind of deceit that was presented to him."

"Except yours, apparently."

"Yes."

"But that wasn't your only reason, was it?"

He shrugged.

"You wanted me to be angry at you. You thought I'd find your departure easier to cope with if I was angry. Maybe you even thought it would help you avoid a row. You could cut and run without a goodbye."

He was ashamed of himself. Until that moment he hadn't completely understood his own motivation. He hadn't wanted to understand it. Apparently he was even more human than he had thought. "It almost worked."

"But it didn't. Because here I am, standing right in front of you. So say goodbye to me, Paddy. Tell me why you're leaving and say goodbye. You owe me that much for saving your life."

He couldn't speak. He was so torn by emotion that he couldn't find words to explain himself. There were tears in Mackenzie's eyes, though he doubted she knew it. Tears and something unspeakably beautiful shimmering behind them. Her words demanded that he tell her goodbye, but her eyes told him something different. She didn't want him to leave. She never wanted him to leave.

"Say it, Paddy!"

He knew that a lie would be kind. He could invent a past that called to him, a past and a situation that she couldn't interfere with. He could tell her of his imaginary family, of the wife whom he pretended to remember and the children who counted on him for support and love. He could make up a story, implausible though it might be, that explained why he had been facedown in the desert dying of exposure when she had found him.

But he couldn't lie to her. And he couldn't tell her the truth.

"I have to leave," he said, turning away from the brilliance of her tear-filled eyes. "I can't tell you why. Don't ask me to."

"You have to? You have no choice? With all your special abilities, you have no say in this?"

"I'm nothing. And I have...people I must answer to, just like all of us."

"Then you've remembered who you are?"

"I can't tell you anything else."

She moved closer to him. She wanted to make him look at her. "Don't tell me you're powerless! I've seen you in action, remember? No one is pulling your strings. You want to leave. Something...someone is tugging at you."

She touched his arm. Reluctantly he turned. She was so close. Too close. By her standards he was powerful beyond imagining, but at that moment he felt no power. He only felt himself drawn closer to her. The power was hers.

"I don't want to leave you," he said. He saw his words reflected in her eyes. He gave a harsh sigh and framed her face with his hands. "I don't want to leave you! But I don't have a choice."

"Why not? Who are you?" She covered his hands with her own. "Why can't you tell me? It can't be worse than not knowing the truth. It can't be!"

"Mackenzie." He uttered endearments in his first language, pulling her close and holding her to him. The sounds glided over her like the rain, but unlike the rain they warmed her. He warmed her.

She lifted her head and looked into his eyes. "I love you," she said softly. "Bloody hell, I love you, Patrick. And whoever you are, I'll love you still. It doesn't matter. Just don't leave me. Don't go away and leave me here without you."

He kissed her. He told himself not to. He told himself that he was changing her world for all time, interfering in a life with which he could have no contact after tonight. But he told himself these things as he kissed her. Because no matter what his thoughts, he couldn't force himself to stop.

She wrapped her arms around his neck and held him close. She tasted his desire and his anguish, felt them in every cell of her body. "Are you married?" she whispered. "Tell me you're not married."

"I'm not." He breathed the words against her cheek. The mating ceremony he had remembered had not been his own. He lived alone; he had always preferred his freedom. Never had he even been tempted to take a mate. Now he knew why. His temptation had dwelled on another planet, in another solar system, in another kind of physical reality. His temptation, his mate, was here in his arms.

"I don't know what I would have done if you'd said yes!" She kissed him again, slanting her lips over his first one way, then another. She stroked him with the palms of her hands, kneaded his flesh with her fingertips, rubbed her thighs against his as she kissed him harder.

He groaned, a man reduced by his own physical urges to animal or angel—he wasn't sure which. He only knew that this time he wouldn't have the control or strength to refuse her unless he left her now.

"We can't." He tried to pull away and found it was impossible. He was as trapped by his desire as if he was caged.

"We are." She was triumphant, woman conquering man, woman reshaping the world to her own wishes. She sensed his reluctance, but more, so much more, she sensed his need and his passion. Whatever stood between them wasn't as important as what united them. He wanted her. Desperately. And that was enough.

The bed in the corner of the room was covered by a quilt. She wondered if it had been the stockman's marriage bed, and if, before leaving the hut, his wife, in a fit of sentimentality, had not been able to bear to expose it to the elements. She led Patrick to it now, bore him there on the tide of their passion.

She was innocent, untutored, but in some strange way, he was more so. He held on to every touch, every kiss, every moment, savoring it in wonder. She unbuttoned his shirt, and she pressed her hands against his chest. He unbuttoned hers and explored each softly padded curve and angle.

"I love you," she whispered again. She lowered herself to the bed and held out her arms. He shut his eyes as if trying to deny himself even the sight of her, but at her touch, he opened them again.

"I love you," he said. "I always will."

She saw the torture in his eyes. "Please, don't worry now," she whispered. "Whatever it is, I'll help you."

He answered her in the language she didn't understand, but the words soothed her. When he lay down beside her, she took him in her arms again and tried to kiss away his fears. His hair was like sunlight against her fingers; his skin pulsed with life. She wondered how she could have denied herself a man for so long and answered in the same thought that if he hadn't appeared, she might have denied herself forever.

He murmured to her again as his lips found the speeding rhythm of her heart. He savored the herbal fragrance of her hair, the warm cream flavor of her skin. He wanted to ab-

sorb her inside him, yet the fact that they were two separate
bodies fascinated him. He explored with more fervor, removing the scrap of cloth that bound her breasts so that he
could experience them in their totality.

When she moaned, he knew he was pleasing her. He could
feel her pleasure emanating in shock waves throughout him.
It increased his own pleasure tenfold. Perhaps he could not
absorb her, but he could know what she knew, feel what she
felt.

He wondered if she could do the same. He wanted to
know, had to know. He couldn't bear that the pleasure, the
communication, might only be one-sided. "Mackenzie," he
whispered, "do you know what you're doing to me?"

Her answer pleased him. She arched against him as he
took the tip of one breast between his lips. He could feel
parts of himself becoming as hot and turgid as the breast he
suckled. He slid his hands under the waistband of her
moleskins, then around to unsnap them. Her response was
to unsnap his.

He could not absorb her, but he could experience her. He
could tell her, without words, thought to thought, exactly
what he wanted.

Exhilaration filled him. He murmured the chant of the
mating ceremony. He remembered every word, and he slid
the words along her skin, filled her pores with them, buried
them in her hair.

She gave a small cry when he had undressed her and they
were flesh to flesh with nothing between them. She was immersed in sensation, so filled with Patrick, his touch, his
kisses, the totality of him, that she felt as if she was in a
dream. Her fears were gone; her doubts had vanished, too.
She was sure that no one had ever experienced this pleasure, that no one could ever understand—even if she could
find a way to explain—that this joy could exist in the world.

Her legs were strong from hours, days, years spent on
horseback. She used them now to bring him closer. She
wanted nothing between their spirits; she cursed the flesh
that was giving her pleasure, because it separated them when
she yearned for them to be one. She could feel the heat of his

arousal as well as her own, more secret heat. There would be an explosion when they merged; she knew it deep inside her. There would be an explosion, and the world would change forever.

She wanted the world to change. She could not bear for it to stay the same. She wanted it to change while she was wrapped around this man, and when they emerged together, she wanted it to create a place for them, a place far from doubts and fears and the mysterious things that were driving Patrick away from her.

She opened her eyes and looked into his. She saw he was waiting for her, for some small sign that she was ready for the earth to stop spinning in quite the same way.

"Yes," she said. "Oh, yes, Patrick. No matter what happens next. Yes."

His eyes closed, but she knew he could still see her. She lifted her hips to his and felt him sliding inside her. All the barriers between them fell away. All the doubts, the fears, their very flesh. She was transported to another world, another reality.

She was transported to the stars and the heavens, through the universe, into infinity, in Patrick's arms.

Chapter 16

There was the faint, pleasant tang of wood smoke, the percussive splash of rain beating on metal and the taste of Patrick's kisses on her lips. Mackenzie absorbed it all without opening her eyes. Her body ached, but the pain was nearly as delicious as the lovemaking had been. She could almost feel Patrick's hands against her skin stroking her, just as he had stroked her as she'd fallen asleep.

He was a man of many special abilities. Now she had been privy to one more.

She turned to her side. A trace of shyness delayed the moment when she would open her eyes. She was shameless, a true wanton who'd had little on her mind except satisfying her animal instincts.

She smiled lazily at the thought.

She and Patrick were destined to be together now, for better or for worse. Their union had been both earthbound lust and a heavenly merger of their spirits. She wasn't experienced—witness the ache in places that would soon grow accustomed to Patrick's explosive sensuality—but she knew that what had happened between them was as powerful as life itself.

She opened her eyes. Patrick was nowhere in sight.

She sat up and looked around the room. The fire had almost died away; she had been asleep longer than she'd thought.

No one moved through the two silent rooms.

She swung her legs over the bed, panic welling inside her. "Patrick?" His name resounded against corrugated iron. There was no other sound. "Patrick?"

She stood and found her clothes. His were gone. Perhaps he was only outside, tending to the horses. But even as she scrambled for some explanation other than the obvious, horrifying one, she knew she was just wasting time.

She pulled on her pants and shirt, barely registering that they had been on the floor long enough to dry. "Patrick, damn it, where are you?"

She heard a whinny behind the hut. One whinny, from one horse. She searched the room for her coat and hat before she saw them neatly folded on a table beside the door. She had pulled on the coat and was fumbling with the double row of snaps when she saw a piece of paper on the table.

She refused to pick it up. She saw her name at the top, but she glanced away, to avoid it. "Patrick!"

Outside the rain was falling harder. Sebastian had left the station just in time. This was no harbinger of things to come. This was the long-awaited Wet, early, but no less dramatic than it had ever been. The drought had ended.

She ran to the back of the hut and found one horse, sheltered, but white-eyed from the steady ping of rain against metal.

"Bounder." She threw her arms around his neck. As if he understood her misery, he stood still for her caresses. "Where did they go, Bounder?"

The horse nuzzled her in sympathy.

Out from under the shelter she scanned the horizon, but what moonlight there might have been was hidden under clouds and sheets of rain. Patrick and Sunfisher had disappeared into everywhere and anywhere.

She had no choice now but to go inside and read Patrick's letter. It was the only clue left her. There was no light to find tracks, even if the rain didn't wash them away minutes after they were made.

She didn't remove her coat. She let it drip on the floor as she lifted the letter and took it to read beside what was left of the fire.

There were only a few sentences. Patrick couldn't tell her why, but he had no choice except to leave her. He loved her; he always would. If there had been a way, any way, he could have stayed, he would have. But staying was impossible.

And under those words, penned in a bold, flowing script, was a map of the station, Waluwara in painstaking miniature, with circles marking half a dozen spots where rich, high-grade deposits of manganese could be found.

And one diamond mine.

Diamonds. She knew that diamonds had been found in the Kimberleys of Western Australia in the 1970s, making Australia the largest diamond producer in the world. Though most of what was mined wasn't gemstone quality, the find produced diamonds for industrial use, millions of carats a year. There had been talk of potential diamond deposits in the Northern Territory. Talk.

Diamonds.

In her hands she held all the solutions to Waluwara's financial problems. With the help of other investors, her uncle could choose carefully what to mine and when. He could prevent an unbridled rape of the land and take just enough from it to insure that Waluwara flourished. Now there would be money to make all improvements, from refurbishing equipment to buying better breeding stock and constructing sturdy paddocks to ensure that a controlled breeding program was successful.

But Patrick wouldn't be there to witness any of it.

She folded the letter with its skillfully drawn map and tucked it deep inside her shirt.

Outside again, she stood on the narrow porch and gazed at the sky. The storm was a constant. Wishing was not going to make it disappear. Trying to follow Patrick to stop him from leaving was foolhardy. She had no light, no tracks. She had nothing but a horse with a steadfast heart and her own instincts.

She rested her face in her hands. She had never felt more alone or helpless. She possessed nothing that would help her find Patrick. No inkling of where he might be heading, no information about his past to help her make calculated guesses. She knew he was a special man, a man with powers unlike any she had seen. Perhaps he even had the ability to disappear into thin air. Hadn't he come from thin air?

She remembered the day she had found him. She had been riding Bounder that day, too, and she had almost passed him by. But Bounder had been stubborn. And when she had used her instincts in conjunction with the horse's, she had been guided to Patrick's side.

Could she do it again? Was she kidding herself? Was she so steeped in the mystery of Patrick's powers that she fancied she had some of her own?

But she had found Patrick that first day. The dust storm had swirled around her like the rain was swirling now. The sky had been dark, not as dark as it was at this moment, but her vision had been curtailed. She had found him because she had allowed herself to believe she could. She had been determined to discover the source of Bounder's nervousness and the shivers creeping along her own spine.

Was she less determined now?

She gathered together the few things that Patrick had unpacked from her saddle. Her swag, her water bag. Outside, under Bounder's shelter, she found his saddle and hoisted it up on his back, taking care to fasten it properly before she added the burden of her few belongings. In a few minutes she was in the saddle, ready to depart.

One thought very nearly stopped her. Was Patrick's leaving a kindness? Was he protecting her from something so terrible that she was better off not knowing what it was? The sudden dampness of her palms had nothing to do with the storm. She felt herself poised on the bank of a rushing river. She might battle to cross it, use every last ounce of energy to reach the other side, only to find that the other side was the outskirts of hell.

In her mind she saw Patrick's face. It would stay with her always; everything about him would stay with her always. If the other side of the river was hell, then hell was where Patrick was. Nothing, not hell, not a terrifying revelation about who or what he was, could keep her from his side.

She nudged Bounder, and willingly, he started into the storm.

The rain wouldn't keep the ship from landing, although it would slow its progress. In comparison to the storms Patrick had seen on other planets in other galaxies, this one was mild. There were no cascades of fire, no bursts of noxious gases, no plagues of insects or purple-eyed predator birds.

There was only rain, soft and wet against his flesh. His flesh. Patrick reined Sunfisher to a stop and looked out over the landing site, where he had been instructed through telepathy to wait. His flesh tingled with memories, tactile memories burned into a living substance that his own people had abandoned millenia ago. What a mistake it had been to ascend to a state where flesh was unnecessary and everything that went with it became unnecessary, too.

There were pleasures in his world, knowledge and warm friendship and love of family. As a boy he had been thrilled to learn all the philosophy, customs and vast stores of information that his people had collected throughout eternity. The master had been his teacher, even though he was a teacher of teachers and hadn't needed even to speak to one small boy. But Patrick's parents had left him while he was still young to take a short voyage through space, and when they had never returned, the master had taken over his education. Later he had taken Patrick on space voyages, too, until Patrick was as accomplished as any of his people at navigation.

All these things had been pleasures. But none of them compared to what he had experienced with Mackenzie. He would go back to his own race now, perhaps even find a way to return to his original form. He would be bathed in the love of those he had always known, continue his intellectual and physical journey through the universe. And all the time, even in years to come, when surely Mackenzie would be dead here on earth, he would think of her and yearn for her. No, not yearn. The word was too weak.

He uttered another, one from his own language. It meant to suffer the darkest torment, to long so desperately for something that everything else in life became immaterial. To waste away. To stop growing. Finally, unfulfilled, to die.

But he could not stay here. He had a human body, but he was more. Even here, almost as far from civilization as man could live on this planet, he had used his very alien powers to change this tiny corner of the world. He had not been able to resist temptation. He had used his abilities to thwart St. Carroll. He had used them to better life for the people of Waluwara. And worst of all, he had succumbed to temptation in the form of one human woman whom he never should have touched, never should have fallen in love with.

He was not strong enough to live here. He would change anything and everything with which he came in contact. And in changing the small things, the seemingly inconsequential ones, he would change human history and the hope that this planet would continue to evolve in its own best way.

He felt Sunfisher move restlessly beneath him. He would miss the horse. He had ridden other, far less appealing creatures, but he had never felt one with their flesh, because he had never understood flesh in quite the same way. Still, Sunfisher would be fine. He would return to the station to be cared for by other stockmen. Intelligent and alert, he would be in demand as a mount, and he would live out his days in relative comfort. Soon he would even forget the human sitting on his back now, the human who had been able to establish a primitive communication with him.

Mackenzie wouldn't forget. She would long for Patrick as he would long for her. She would not marry, not bear children . . . unless they had created a child together tonight.

Had he repeated the sin of Mackenzie's father? Had he left her to swell with his baby, to raise it without his participation? Somehow he knew that if that was the case, she would not repeat the mistakes of her mother. She would raise the child at Waluwara, teach it everything she knew, shelter it, love it, give it the best inside her. She would be devastated by the loss of the child's father, but she would love the child just as fiercely.

There were no stars in the heavens tonight. The rain fell harder, and the clouds only seemed to thicken. But behind one cloud Patrick saw a faint glimmer of light. It was not a star. He felt its identity deep inside him.

His hands tightened on the reins. For a moment his human flesh rebelled. He yearned to turn Sunfisher toward the homestead, toward the two-room hut where Mackenzie lay dreaming of him.

The light grew brighter. Sunfisher danced beneath him. Patrick drew the reins tighter. Then he dropped them and bowed his head.

He uttered the word that expressed the longing he would feel from that moment forward.

It mimicked the sound of tears.

At first Mackenzie hadn't been able to decide what direction to take. She had sat at the top of a low hill, holding Bounder still to keep him from bolting. There had been lightning far in the distance, just the occasional flash followed by the low rumble of thunder. But the worsening weather had made the horse nervous—or at least something had. She had reined him tight and freed all her senses to make the decision for her.

Then, without understanding why, she had chosen the route that seemed to lead into the heart of the storm. With Bounder steadier beneath her, she had ridden into it.

Nearly an hour had passed. She was so numb with cold that the rain was no longer a torment. She had no clues that she was heading in the right direction. She knew where she was, and where she was going. She knew that there was a dry streambed not too far in the distance, and that it might be filling with water even as she rode toward it. If it was, and she crossed, she might not be able to return for days, even weeks.

She wanted to shout for Patrick, but she knew how foolish that would be. He wouldn't answer, even if he heard her. He would ride faster, harder, farther. Even now she struggled to block him from her mind. She sensed that there were things she could do to keep him from discovering that she was trailing him. That sensation, that knowledge, was new and wholly untried, but she struggled to follow her instincts in this, too, just as she struggled to follow the course she had chosen.

She was nothing but instinct now. She wondered if making love to Patrick had somehow taught her what she needed to know to find him. Or had their lovemaking only opened her up to a wealth of feelings and instincts that she had covered up all her life? Whatever the answer, she knew she had to trust herself now.

She urged Bounder on. In another half hour they neared the stream. She dismounted and walked to the edge. There was so little light that at first she couldn't make out the state of it; then, as she tugged her hat over her face to shield her eyes from rain, she got her answer. Water was filling the wide bed. There was nearly a foot covering the bottom, and it appeared to be rising fast. She and Bounder could cross, but if the rain continued, and it likely would, the stream could rise and become a rushing torrent. Then it would separate her from the homestead.

Now it separated her from Patrick.

"Come on, Bounder." She stepped into the stream and felt the water rush over the tops of her elastic-sided boots. The bottom was already spongy, and each step was more difficult than the last. She tucked the reins under her arm, and Bounder followed reluctantly.

The water rose higher as they approached the center of the stream. A large branch rushed past her, catching her with the tip of a spidery limb that almost knocked her off balance. Bounder, frightened by the object, reared up and jerked her backward off her feet. She recovered, soothed him and started once again for the other side. They were almost to the opposite bank when she heard the pitiful bawling of a calf.

Intuitively she knew what had probably happened. The mother cow had gone to the streambed to drink, perhaps before the water began to flow so rapidly. Her calf had followed and ventured too far. Then, when the calf tried to climb out, its feet had bogged in the mud. The harder it had struggled, the more it had bogged. Now it was just a matter of time before the pitiful small body would be covered with water.

She had to let it die. She was probably far behind Patrick as it was. If she didn't keep searching now, she would never find him.

The calf bawled louder, its terror readily apparent. From somewhere farther up the bank she heard its mother reply. Unconsciously Mackenzie's hand rested on her belly. Her head bent, and she gazed at her hand.

She could be carrying Patrick's child. She hadn't thought of it until that moment. They hadn't used any form of birth control; she hadn't even considered it. She could be pregnant with Patrick's child!

The calf bawled again, its mother answered, and Mackenzie could hear the cow's distress. She was an animal, but her feelings were strong. Her instincts told her to do what she could to save her offspring. She might even die in an attempt to lead the calf to safety. Mackenzie had seen it before. If necessary the cow would die for her calf just as Mackenzie would die to save the child inside her.

"Bloody hell," she whispered fiercely. She grabbed Bounder's reins with both hands and led him safely across.

Then, still leading him, she went in search of mother and child.

More than half an hour passed before she and Bounder were on their way again. The calf and its mother had been reunited and shooed toward higher ground. Mackenzie was covered with mud that even the hard rain couldn't entirely wash away, and she was physically exhausted from wrestling with the stream and the calf.

She dug her heels into Bounder's sides, but he had little to give her in the way of speed. He had borne much of the burden of pulling the calf from the streambed, and he was exhausted, too.

An impending sense of loss filled her as she rode into the storm again. Her instinct was blurred by fatigue. Waluwara was thousands of square kilometers. What had made her think she could choose the right direction? And even if the general direction was correct, missing Patrick by half a kilometer was the same as missing him by a hundred.

She was not going to find him. She reined Bounder to a halt to try to clear her mind and find the trail that had seemed so right to her before. But all she could feel was fear.

Patrick would soon be gone. She knew it as surely as she knew her own name. Soon it would be too late to find him. He would disappear forever, and she, like her mother, would be left to mourn the absence of the man she loved.

But she was not Mary Kate. She would not give up without a fight. She had only the dimmest vision of where to go, but she would follow it. She would follow it until there was no vision at all, until the moment when she was certain Patrick was gone for good.

"Come on, Bounder." She kicked him again. He moved a little faster. She leaned forward to encourage him, and he moved faster still. In the distance, in line with her path, the clouds parted to reveal a glow. For a moment she thought the storm was abating and the glow was the hidden moon. Then she realized it was too bright.

She kicked Bounder again, apologizing silently for asking so much of him on the treacherous, spongy earth. He gave her more, as if he, too, realized the importance of speed.

She had no idea what the light might be, but every part of her knew it had something to do with Patrick. She guessed it was a plane, perhaps some sort of vessel from one of the controversial outback military bases. Her mind sorted through explanations, each more impossible than the one before. Patrick had been part of a military experiment in extrasensory perception. Patrick was a spy from another country, perhaps one who had been left for dead.

The light grew brighter, then began a descent. Fear filled her, and beneath her Bounder slowed, then, despite all her efforts, came to a halt. He reared, almost unseating her. As he did, he gave a terrified scream.

She succeeded in calming him enough to dismount. He was no good to her now. His ears were flat against his head, and his eyes were wild. As soon as she was on the ground again, he reared once more.

The light seemed to be approaching earth almost half a kilometer away. Half a kilometer, and whatever the light was, she knew it had to do with Patrick. In an instant she weighed her options. Bounder would not be persuaded to go on without a fight, and she had no time to fight. She had to get to the light, whatever it was. She had to find Patrick now.

She began to run. Behind her she heard the sharp clack of horseshoes against stone and knew that Bounder was on his way back to the homestead. She had no time to worry about what that meant for her. She ran on, stumbling once in the darkness, then, almost at her destination, again. Pain shot through her leg the second time, but she ran anyway, although now each step was a torment.

The light sank closer toward the earth. She ran, stumbling again and again as her leg gave way beneath her. She was so tired that for a moment, as the light seemed to touch ground, she thought she was floating. She wanted to close her eyes, to rest for a moment, but a voice inside her demanded that she not give in.

She slowed to a hobble, because now she was dragging her leg behind her, but she moved as fast as she was able.

"Patrick." Her voice was nothing but a rasp. "Patrick!"

She looked up and saw that the light was a glorious display of colors pulsing through the air to lap at the ground just meters away. She could barely breathe, not just from exhaustion, but from the magnificence of the spectacle. She had concentrated so hard on reaching this place that she had shut her mind to everything else. Now she heard music, an array of sounds unlike any she had ever heard before.

Tears sprang to her eyes, and she dragged herself on. She knew she had to reach the light, that if she didn't, couldn't, she would never see Patrick again. Her leg gave way beneath her, and this time she couldn't stand. She dragged herself across the ground, clawing her way toward the light, which seemed to be receding now.

"Patrick!" She clawed onward, lifting herself on her good leg to propel herself forward. Tears streamed down her cheeks.

Her fingertips touched the light's edge. She could see the rainbow hues dance along her nails. She rose again and propelled herself forward once more. Now her hands were bathed in color, then her wrists.

"Mackenzie!" She heard Patrick's voice from far away. She shouted to him, but the sound seemed to catch in her throat.

She felt herself being lifted, and suddenly she was in his arms. The torment in her leg disappeared as if she had never been injured.

"You weren't supposed to see this!" He held her tighter, as if his mere human strength could save her from what was to come.

"What is it?" She could barely whisper the words.

"You know what it is."

She did know, but her mind refused to move one step farther. "But why are you here? Why do they want you?"

"I'm one of them." He held her tighter and felt her jerk at his words. "I'm one of them, and they've come to take me back."

"But you're human!"

"That, too."

The music grew louder. She slipped her arms around his waist and locked them. "Patrick, don't go. I don't care what you are, who you are! Stay with me!"

"I can't stay."

The music seemed to slip inside her, and even though her eyes were shut, the colors seemed to slip inside her, too. She held on tighter and pushed the music and colors away. She knew, without knowing how, that she had to resist.

"You'll go to sleep," he said softly, "and when you wake up, this won't even be a dream. You'll forget what you saw."

"I'll never forget!" She opened her eyes. "I won't forget! Not any more than you'll forget me! Can you promise that a little magic will change everything? That I'll forget I loved a man from another..."

"Dimension? Planet?" He kissed her, because there was nothing left to say. He felt the warmth of her lips, the terror in the way she clutched him. He had a sudden, perfect vision of how she had looked and felt when she was naked against him.

He shut his eyes and felt the ship land. Then he loosened his grip on her and tried to push her away. "You'll forget you saw this."

"Then what shall I tell our child? That his father disappeared one night, and that I don't remember anything more?"

"There may not be a child."

She grabbed his hand and set it against her belly. She knew the truth now, had known it since crossing the stream. "Feel your son come to life under your hand!"

His throat closed. He couldn't breathe or swallow. He felt the stirring of life inside her just as surely as she did. She would have his baby. His son. He would leave more than a legacy of sorrow in this desolate, savagely beautiful place. He would leave part of himself.

He heard the soft purr that meant he would soon be drawn into the vessel. He tried to move away from her, but he could not. She locked her arms around his waist again. "You'll have to use force to make me leave you," she said.

The purr became a roar. He clutched her against him. In that moment he knew he could not use force. He couldn't even give her a gentle push. He did not want to leave her or their child. There were no universal laws that were more important than protecting her. "Hold on!"

She felt herself being lifted in his arms. The ground disappeared beneath her feet. They were drawn through the air together in a pathway bathed in light and pastel, welcoming colors. Terror filled her, but she held on to him, because she knew that if she loosened her grip, she would never see him again.

When she opened her eyes she was inside a room like none she had ever seen. The walls were shimmering, iridescent light. Patrick was still holding tightly to her. She felt him steel himself, as if for battle.

Then a being like none she had ever seen appeared in front of her. She gasped, but not in terror.

"You were always the child who did what he thought was best," said a voice, emanating from the being in front of her.

"And now I am a man who does what he knows is right," Patrick said in his own language. "I cannot, will not leave her!"

As Mackenzie watched, stunned, the being transformed until its substance, little more than radiant light, became flesh. The being, now in the form of a man, moved toward her.

He was silver-haired, but his face was unlined, and his eyes were the brown of Waluwara's earth. "You have unusual courage," he said in English. "How many humans would have faced the odds that you did to come here?"

"I'm not leaving." Mackenzie felt herself being drawn toward the man. She grasped for Patrick's hand. "Don't try to make me leave."

The captain held out his hand, but he didn't touch her or motion her closer. "You won't be asked to leave. You have always been welcome here."

She stared at him. "Always? What does that mean? Do you think I knew about you before this?"

"Didn't you?"

She felt Patrick's fingers thread through hers. They gave her courage. "No."

"Look deep inside yourself. To the nights as a child when you gazed into the heavens and wondered what was beyond the nearest star."

"Now I reckon I'm standing inside the nearest star."

"You're standing on a threshold, daughter."

She felt Patrick's fingers tighten spasmodically. "Why do you call me daughter?"

"You're much like your mother, Mackenzie. But you have more spirit."

She stared at him.

"I was on a mission here. I wasn't supposed to encounter anyone, but Mary Kate was riding by herself one night far from this place, out enjoying the stars. And we met by accident."

She remembered her uncle's story. "In New South Wales," she said wonderingly. "When she was visiting friends."

"She was beautiful," the captain said. He dropped his hand to his side. "Sweet, kind, and when we joined together, we broke almost every law of the universe. I wanted to break them all. I wanted her to come with me, to transform and become as I truly was. She would not. She was earthbound in a way that you aren't, daughter. You are truly a child of two worlds. She was a child of one. She chose to stay behind and give birth to you, although she shielded your existence from me. For a human, she had great strength."

Mackenzie's universe spun again. She stared at the being, her father. The father she had never known; the man—
who was not a man—who had destroyed her mother's life.

"She died for love of you," she whispered. "You killed
her with your love!"

"She would not come. I could not stay. When laws are
broken, tragedy is the aftermath. I have mourned her and
will mourn her every day for the rest of my existence."

Tears filled her eyes. She held tighter to Patrick's hand.
"You didn't know about me?"

"Not until...Patrick...disappeared. He was drawn to
this place by your spirit. The two of you were destined to
meet. Like you, he is almost human now, but for different
reasons."

She turned to Patrick. "But your powers. I have no powers to equal yours."

"You have all his powers," the captain said. "You have
only begun to use them."

The truth whirled in her head. She had found Patrick in
one storm and traced him to this place in another. She had
read his thoughts and shielded hers from his when she
needed to. She had show great aptitude for tracking and for
all the station chores that necessitated a special instinct with
animals. Her capacity to absorb knowledge had so outdis-
tanced that of her classmates that school had never been
anything but a waste of time.

"I discovered your existence at the same time I found
Patrick," the captain said. "My daughter. The child I never
knew I'd had."

She was afraid to let go of Patrick's hand, afraid to embrace the man standing before her. She felt Patrick's arm
slip around her waist.

"I am not my mother," she said. "I will transform. I'll
turn myself into a bloody kangaroo if that's what it takes to
stay with Patrick. But I'm not leaving him. I don't care
about your universal laws. I didn't vote for them."

The captain smiled. "I can easily understand why the two of you were attracted to each other."

"I won't leave Mackenzie," Patrick said. He felt her flesh against his, flesh *like* his, and knew that he spoke the truth. Everything that had ever existed for him in the past slid away. Only the moments that were left to them were important now. "I choose to die here with her, if that's what must be."

Mackenzie faced the man she had risked everything for. She saw love shining in his eyes, love exactly like that in her heart.

"You can't stay here," the captain said. "And you can't come with us."

"Dying seems a poor third choice," Mackenzie said. She could not pull her gaze from Patrick's. She felt completely calm now. Whatever happened, they would be together.

"When our race transformed and abandoned the flesh, we lost something very important. It's an error that you two, and others like you, will correct for us," the captain said.

"Others like us?" Patrick asked.

"There are others like you. Others who, for one reason or another, are human and not human. And there is a colony—" he uttered a long, melodious name in the language that Mackenzie could not understand "—that is beginning far from here. You may go there and be settlers with the others. You can build a new world, add your own unique signature to the universe."

"Be a pioneer? An explorer?" Mackenzie asked. She thought of the dreams she had always had. Even the outback had been too tame.

"You are uniquely suited, daughter."

She turned to her father then. She saw his yearning to hold her. With a sob, she went into his arms. A lifetime of questions and anger dissolved as he held her. When he gave her back to Patrick, her tears had finally dried.

She looked into the eyes of the man who would be her mate for millenia. "Am I robbing you of your life? Of what you could have had if I hadn't come after you?"

"You are giving me life." He unsnapped her raincoat and touched her belly, warm even through her trousers. He felt the movements of his son and the other children they would create together. He felt generations created by them, from them, children with Mackenzie's courage and intelligence. Children of the universe. "You are my life."

She kissed him, aware that her father still watched. Patrick's lips, the warmth of his fingers against her, were all the promises she needed. "I want to go," she said fiercely. "It's all I'll ever want."

His voice was just as fierce. "And I want to go, too."

"Will we ever be able to come back?" Mackenzie asked. "Will I ever see Waluwara again?"

"I don't know."

She turned to her father. "Will we?"

"As you humans say, stranger things have happened."

"The map." Mackenzie reached inside her blouse and drew it out. "Uncle Clint . . ."

"I think there are some things I would rather not witness." Her father touched her shoulder. She felt the warmth radiate through her. Then he was gone.

"Patrick?" She turned to him, still afraid of what she might see.

He kissed away her fears, her questions, her apologies. He told her, without words, what she meant to him. She felt his warmth, his hunger, his proud humanity and the core of him that wasn't human at all.

And when he was finished, she was at peace.

Waluwara was lush and green, and finally, after weeks of rain, the Territory was between storms. The garden that Mackenzie had always loved so well was heavy with blooms. At sunset Edwina and Clint stood on the homestead veranda gazing out at the land that would nurture them and, God willing, their children, for the rest of their days.

"I know she's gone forever," Clint said. "There's no sign of her anywhere. Or Patrick, either."

"Wherever she is, she's safe," Edwina said. "I feel it."

"Her horse came back. She didn't."

Edwina put her hand on his arm. "But Patrick's horse didn't return."

Clint stared at the horizon. A small dot marred the view. A cow escaped from a nearby paddock, perhaps, or a brumby straying too close to civilization.

The dot grew steadily larger. He watched it, without taking his eyes off it once. When he saw that the dot was Sunfisher, he stepped off the veranda and went to unsaddle the horse himself.

There was little enough there to tell a story. A saddle, which was out of character for Patrick, and a tired horse who stood quietly under Clint's stroking. Clint reached for an unusual waterproof pouch tied to the saddle's Johnny strap. The map he found and the few scrawled sentences at its top were the story's ending.

"What is it?" Edwina asked, coming out to join him.

"Mackenzie's gone," he said. "She's safe, and she's with Patrick. She says she's happy and that . . . she loves us and hopes she'll be able to see us again one day."

"That's all?"

He folded the map and slipped it inside his shirt. "There's more. Come inside. I'll show you the rest."

"Do you think she's really all right?"

He turned and gazed into the distance. The sky was quickly growing dark. Some instinct told him that no matter how hard he searched the horizon, he would never find her there.

"Clint?"

"Yes. I think she's all right," he said.

He turned his eyes to the heavens and gazed at the gathering clouds, wishing that he could see beyond them. A strange tranquility descended over him as a lone star appeared between clouds. It shone more brightly than it had a right to, a beacon in a twilight sky.

He could not tear his eyes away, not until the star was finally smothered by clouds. Then he looked at Edwina. "Mackenzie's all right. Wherever she is."

He put his arms around Edwina's waist and held her tightly against his chest. The sky was black and the rain was beginning to fall again when, hand in hand, they went inside together.

*   *   *   *   *

AMERICAN HERO

You have spoken! You've asked for more of our irresistible American Heroes, and now we're happy to oblige. After all, we're as in love with these men as you are! In coming months, look for these must-have guys:

In COLD, COLD HEART (IM #487) by Ann Williams, we're looking at a hero with a heart of ice. But when faced with a desperate mother and a missing child, his heart begins to melt. You'll want to be there in April to see the results!

In May we celebrate the line's tenth anniversary with one of our most-requested heroes ever: Quinn Eisley. In QUINN EISLEY'S WAR (IM #493) by Patricia Gardner Evans, this lone-wolf agent finally meets the one woman who is his perfect match.

The weather starts to heat up in June, so come deep-sea diving with us in Heather Graham Pozzessere's BETWEEN ROC AND A HARD PLACE (IM #499). Your blood will boil right along with Roc Trellyn's when he pulls in his net to find—his not-quite-ex-wife!

AMERICAN HEROES. YOU WON'T WANT TO MISS A SINGLE ONE—ONLY FROM

Take 4 bestselling love stories FREE

Plus get a FREE surprise gift!

Special Limited-time Offer

Mail to Harlequin Reader Service®

3010 Walden Avenue
P.O. Box 1867
Buffalo, N.Y. 14269-1867

YES! Please send me 4 free Silhouette Intimate Moments® novels and my free surprise gift. Then send me 6 brand-new novels every month, which I will receive months before they appear in bookstores. Bill me at the low price of $2.71* each plus 25¢ delivery and applicable sales tax, if any.* I understand that accepting the books and gift places me under no obligation ever to buy any books. I can always return a shipment and cancel at any time. Even if I never buy another book from Silhouette, the 4 free books and the surprise gift are mine to keep forever.

245 BPA AJCK

Name _____ (PLEASE PRINT)

Address _____ Apt. No. _____

City _____ State _____ Zip _____

This offer is limited to one order per household and not valid to present Silhouette Intimate Moments® subscribers. *Terms and prices are subject to change without notice. Sales tax applicable in N.Y.

UMOM-93   ©1990 Harlequin Enterprises Limited

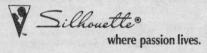

INTIMATE MOMENTS® *Silhouette*

CONARD COUNTY continues...

Come back to Conard County, Wyoming, where you'll meet men whose very lives personify the spirit of the American West—and the women who share their love. Join author Rachel Lee for her fourth exciting book in the series, IRONHEART (IM #495). Gideon Ironheart didn't expect his visit to Conard County to embroil him in a mystery...or entangle his heart. But the magnetic half-breed with a secret hadn't counted on wrangling with Deputy Sheriff Sara Yates. Look for their story in May, only from Silhouette Intimate Moments.

Celebrate our anniversary with a fabulous collection of firsts....

Silhouette Books is proud to present a FREE hardbound collection of the first Silhouette Intimate Moments® titles written by three of your favorite authors:

NIGHT MOVES
by *New York Times* best-selling author **Heather Graham Pozzessere**

LADY OF THE NIGHT
by Emilie Richards

A STRANGER'S SMILE
by Kathleen Korbel

This unique collection will not be available in retail stores and is only available through this exclusive offer.